DD

Items should be returned on or before the
been he Items not already requested i
d in person in wri

MATHILDA SAVITCH

VICTOR LODATO

Mathilda Savitch

FOURTH ESTATE · *London*

First published in Great Britain in 2009 by
Fourth Estate
An imprint of HarperCollins*Publishers*
77–85 Fulham Palace Road
London W6 8JB
www.4thestate.co.uk

Visit our authors' blog: www.fifthestate.co.uk

Simultaneously published in the United States by
Farrar, Straus and Giroux

1

A catalogue record for this book is available
from the British Library

HB ISBN 978-0-00-732222-0
TPB ISBN 978-0-00-732221-3

Set in Sabon by Palimpsest Book Production Limited,
Grangemouth, Stirlingshire

Printed in Great Britain by
Clays Ltd, St Ives plc

Mixed Sources
Product group from well-managed
forests and other controlled sources
www.fsc.org Cert no. SW-COC-1806
© 1996 Forest Stewardship Council

FSC

FSC is a non-profit international organisation established
to promote the responsible management of the world's forests.
Products carrying the FSC label are independently certified
to assure consumers that they come from forests that are managed
to meet the social, economic and ecological needs
of present and future generations.

Find out more about HarperCollins and the environment at
www.harpercollins.co.uk/green

for my mother, Sophie, always present

*For children are innocent and love justice, while most of us are
wicked and naturally prefer mercy.*

G. K. CHESTERTON

PART ONE

1

I want to be awful. I want to do awful things and why not? Dull is dull is dull is my life. Like now, it's night, not yet time for bed but too late to be outside, and the two of them reading reading reading with their eyes moving like the lights inside a copy machine. When I was helping put the dishes in the washer tonight, I broke a plate. I said sorry Ma it slipped. But it didn't slip, that's how I am sometimes, and I want to be worse.

I've hurt things, the boys showed me this. Pulling legs off spiders and such. Kevin Ryder next door and his friends, they let me come into their fort. But that was years ago, I was a child, it didn't matter if I was a boy or a girl. It would be against the law to go into their fort now I suppose. The law of my mother. Why don't you stay home? she says. Be careful out there, every time I walk out the door. But is it just words I wonder, how much does she really care? Who is she really thinking about when she thinks about me? I have my suspicions. And anyway, do the boys even have a fort anymore? It was probably all destroyed a long time ago. It was a fort in the woods made from sticks and blankets and leaves. Things like that don't last forever.

And besides, now I know things about my body I didn't know back then. It's not the innocence of yesteryear, that's for sure.

Awful is easy if you make it your one and only. I pinch Luke sometimes. Luke is our dog. You can't pinch all dogs, some will bite. But Luke is old and he's a musher, he's all about love love love and so he'd never bite you. I pet him for a few minutes all nice and cuddly and then all of a sudden I pinch him and he yelps and goes circling around the room looking for the mystery pincher. He doesn't even suspect me, that's how blind with love he is. But I suppose if you held a gun to my head—did I love him, didn't I love him?—I guess I would have to say I loved the stupid dog. He's been with us forever and he sleeps on my bed.

If you want to know, I was born in this house with this dog and those two, teachers of all things. A blue house. If you look at it from the outside, you'd swear it had a face, the way the windows are. Window eyes, a window nose, and a door for a mouth. Hi house, I say whenever I come home. I've said this for as long as I can remember. I have other things I say, better than this, but I don't tell anyone. I have secrets and I'm going to have more. Once I read a story about a girl who died, and when they opened her up they found a gold locket in her stomach, plus the feathers of a bird. Nobody could understand it. Well, that's me. That's my story, except what are they going to find in my stomach, who knows? It's definitely something to think about.

For a second as I watch them reading, I think Ma and Da have turned to stone. So where is the woman with snakes in her hair, I ask myself. Is it me? Then I see the books moving up and down a little and so I know Ma and Da are breathing thank god. Luke is a big puddle of fur on the carpet, off in dreamland. Out of nowhere he farts and one eye pops open. *Oh what's that?* he wonders. *Who's there?* Some guard dog, he can't tell the difference between a fart and a burglar. And he's too lazy to go investigate. As long as they don't steal the carpet from under him, what does he care. I can pretty much read his mind. Animal Psychic would be the perfect job for me. The only animals I'm not good at getting inside are birds. Birds are the lunatics of the animal world. Have you ever watched them? Oh my god, they're insane! Even when they sing I don't a hundred percent believe them.

I hate how quiet it is. One smelly dog fart and then nothing, you almost think you've gone deaf. A person in my position begins to think about things, death even. About death and time and why it is I'm afraid sometimes at night sitting and watching the two of them reading and almost not breathing but for the books moving up and down like something floating on top of the ocean. And is Ma drunk again is the other question, but who's asking. Shut up and mind your own business, I think. She's a free man in Paris. Which is a song Ma used to sing when there were songs in the house. Ancient history.

Oh, and infinity! That's in my head again. That will keep

you up all night, the thought of that. Have you tried to do it? Think of infinity? You can't. It's worse than the thoughts of birds. You say to yourself: okay, imagine that space ends, the universe ends, and at the very end there's a wall. But then you go: what's behind the wall? Even if it were solid it would be a solid wall going on forever, a solid wall into infinity. If I get stuck thinking on this, what I do is pull a few hairs from the top of my head. I pull them out one at a time. It doesn't hurt. You have to have the fingers of a surgeon, separating the hairs and making sure there's only one strand between your fingers before you pluck it. You have to concentrate pretty hard on the operation and so it stops you from thinking about other things. It calms you down.

He's reading a book about China and she's reading the selected prose of Ezra Pound, that's the long and the short of it. She's got her shoes off and he's got them on. Venus and Mars, if you ask me. And I'm the Earth, though they don't even know it.

When I get a little bunch of hairs what I usually do is flush some of them down the toilet and then the rest I keep in a jar. I know this is dangerous because if someone found the hair they could use it to make a doll of me and then I would be under their power forever. If they burned the doll I would die, I would disappear. Infinity.

"What are you doing?" Ma says. "Stop picking at yourself." She crosses her legs. "Don't you have something to read?"

Books again. I could scream. I mean, I like books just fine but I don't want to make a career out of it. "I'm just thinking," I tell her.

She says I'm making her nervous staring at her like that, why don't I go to bed.

Ma was beautiful once, before I knew her. She's got pictures to prove it. She was a beauty nonpareil, my Da says. Now she looks like she's been crying, but it's just the reading, and the writing too. Grading papers all the time and scribbling her notes. If she cries I don't know anything about it, I'm not the person to ask about that. If she wanted to cry I wouldn't hold it against her. She has plenty of reasons.

"What are you writing?" I said to her once. "The great novel," said she. I didn't know she was joking. For a long time I thought maybe she really was writing the great novel and I wondered what sort of part I had in it.

"Go upstairs," she says. "Your hair could use a wash, when was the last time you washed it?"

She likes to embarrass me in front of my father, who has managed to keep his beauty, who knows how. He doesn't care if I have dirty hair or not but still, you don't want to be pointed out as a grease-ball in front of someone like him. Impeccable is what he is, like a cat.

"I washed it yesterday," I say.

Ma turns to me and does that slitty thing with her eyes, which means you're a big fat liar, Mathilda.

"Good night Da," I say, running up the stairs.

"Good night," he says, "sweet dreams." This is his standard but it's still nice to hear it. At least it's something.

"And wash that hair" is the tail of Ma's voice following me up the stairs.

Ma is funny, she either says nothing or else she has to get in the last word. You never know which Ma to expect and I can't decide which one is worse. Lately it's mostly been the silent Ma. Tomorrow I'm going to break another plate. It's already planned.

———

In my room I look in the mirror. It's amazing how you have the same face every time. Or is it only a trick? Because of course you're changing, your face and everything. Every second that goes by you're someone else. It's unstoppable. The clock ticks, everything is normal, but there's a feeling of suspense in your stomach. *What will happen, who will you become?* Sometimes I wish time would speed up so that I could have the face of my future now.

After the mirror I line up a few papers and books on my desk so that they're even with the edge. I also make sure not one thing touches another thing and that everything is equal distance apart. It's only an approximation, I don't use a ruler or anything. I've been doing it for about a year now, the lining up of things. It's like plucking the hair. Basically it's magic against infinity.

When Da comes in my room I'm sitting on the bed. Maybe I've been here for an hour, who knows.

"I meant to take a shower," I say. "I forgot."

He sits next to me and he tries to look at me, except he's not so good at it anymore. His eyes go wobbly, almost like he's afraid of me. He used to pet my hair, but that was practically a million years ago, when I was a baby. Still, it's a nice moment, just the two of us sitting next to each other. But then all of a sudden she's there, sticking her head in the door.

"I know," I say, without her having to say anything. *I know, Ma.*

"Are you okay?" she says. But it's not even a real question. I wish it was but it's not.

Da gets up to go and he pats my dirty hair and I suppose I should be ashamed, but what do I care about anything anyway. That's part of being awful, not caring. And then what's part of it too is the thought that suddenly jumps into my head. The thought that it could be a person's own mother who might make a doll with her daughter's hair and throw it into a fire. She'd watch the flames eat it up and then she'd dance off to bed laughing and having sex and bleeding little drops of perfume all over the sheets as if there was nothing to it. I wouldn't put it past her.

But don't get me wrong. I love her. This is another one of my secrets.

The thing is, I *can't* love her, not in the real world. Because this would be degrading to me. To love someone who despises you, and she just might. You should see her eyes on me sometimes. Plus she's not even a mother anymore, she's just a planet with a face. Da at least has hands.

"Good night Ma," I say. "Good night Da." And they just leave me like that and they don't make two bones about it. Walk out, *whoosh*, and where do they go? All I know is I'm not tired and I'm not taking a lousy shower and I'm not reading a stupid book for school about the King and Queen of Spain. I'm just going to sit on this bed and if I want to pull a few hairs from my head I will, and no one can stop me.

Six hairs. Brown, but when I look close I can see it's almost red where it comes out of my head. Like the hair of another person. Like another person inside me, and she's just starting to squirm her way out like a sprout. This is not in the least bit frightening. I've actually been expecting her.

I know you can't see anything from where you are.

You just have to believe me.

2

School started again a week ago and I'm very happy to report that Anna McDougal, my best friend, is in my class. Overall it's an interesting mix of people this year. No one but Anna has any relevance to the story of my life, but a list is always a good thing. I'll give it to you with thumbnails.

Libby Harris has a disastrous mole on the tip of her nose. A shame really because she's very quiet and nice. Her father is a lawyer and so she'll probably have plastic surgery eventually.

Sal Verazzo is pretty much the fattest person in the school. Black hair, possibly shoe polish. Thinks he's a rock star. Completely deranged.

Sue Fleishman is tall and has curly hair. She doesn't walk, she sort of slides across the floor like she's wearing slippers. A stupid way to move but the boys drool over her.

Barbara Bradley always has snacks. She's allowed to eat them during class. Supposedly she has a disease.

Jack Delaney is an admirer of mine, but we've never spoken. He has a shirt with a rude monkey on it. Sex addict or will be.

Mimi Brockton is crippled! I'm always watching her, I can't get enough of her. Red hair. I know I'm not supposed to say crippled, but it's really the best word.

Donna Lavora has thrown up several times since she's come to this school. Will not do well in life.

Max Overmeyer looks like he lives in a shack. Doesn't smell right. Probably a victim of poverty.

Eyad Tayssir has perfect white teeth but you hardly ever see them. He's not a big smiler. Middle Eastern, I'm not sure exactly what country.

Mary Quintas supposedly has a great singing talent but I've heard better. She wants to be snob sisters with me but I'm not interested.

Lonnie Tyson still thinks he's going to be an astronaut. Good muscles.

Carol Benton is the worst. Conceited, big breasted, and loud. Unattractive but worshipped by men. Doesn't like me apparently.

Bruce Sellars is funny and I hear he knows magic. I've seen him speaking to Carol Benton unfortunately.

Chris Bibb, known as Dribble, came back to school with a tan. It doesn't make sense on him.

The lovely Anna McDougal of course. With whom I have an important but stormy relationship. More on this later.

Kelly Graber has bad teeth. I suspect she's unloved. Good at sports.

Lisa Mead eats liverwurst. Every day!

Lucas London is very pale but I don't think albino. When he talks his hands shake. He's like a lamb. He's so small you almost want to carry him.

Avi Gosh is the one person smarter than me. He has the eyes of a girl, but he's very confident. Rich. Sometimes wears sandals.

I'm probably forgetting a few people but if I am there's probably a reason. Some people are like ghosts, you can't capture them, or if you do it's nothing but a blur.

But really it's amazing to be around so many different kinds of people every day. Sometimes I watch them and it's like Animal Planet. Everyone's alive and hungry and sometimes Sal Verazzo is so crazy to tell a story that spit starts flying out of his mouth. And in the morning just before class begins, when everyone's talking at the same time, it's like a radio caught between stations. But not two stations, more like a hundred. You can't make heads or tails of what anyone's saying. It doesn't even sound like English, it sounds like bubbles coming up out of boiling mud. If I listen too long, it starts to bother me. It's probably what hell sounds like. I saw hell once in a movie, and it was pretty incomprehensible. I had to turn it off.

3

I have a sister who died. Did I tell you this already? I did but you don't remember, you didn't understand the code.

My sister's name was Helene. Helene and Mathilda. Everyone always said we were the opposite of each other. Night and Day was the famous expression. I'm the younger one, but it still feels backwards that Helene died first.

She died a year ago, but in my mind sometimes it's five minutes. In the morning sometimes it hasn't even happened yet. For a second I'm confused, but then it all comes back. It happens again.

She was sixteen at the end. Practically seventeen, just a few months to go. But sometimes, the way she dressed, you'd think she was even older. Plus she had an excellent way of moving. A person who didn't know her might think she was showing off, but the truth is she just had a natural sway to her. And then add to that her legs. They went from here to

Las Vegas, which is how Ma once described the length of them.

Some of the memories I have of Helene are from the beginning of my life, when I was a baby. Ma looks at me like I'm crazy when I tell her I remember the day Helene was carrying me, and then she started running and she climbed over a fence with me still in her arms.

"What fence?" my mother says.

"A white fence," I say.

When I say this my father puts his hand on my arm. "Stop," he says. Lately that's getting to be his favorite word.

I think about Helene a lot, but basically I'm not allowed to talk about her. To Ma and Da, I mean. Not that this is a rule. It's more like a law, I suppose.

The other memory I have is Helene and I are in a hole and it's dark and wet. Somehow we're upside down. I remember water getting in my mouth. Maybe we're in a well is my first thought.

"You never fell in a well," Ma says.

"What about a grave," I say, "or a ditch? People fall in holes all the time," I say.

Ma goes white like I'm the vampire of questions. My beautiful Da looks at me and I stop.

The thing is, Helene died from a train. That's the problem. She didn't jump, a man pushed her. We don't know who this man was and the police say, at this point, we probably never will.

I wasn't there when it happened. Neither were Ma and Da. Why she was at the train station is still a big question. A boyfriend is what I think. Helene had lots of them, sometimes even boys from other schools in other towns. She was pretty popular. She had red hair, it was the most amazing hair in the world.

It happened on a Wednesday, which is such an ordinary day. It happened in the middle of the afternoon. A man pushed Helene in front of a train, it's unbelievable. I always think it's a mistake. But then it proves to be correct.

Do you believe in curses? That there can be a curse on a person or on a bunch of people at the same time, like a family curse? How will we all die? I wonder. And when?

Helene was going to be a singer. She was a singer. There are recordings. Da made them on his old tape recorder. No one can listen to them now, they're the most dangerous thing in the world. On one of the tapes it's Da singing some stupid song with Helene. Both of them are laughing as much as singing. If you listened to it now, it would be Da singing with a ghost. The laughing would kill you.

Ma says the recordings are lost but I know where she keeps them. Plus, I have things hidden too. In my room, under my bed, I have some of Helene's school notebooks. I have letters and drawings and birthday cards. I also have some e-mails she printed out. And there's tons of stuff still left in her room. A person, even a sixteen-year-old, leaves a lot of stuff behind. For a long time I couldn't look at any of it, but then I realized there might be clues. I've started to spend more time in H's room, but only when I'm alone in the house. It's a better room than mine and I wouldn't mind living there. Ma would never allow it though. Sometimes I leave the door to H's room open, even though I know it irritates her.

I remember once, when I was little, I was looking out H's

window and I saw a hummingbird. Come quick, I said, but by the time Helene came over it was gone. Maybe it'll come back, she said, and we both stayed by the window for almost a minute, waiting. I guess we didn't have anything better to do. When I think of the two of us standing there, waiting for that stupid bird, it drives me crazy for some reason. I feel like screaming.

Why does a person push another person in front of a train? Does it have a meaning for the person, the pusher? The explanation of most people is madman. The voices of demons telling him to do it. But how did he get away is my question. It doesn't make sense. Two men at the train station said they tried to grab him but he slipped away. He just pushed her and then he took off. The police say it happens all the time.

In my mind it's almost as if the man disappeared after he did it. Like he had one job on Earth. To kill Helene. And after that there was nothing left for him to do but vanish.

I hate him. The feeling is tremendous. I've never felt anything like it. If we knew who the man was he'd be in jail. We could go to the jail and ask him questions. Ma and Da wouldn't but I would. I would be all over him. Even if it was the voices of demons I would pull the demons out of him and make them explain. I would use every bit of my magic.

Next Thursday it will be the day Helene died all over again. It'll be exactly one year. I marked it in my calendar like this: H.S.S.H. Which is Helene's initials the right way and then backwards. If you stare at the letters it's almost like someone telling you to be quiet. Ma and Da haven't said anything about the big day. I want H.S.S.H. to be a day we'll all remember. If Ma and Da think I'm going to ignore it, they've got another thing coming.

The thing is, Helene was supposed to live forever. That's just the kind of person she was. You always felt she had some secret power that was going to make her immortal. I wish I could describe to you the color of her hair but there's nothing to compare it to.

If the man was caught he'd probably be electrocuted. But electricity doesn't kill demons as far as I know.

People say the hair was like pennies, but it was better than that.

And she smelled like lemons. When I said this out loud once, Ma looked away, but Da said he had to agree. He whispered in my ear. He said I was right. He said it was lemons all the way.

4

I said to my friend Anna how I want to be awful and Anna said, "What about your soul?"

"What about it?" I said. "Why should I care about my soul?"

"If I even have one," I added, "and nobody knows for sure."

"It can't be proved," I said. It made me a little mad that Anna brought up the subject of souls, considering everything she knows about me.

"And if it is real," I said, "*where* is it?" Stuck up inside me like a baby all white and pudgy like a piece of dough? And what does it do anyway except stay inside you for your whole life and then it's not born until you're dead.

I said all this to Anna and she didn't have an answer. But it got her thinking. I could tell by the way her face (which for the record is quite beautiful) went ugly with wrinkles. It's hard for Anna to think, for her it's like climbing a mountain. She's in the remedial reading group, as well as slow math.

Finally, after a minute, Anna's face came back and she said, "But the baby is you, Mattie, your soul is you, there's no difference."

And then she said she didn't think it was at all like a piece of dough but more like a silk dress in the shape of your body, your head and your hands and your feet and everything.

"And see-through," she says. When she says things like this you realize what a child she is. Religion has a way of making people into idiots is what my father says.

"If it's see-through," I say, "does that mean I can see your titties?"

"No," Anna says, the total nun now. "The dress is on the inside," she says, "and so who could look through it, no one but god."

If Anna gets too smart I might have to stick pins in the head of a doll lumped up into the shape of her. If you added brains to Anna's beauty it would be unbearable.

And by the way, Anna doesn't even have titties. She basically has two anthills on her chest.

"Don't you want to live forever?" she says.

"Heaven and everything," she says. "A person like you has to believe in heaven, don't you Mattie?"

I had started up Anna's thinking engine and now she wouldn't shut up. Plus I didn't like where she was going with this conversation. Trying to get me to talk about private things.

Personally, I don't believe in god. I never had any lessons in him like Anna. She got a bunch of information from her family and from Sunday school. I have my own beliefs, self-invented. What I believe is that there are people watching us,

I don't know who they are, they didn't give me their names. The watchers I call them. They could be anyone. Who's to say if they're even human.

Anna kept talking but I just stopped listening and stared into the blue magic of her eyes. Anna has eyes, not everyone has them. Most people just have holes in their faces, it's just biological, like pigs or fish. Plain ordinary eyes that don't mean very much. Anna's eyes are from outer space, they're not animal and they're not human either. I could kiss Anna sometimes she's so beautiful. Blonde hair too. I only want beautiful friends, even though I'm not beautiful myself. My mother says I'm handsome. I look sort of like a baby horse. Striking is what I am.

I'm looking at Anna going on about her soul, but in my head was still that word. Awful. Awful Awful Awful Awful. Lufwa, if you write it backwards. I figure this out in my head and then I say, "Anna, shut up, listen. From now on," I say, "I want you to call me Lufwa."

Does she understand? Of course not.

"Why?" she says. "What does it mean?"

"Just do it," I say. "Okay?"

"But what does it mean?" she says again.

If only she could have figured it out, that would have been the perfection of the moment. In my fantasy, the light-bulb goes on in her head and her face just starts beaming from the miracle of understanding. Lufwa, she'd say, winking at me with her magic eyes. *Lufwa.*

And by the way I'm not a lesbo. I've been told I have an "artistic temperament" which means I have thoughts all over the place and not to be concerned, Mr. and Mrs. Savitch, who are my parents. The doctor who said this was old and looked like a tree and he's famous at the college where my parents teach and so they had to believe him. My parents have tried to become famous too, but they haven't gotten very far. They've written one book apiece (academic not creative), but neither book made much of a splash. Both of them meant to write a second book, but they never did. Apparently they had a lot of hopes and dreams back in the old days.

When my parents took me to see the Tree, I didn't say much. I kept what they call a low profile.

"Is she an only child?" the Tree asked.

Da said nothing and Ma said, "What about medication?"

The concern was over my tip-top magical thoughts. And because of the nightmares.

"It sounds French," Anna says.

"What does?" I say.

"That word," Anna says. "What you said to call you."

"It doesn't sound French," I say. "Don't be stupid."

Anna sulks when I say this.

"Well it doesn't sound English," she says.

"It's not English," I say. "There's more languages in the world than just French and English."

"What language is it then?" she asks.

I can't even answer her when she gets like this.

"It's probably not even a real language," she says.

"Probably not," I say. "You'll never know."

There is so little imagination in the world. A person like me is basically alone. If I want to live in the same world as other people I have to make a special effort.

I take Anna's hand. It confuses her because she thinks we're having an argument.

"What?" she says. She doesn't trust me.

"Nothing," I say. "Don't be afraid."

"I'm not afraid," she says.

"Good," I say. I'm looking at her dead in the eye.

"Just say it, okay?"

"Please," I say.

She closes her eyes. There is a pause a person could die in.

"Lufwa," she says.

When she says it I have to laugh.

"Oh my god," I say, "it does sound French."

Anna opens her eyes and smiles like someone's given her second prize.

"I told you," she says.

"Lufwa," I say. Suddenly I am the king of France. *"La fois,"* I say. *"La fois!"*

We are both laughing now and it's almost like being a child again. Anna is only eight months younger than me but sometimes she's like a magnet pulling me backwards. It is the glorious past of childhood and no one is ever going to die. It doesn't even matter that Anna is a little slow. And really she's not much slower than most people.

And besides, very few people have eyes from outer space, and it doesn't matter if these people are smart or not. Angels, I bet, are not smart. I bet angels are dumb. But it's not even relevant, the smartness of angels. The point of angels, as far as I understand, is something even greater than smartness. Supposedly it has more to do with brilliance. Which is light beyond anything we can understand. Like diamonds everywhere, in every bit of the air, and colors you wouldn't even have names for.

Anna stops laughing and wipes the tears from her cheeks. "I have to go home," she says.

It is the completely wrong thing to say.

Because we are standing in that place where two people could stand forever, staring into each other's eyes. And how often does that happen? And will it ever happen again?

5

At school today, first thing, I was told to go to Ms. Olivera's office. She's the principal of the penitentiary but you wouldn't know it from the way she dresses. Beads and bracelets and scarves in her hair. She really should be out on the street selling incense.

"Look at me," Ms. Olivera says.

I only look at the lips.

"How have you been doing lately?" the lips say.

Oh brother, I think, now we're going to have to go through the whole story of my life, when all she really wants to know is why I slapped Carol Benton in the face yesterday. Which I did without really meaning to do it. It actually surprised me when it turned out to be a real slap and not just the thought of a slap.

"Why are you so angry?" O says. Who does she think she is, the Tree?

"I'm not angry," I say. I wonder if she's recording me.

"You slapped someone, Mathilda. That's an act of anger," the lips say.

The truth is, Carol Benton is the kind of person who inspires violence. Just the bigness of her face. And more than once I've seen her whispering with her friends and then they look at me. What's the big secret? As if everyone doesn't already know.

"Mathilda," O says. "*Mathilda*. Are you listening to me?"

"I'm giving you a chance here," she says, and she reaches for my hand like a pervert. I pull away and pretend I have an itch.

"Is everything okay at home?" she says. The same old questions.

"How are your mother and father doing?"

"Is your mother doing a little better?"

"Fine," I say.

O looks at me with her X-ray eyes but I don't let her in. I don't know that I can trust her. I'd like to tell her how it's been almost one year, and how I still haven't seen my mother cry in the way mothers are supposed to cry after the death of a child. Ever since Helene died it's like Ma's joined the army. Is that normal? I'd like to ask.

"Can I use your bathroom please?" I say.

O nods and I get up and go through the door.

O has her own private bathroom. It's not as clean as it should be. There's a hair in the sink. I pick it up with a piece of toilet paper and put it in my pocket, just in case. On a little shelf there's some air freshener, plus a tin of mints and a candy bar. Who keeps food in the bathroom? Disgusting, if you ask me.

Interesting as well is a bathtub filled with potted plants. All leaves, no flowers. Jungly. I pretty much have to force myself not to make the sounds of monkeys and tropical birds.

I flush the toilet so as not to arouse suspicion. I open the medicine cabinet. Inside there's a hairbrush, lipstick, a bottle of pills, a toothbrush, and toothpaste. I take the pills, which are called Exhilla, and I put them in my pocket. According to the commercial, Exhilla helps you get through your day with a lot less worry. But the thing is, I remember last year, right after the explosion at the opera house in New York that killed a lot of bigwigs including a senator, Ms. O gave a special talk to the whole school and by the end of it she was crying into her scarves.

When I come out of the bathroom, O is smiling. As far as I can tell it's not a lie.

"I'm sorry," I say.

"I won't do it again," I say. And I ask her to please not tell my parents.

"You have to ignore people," Ms. Olivera says. "You can't let them get under your skin."

It's a sad smile. Like my father's.

"You're a smart girl," she says. She stands up and I'm afraid she's going to try and touch me again.

"Go to class," she says.

"Yes," I say, but I don't move. I don't move for about ten years. At least that's the feeling. Time is funny lately, nothing to do with clocks.

––––––––

After school Anna and I decide to go to Mool's for a soda and curly fries. Walking there Anna doesn't bring up Carol Ben-

ton, which is a big relief. Instead she asks me what I think of
the boys this year in our class.

"Not for me," I say.

"No one?" she says. Obviously she must have her own
eye on someone.

Anna and I haven't started with boys yet, not professionally anyway. But I have noticed that Anna is becoming a bit
of a flirt. She has this new thing she does with her hair, a kind
of a toss. It's pretty impressive actually. If there's one way
Anna's ahead of me it's in this department. Flirting isn't a
brain thing, it's an animal thing. But so is slapping people, I
guess. And so if I can slap people I should be able to flirt with
them. Probably I should give it some attention. I've learned
a few things from Helene's e-mails, most of which are from
boys. The language gets pretty explicit sometimes. I can't
believe she printed them out, considering the possibility of
Ma finding them. I'm adding bravery to the list of Helene's
virtues.

When you think about your body you barely know where
to begin. Even just the words for it. Your bum is your bottom
is your butt. Is your ass if you want to get crude about it.
There's a ton of expressions for everything down there. Your
vaj is your cooz is your crack. Or your cunt if you're really in
the mood or you're a slut or if someone's trying to insult
you. Boys have more words for theirs than girls, according to
my calculations. Penis and pole and peter and prick, but it's
not just Ps. You also have dong and cock and stormtrooper
and willy and sausage and you could go on and on if you had
all day. Breasts and tits and knockers and boobs and if you're
an old lady you have a bosom, which is hysterical. If I ever
say *bosom* to Anna she nearly pees her pants.

Once, a long time ago, I saw my father come out of the shower and he was naked. Ma was in the bathroom with him. I saw my Da's thing and it looked like a carrot pulled out of the ground with all its roots and hairs sticking to it. I thought of it inside my mother, like putting a carrot back into the ground, back into the dirt. A woman is a garden, they say. I used to think flowers but now I think vegetables.

"Lonnie's not bad," Anna says.

"The astronaut?" I say.

"He doesn't want to be an astronaut anymore," Anna says. "That was like three years ago." She grabs my arm and drags me into Mool's. Nobody's there but us and we take the booth in the corner, which is our favorite.

"What'll it be?" Mool says, even though he knows it's always curly fries and cokes. He comes over to us, practically dancing from the pleasure of our company. Mool is the happiest old person I've ever met. Old people are funny, they're either lizards or birds. Mool is a bird. When he drops the basket of fries into the oil, he goes *squawk squawk*, he can't help himself.

To tell you the truth, I wouldn't mind living at Mool's. I wonder if there's a Mrs. Mool hiding in the back. I've never seen her. Maybe she's the reason for his happiness. Maybe they have the kind of love that lasts forever. Did you ever read "The Gift of the Magi"? Picture that couple about fifty years down the road, that would be Mool and his wife.

"Do you want to sleep over this weekend?" Anna says. This is another one of Anna's skills. Mind reader.

Anna's house isn't as happy as Mool's restaurant but it's not unhappy, it has its charms. "Yes," I say, "I would love to." And suddenly I'm feeling so good that I think to tell Anna about H.S.S.H., but for some reason it won't come out of my mouth. Maybe I'll tell her tomorrow. Timing is everything, they say. I want Helene's anniversary to be a special day. Who knows, maybe I'll throw a surprise party for Ma and Da, just to wake them up. Ma and Da need a slap in the face even worse than Carol Benton.

Mool brings over the fries and suddenly I want to kiss him. I want to throw my arms around him and give him the smooch to end all smooches. I know it's out of character but the thing is, it's probably better to save my awfulness for the people who deserve it. It'll just get stronger and stronger like the venom inside snakes. You don't want to waste it on the wrong person.

6

When I got home from school, Ma was in the kitchen staring out the window. She had on her Chinese robe with the bridges and the dragons.

"What are you looking at?" I said.

There was a pecan ring on the table. Ma had already eaten a good chunk of it. Ma's always been skinny and I want her to stay that way. Fat wouldn't make sense on her, she doesn't have the bones for it. Plus fat people are liars, have you noticed that? They hide things.

"What are you doing?" I say. She was just standing there.

"Pecan ring," I say. "From Kroner's?"

"You want a piece?" she says.

I tell her no, even though I'd love a piece. Pecan rings from Kroner's are pretty amazing. My plan is to eat it later when she's passed out.

I sit at the table and wait to see what happens. It takes about two hours but then finally Ma comes over to me.

"Your hair's getting long," she says, and she touches it. The feeling is electricity, warm, and maybe it wouldn't have felt half bad if Ma's lousy hands weren't shaking. Plus the kitchen smells like cigarettes, which is her old habit back again.

I pick a nut off the ring, but I don't eat it. I examine it like a scientist until Ma moves away. Suddenly all I can hear is the humming of the refrigerator. It's like the sound track to infinity. I get up and whack the stupid thing. Ma flinches a little, it's almost funny.

"Your father and I are going to the theater next week," she says suddenly out of left field. The two of them never go out anymore, so it's a little suspicious.

"What day are you going?" I ask her.

"Wednesday," she says.

Which is the day before. The day before H.S.S.H.

"Is it a special occasion?" I say. Maybe Ma and Da have the day marked in their calendars as well, maybe I've underestimated them.

Ma makes a disgusted face and backhands an invisible fly. "Someone gave your father the tickets," she says.

I ask her if I can come but she says they only have two seats.

"Can't you buy another one?" I say.

"You wouldn't like the play," she says.

I ask what's the name of it and she tells me, *The Moons of Pluto.* She says it like it's the worst title in the world.

"I want to go," I say.

I bet Ma doesn't even remember that planets used to be one of my big obsessions. I used to have the whole solar system up on my ceiling. Glow-in-the-dark stars as well.

"I want to go," I say again, but Ma doesn't answer me. She probably wants me to beg, but I'm not in the mood. I'll do the begging routine later with Da.

"I'm sleeping over at Anna's this weekend," I say.

"You're not the only person with plans," I tell her.

Ma just nods. She's at the window again. I don't know what she's looking at. Is it trees she's interested in now?

The silence again, I'm telling you, you can't imagine it. All of a sudden I wish I hadn't punched the stupid refrigerator. It's the perfect moment for some refrigerator screaming.

Before I know what I'm doing I'm eating the pecan ring. I sort of make a pig of myself. I eat more than I mean to. Ma's still turned away from me, and when she breathes it makes the dragon on her back look like he's getting ready to shoot a big load of fire. I wish I knew what was inside her head. For some reason my ESP doesn't work when it comes to Ma. I keep counting the breaths of the dragon and when I hear Da's car, it's music to my ears.

Ma moves over to the stove, pretending to be normal. She stirs something in a pot. Dinner, I suppose, though she hasn't been too creative lately. Lately she's the one-pot wonder. Throw everything in and hope for the best.

The front door opens. Luke barks from somewhere in the house.

"We're in the kitchen," I say, careful not to shout. But then I can't help myself, I say it again and this time I shout. *"We're in the kitchen, Da."*

Just get him in here is my thought. Save me from the dragon.

———

Once or twice I've heard my mother and father having relations in their bedroom, but not in a while. Ma sounds like an owl and Da sounds like a sheep. When Helene and I were kids, we would catch them kissing in every part of the house. Da gave Ma the kind of kisses that linger, and afterwards she looked like someone who'd just had a bath. Recently Da has been trying to put his hands on her again but she's not too interested. He makes jokes and tries to touch her but he mostly misses. Ma's pretty fast when she wants to be.

Every night after dinner Da takes a walk with Luke. "Anybody coming?" he always says. My standard excuse is homework, and Ma is Ma. Other than work she hardly ever leaves the house. Lately she doesn't even answer him. But my Da can't help asking, he's always been the optimist in the family. He's definitely the one who could save the world, but will Ma let him is the question. Maybe she wants everything to come down in fire.

Tonight when Da asked if anyone was coming, I said yes. Ma looked at me like I was an impostor.

"What?" I say to her. "I used to walk Luke all the time when I was little." I wanted her to know that some people can do more than just sit around and smoke cigarettes. A person can wake up if she wants to.

"Get your coat then," Da said. He didn't seem terribly excited by my company. It struck me that maybe he goes somewhere private on his walks and now that I was coming he wouldn't be able to go there. Or maybe it was just his private thoughts I'd be interrupting.

We only walked around the neighborhood, it wasn't anything special. A few people waved at us and we waved back. Luke barked at some dogs. One house still had a BRING BACK OUR TROOPS sign on the lawn and I couldn't even remember if we still had troops over there. I guess we always have troops somewhere, due to the fact that it's an age of terror. And then the funny thing was, I completely blanked out as to where "over there" was. Helene would know, she was very political for a person her age. Ma and Da used to be political too, they were big marchers once upon a time. But I guess they're more selfish now. Death does that to people apparently.

When Da bent down to scoop up Luke's poo I noticed a tiny bald spot on the top of his head. I realized I wasn't exactly sure how old my Da was. I know he's not too old but a bald spot, even a tiny one, is definitely a sign of time passing. I tried to picture my Da bald but I had to stop because it was like a monster movie in my head.

Luke stopped to smell something and Da and I waited. We were like two strangers at a bus stop. Finally I kicked Luke, not hard, just a love tap. "Get a move on," I said.

"Be nice," Da said, and so I gave Luke a make-up smooch right on his nose, which made his butt wiggle. And then I wiggled my butt the same way and Da laughed. When a plane flew by overhead Luke barked. It was dark up there and the plane's lights were on. It's still something that scares me. I wouldn't mind if I never saw an airplane again my whole life. In our history book, there's a picture of the burning towers.

I was only a kid when it happened, but they don't let you forget stuff like that.

I wondered what Ma was doing, if she was already in bed, safe and sound. I could picture her under the covers, naked. And I could picture Da slipping in later like a mouse. Ma sleeps on the left and Da sleeps on the right, and on both sides of their bed there's a little cabinet. On top of each is a lamp for them to read by. And then there's the inside of the cabinet for their personal stuff. When you're married you can't hide things under your bed anymore because the bed is shared property.

In Da's cabinet there are books and also some photographs from a trip we all took to Concordia Farms to pick pumpkins. And every now and then there's a magazine of perversion in there, mostly about breasts. Pretty much the women are alone and when they touch themselves they look like they're in pain. Sometimes the women look right at you. Some of them look insane. In Ma's cabinet are cigarettes and notebooks and sometimes a bottle. I don't know why they don't put locks on their stupid cabinets to keep people from snooping.

When people came to see the display of Helene in her coffin, they didn't see Helene because the coffin was closed. Locked. I wonder who had the key. Apparently Ma and Da got to look at her before they closed it but I wasn't invited. Supposedly her body was pretty bad. I don't know if it was or it wasn't. Everyone went up to the stupid box as if Helene was inside. But I wasn't convinced. Death is a joke almost. You can't honestly believe it.

Ma wore red lipstick to the funeral because that's the only color she has. I sat next to her and she kept saying the same thing over and over again, but I couldn't make heads or tails of it. *Oh god oh god oh god* it could have been. But probably not, because she doesn't even believe in him. Capital Him.

It's funny, it didn't even rain the day of the funeral. Nothing was right about it. Da's brother made a speech but he barely knew his lines, he kept looking at a piece of paper. I'm telling you, the whole day was completely unbelievable. I know what funerals look like from movies, and Helene's was a total sham. If it rains on H.S.S.H. I'll be happy.

Well, not happy exactly. I'll just have the feeling someone's been listening. One of the watchers maybe. Rain is the least they could give me. I'm not asking for a miracle, just a little lightning, a few cracks of thunder. Is that too much to ask?

7

This morning, after breakfast, I went outside to smoke a cigarette. It was from my mother's stash, which she keeps in various hiding places around the house. Ma doesn't smoke anymore, that's the story we're supposed to believe. The lie of the universe, one of many. Ma doesn't drink either, if you want to have the whole blanket over your head.

The cigarette is extra long. I decide not to light it, Ma will smell it. It's just as good to hold it in your hand. I haven't actually smoked a cigarette yet but I'm going to at some point, and how you hold it is significant. My way, I've decided, will be to hold it between my forefinger and my thumb, like a man. When you hold it like this you have a kind of power.

The family next door, the Ryders, are having a new swimming pool put in. I don't know what was wrong with the old one. There's a bulldozer going, the noise is amazing. When the sun comes through the dust, it's weird, like poison gas.

On a hill above the pool is a white gazebo. It belongs to the Ryders but they let me have a birthday party there once. When I was ten. I wore a blue dress with yellow ribbons on it. The gazebo doesn't have any walls, just columns and a roof, and with the dust from the bulldozer blowing through it, it's like a postcard from Ancient Greece. I hope they're not going to knock that down too.

Kevin Ryder is by his back door watching the destruction. I go over toward the fence to make him notice me, but he doesn't. Kevin's brother was one of Helene's lovers, by the way. They used to make out in the gazebo.

"Kevin!" I practically have to shout to get his attention.

We both move a little closer to the fence.

"Do you have a light?" I ask him.

He puts his hand up to his ear. *I can't hear you.*

I tap the cigarette against my mouth to make him understand.

Kevin looks confused. He shakes his head. He's wearing a big silver chain around his neck and his hair is blue. It's a completely different person from when he was little. He also has black fingernails. But his face is still the face of a baby, even though he's probably thirteen already. I wonder what his mother thinks of his hair. She probably fainted when she saw it. God, I'd love to make Ma faint. Just once, just to teach her a lesson. But the truth is people don't faint as much as they used to. In the old days people fainted all the time.

Suddenly the bulldozer stops, it's like a waterfall of silence. Kevin and I stand under the roar of it.

"You smoke?" he says. "You're allowed to smoke?"

"Oh yeah," I say, "just not in the house."

Kevin nods his head, maybe he's underestimated me.

"What did you do to your hair?" I say.

"I'm not gonna keep it," he says.

I tell him I like it.

"I don't know," he says. He turns away from me and looks at the destruction again. He starts to play with the chain around his neck.

"I have to get going," he says.

I ask him does he want to go up and hang out in the gazebo. I fake puff on my cigarette. He just stares at me.

"Come on," I say, "like the old days."

"I can't," he says, "I have homework."

Homework? I think. A boy with blue hair should not have to do homework.

"How's your brother?" I say.

Kevin nods his head and then looks at his boots. I wonder is he afraid of me. A lot of people are funny around us, Ma and Da and me. They don't want to get too close to the curse of the Savitches.

I have a letter from Kevin's brother under my bed, an e-mail he sent to my sister.

"Does he have a new girlfriend?" I say.

"You shouldn't smoke," Kevin says.

I fake puff on the cigarette and blow the invisible smoke in Kevin's face.

"See you Mathilda," he says, and then he walks away like a cowboy.

I want to fuck you, is one of the things in the letter.

Also, *I am in love with you*.

Isn't language amazing? I can't get over it. Sometimes you can just say things and it's like a bomb that blows all your clothes off and suddenly there you are naked. I don't know if it's disgusting or beautiful.

The bulldozer comes back to life and when I look up at it I see there's a man inside. I didn't even notice him before. He's in a little cage, like a rat or an astronaut. When I look at him he winks at me.

I turn away but I can feel his eyes still on me. Probably because I'm wearing a skirt. I throw the cigarette on the ground and crush it with my foot. I swoosh my foot back and forth three times. It's the classic way to put out cigarettes. Watch people if you don't believe me.

———

A lot of Helene's boyfriends looked the same. They had dark hair. They were skinny but they had shoulders. Mostly tall, pale skin. They never carried books. They swaggered. You would have to say they were good-looking.

Helene wasn't a saint. Have I given you that impression? She definitely had a body. It's weird to think a dead person is the same person who once had a lot of desire. It's weird because you don't want to think too much about the bodies of dead people.

The last few months before the train she was always back from school later than usual and at night she pretty much always came home past her curfew. She had ways of sneaking in and out. She was clever. She knew how to get into bars just from wearing the right shirt and from the way she moved. The funny thing is, she still got all her homework done and passed every test at school. I think that's why Ma and Da couldn't say much about what she did at night, they couldn't really prove it was hurting her. Besides, no one could ever say no to Helene. Imagine the beauty of Anna and add to that a brain.

Sexy and brainy, that's the best combination. That was Helene for sure, and I bet Ma was like that once too. The librarian who takes off her glasses and lets down her hair. She wears a white blouse buttoned to the neck but suddenly she undoes it a little and it's devastating. You see her in a whole new light as she makes herself comfortable on the bed. Even her voice goes deeper.

Ma and Da used to be great sleepers and so it was always me who woke up if there was a creak when Helene snuck out. One night around three in the morning she climbed into my bed. When I clicked on the lamp, I saw she was still in her dress and her face looked blurry like someone had tried to erase it. And her mouth was like the mouth of a little kid when they eat too much jelly. I asked her what was the matter and she said, nothing, go back to sleep. I kept looking at her though because I was pretty sure she wanted to tell me something. She kept staring right back at me and finally she sort of smiled and said, *salagadoola mechika boola, bibbidi-bobbidi-boo*, which is the magic song from *Cinderella*. The lyrics don't make a whole lot of sense but for a long time it was my favorite song in the world. Helene was hugging me so tight that I didn't think I'd be able to fall back asleep, but I did. I think the words of that song do something to you, especially late at night when you're in bed with your sister and suddenly she loves you. Which wasn't always the case.

Sometimes Helene seemed mad at all of us and we hadn't even done anything. Other times it was fits of crying. She was very emotional. Her and Ma used to get into some big fights. For some reason Ma didn't like it when Helene fell in love, which she did quite often. I guess Ma didn't want Helene running off and ruining her life. "I'm not you," Helene yelled at her once, and Ma yelled right back, "Yes you are!" The fighting used to scare me, but when I think of it now I'd give them both Academy Awards. In my mind the fights are like a beautiful movie I wish I could watch again. Sometimes Helene would end up crying in Ma's arms. And every once in a while I'd catch them on the couch downstairs, whispering to each other and laughing. Half the time they'd go mute when I walked into the room. It used to drive me crazy. What did they think I was, a spy trying to get at their secrets? "Come here," Ma would say, "sit with us," and of course I would, but it always felt like a test. I used to try to come up with something really funny just to impress them.

When I have a fit now, Ma just walks away. She won't fight back like she did with Helene. Sometimes my fits are real, sometimes I make them up, but I don't think Ma can tell the difference. The nightmares were real, the first few months, but it was always Da that came into my room. I still have bad dreams every once in a while, but my parents don't know because I don't cry out for them anymore. The Tree taught me how to breathe when I wake up from a bad dream, and how to train my thoughts. When you learn things like this, you can pretty much get along by yourself. You don't need other people waiting on you hand and foot.

I spend a lot of time in H's room. Sometimes I picture myself sleeping in there and Ma comes to the door and sees me under the covers and for a second she doesn't know it's me. She thinks it's you-know-who. If that ever really happened, I wouldn't say boo or anything, I wouldn't want to give her a heart attack. I'd just lie there and keep the covers over my head and let Ma sort it out for herself.

A few weeks after Helene died, there was a night Ma and Da and I were having dinner and the phone rang. Except it didn't come from the kitchen, it came from upstairs. It was the phone in Helene's bedroom. Her princess line, as Ma called it. It rang like twenty times but nobody moved. The next day Ma had it disconnected. Did you ever see the movie where that grown woman goes back in time to the house she grew up in and the telephone rings and it's the woman's grandmother calling? And the two of them talk about nothing special but you can see the woman is crying because in the future where she came from the grandmother is dead. Movies can do stuff like that, that's why they're so important. Movies don't have a problem with time and space. They're not as restrictive as real life.

Even H's cell phone is dead because it was crushed by the train. Apparently it was given to Ma and Da in a plastic bag. At least I have the love letters, if you can call them that. Based on my calculations there were about ten boys Helene was involved with. Not all at the same time of course, but in the last few years. Most of them I can picture because they've been to the house. But the most interesting one is a boy I've never seen, the boy of the last six months. He writes in full sentences and they're good sentences too in my opinion. Louis is his name. LDM@blueforest.com. I'm almost a little in love with him and I don't even know who he is. I can't find a single Louis in H's yearbooks so he's probably from another school. He's a bit of a sad sack in his messages, but he also has a sense of humor. I'm really quite fond of him.

I keep thinking to write him from my own e-mail but I've

never done it. The funny thing is, H's e-mail is still alive. Ma and Da set up Helene and me on the same account. When I sign on I always see H's screen name right above mine, but I can't get her mail because I don't know the password. I've tried about a million words. I haven't given up, though. I still make lists of words in my spare time.

Helene's screen name is HeyGirl. I'm MattieSays. We're both at mindfield.com. If you ever want to find us, that's probably the best way to do it.

8

Anna and I are sitting in her living room. The TV is on but we're barely watching it. Anna's trying to get a splinter out of her finger and I'm making a tattoo of a snake on her ankle with a blue ballpoint.

"Don't press so hard," she says.

Helene used to draw tattoos on me. One time she made a masterpiece of red lips on the side of my shoulder. For a while I was really crazy about tattoos and I made Helene do a new one on me every week. Mostly we did it in secret because Ma worried about blood poisoning. But once, in the summertime, I was sunbathing on the lawn and she drew a giant flower right on my stomach, with the petals coming straight out of my belly button. When she was finished she sealed it with a kiss. "You're a rock star," she said, and I pretty much believed her.

The snake I'm doing on Anna is coming out pretty crappy and I consider turning it into an octopus. On television a man is having a conversation with a deaf boy. The boy is doing signs with his hands and grunting. Anna sighs and changes the channel with the clicker. She goes past a hundred things until she gets to the plastic surgery. At first I don't even know what it is, for a second I think it's a cooking show.

"Look," Anna says, but I'm already looking. A doctor is pulling a loose piece of someone's face, you can't even tell if it's a man or a woman.

"Gross," Anna says, but she doesn't change the channel. "Oh my god," she says. An assistant to the surgeon is sucking up blood with a tube. I get a funny feeling in my stomach. I used to be able to watch gross-outs but lately it's not so appealing.

"I'm going upstairs," I say.

Anna doesn't move, she can't take her eyes off the stupid television.

I really can't stand it when other people have control over the clicker. No one ever watches what you want to watch. And then they always shut the TV off at the wrong moment. When I'm watching TV by myself my rule is to shut it off only after something good has happened, or when the last words you hear are not going to hurt you. You don't want to shut it off in the middle of two people having an argument or someone saying *pig* or *death* or *my car broke down*. You want to make sure the last words are something like *that would be great* or *world of your dreams* or *magically delicious*.

When you go up the stairs in Anna's house, you pass all these pictures of gardens painted by Anna's mother. The flowers are good but the people are just blobs in the distance, they don't even have faces. The blobs are standing under trees or sitting down to blobby picnics. Why even paint people if you're not going to give them some character?

Anna's bedroom is the perfect room of a girl, pink and white and fluffy. Everything is in its place. It's easy to imagine people visiting this room in a hundred years. It would be like a museum. THE BEDROOM OF A GIRL would be the exhibit. This would be in the future when people sleep in pods and live forever. But I bet the room would still make them jealous. A huge bumblebee is knocking on the window. I kick off my shoes and sprawl on the bed.

"What are you doing up there?" Anna shouts. "Are you coming down?"

"No," I say, "you come up here."

I arrange myself on the bed like pornography but when Anna sees me she doesn't get it.

"Why are you lying like that?" she says.

"I don't know," I say, and I close my legs.

The bumblebee is still doing a number on the window, bonking its head. You have to feel sorry for animals like that, you really do.

Anna comes and sits next to me on the bed. She tilts her head like a doll. Suddenly she's my nurse. She pushes the hair out of my face. Around us on the bed are pillows shaped like hearts. It really is another world.

———

You're probably wondering how a person like me could have a friend like Anna. Why am I not surrounded by other brains?

Why would Anna choose me is your question. But it's not even the right question.

Beauty is not the boss. The mind is. The truth is, I chose Anna.

The beginning of Anna and me is historical. The place is the pool club at Randolph Park. The time is only five months ago.

I was sitting on a chaise longue, reading a novel. *The Straw Hotel.* It wasn't on the summer reading list, I found it at a garage sale. The story concerns a woman with amnesia who might also be a killer, I won't say in case you ever want to read it. Highly recommended.

Anyway, Anna was in the pool. She had on a yellow bathing suit. She was treading water and talking to another girl. I think it was Cheryl List but the other girl isn't important. The two of them are whispering and laughing. Their hair is perfectly dry.

Standing at the side of the pool there's a group of boys, also whispering. There's a lot of intrigue at the pool club if you're into that sort of thing.

This was the first time I noticed Anna's eyes. They were like something you wanted to steal.

Suddenly one of the boys, Michael "Bigtooth" Flatmore, jumps in the water. His jump splashes Anna and so she splashes him back. Then Michael moves toward Anna and he dunks her. He lets her up for air and then he dunks her again. He has complete control over her, it's disgusting. For sure, Michael is in love with Anna but all he can think to do is push her underwater. That's how boys are. Probably he's sexually frustrated.

Anna is gulping for air. Cheryl List doesn't even help. When I jump in the water, Michael Flatmore turns and I pull him away from Anna. I call him a fucking idiot, even though that's not an expression in my vocabulary. It just comes out of me. By accident I scratch his face. Anna is coughing and I lead her over to the edge. I was suddenly madder than I'd ever been in my whole life.

"Fucking idiot," I scream back to Michael. The fat lifeguard finally wakes up and blows his silver whistle. "Keep it down," he says.

I help Anna out of the pool. I ask if she's okay, and she nods. But I can tell she's suspicious of me. Why am I helping her? She can't figure it out.

Michael Flatmore is out of the pool now. He walks past us. He's completely humiliated. There's even a little bit of blood on his face.

Anna and I stand there dripping for a long time.

"Do you want to get something to eat?" she finally says. "At the snack bar?"

In *The Straw Hotel*, Beatrice, the woman with amnesia, will only eat fruit.

"Let's have smoothies," I say.

"I'll be right back," Anna says. She goes into the bathroom and I wonder if she's really going to come back out again. I can see Cheryl List on the other side of the pool talking to Michael Flatmore. Unbelievable. I'm still dripping and it almost looks like I'm peeing. Suddenly I think maybe someone is playing a trick on me. I start to feel sick. This still wasn't the best time for me, as you can imagine.

But Anna did come out of the bathroom. Her wet hair was parted and combed. She even smiled at me. When I think of that day it was like Anna just *appeared*. Someone had to, and it was her.

————

When I sleep at Anna's I always sleep in her bed. It's huge. The sheets smell like milk. Hours after the bumblebee that's where we were again, talking with the lights out. I noticed there was a lot of moonlight coming in the window, there was a nice patch of it on the carpet. We were talking about fall projects at school but neither of us were coming up with any brilliant ideas. I suggested we take off our clothes and lie in the moonlight.

"For fall projects?" Anna said. She gets confused if you change the subject too quickly.

"No," I said, "just for tonight."

"Why?" she said.

But I didn't really have a reason.

"I'm not stripping," she said. But she laughed.

"Nymphs do it," I said.

"Do what?" she said.

"Bathe in the moonlight," I said.

Anna's eyes were glowing in the dark. "I don't even know what nymphs are," she said.

I told her that nymphs were beautiful young girls that live in the woods. "Spirits," I said.

She said she didn't want to be a ghost and I told her they weren't ghosts exactly. I mentioned how they were related to the Greek gods.

"Are they immortal?" she said. Boy, did she know how to irritate me.

"Sometimes," I said, "not always."

51

"Most of them live for a long time," I explained, "unless they have an argument with one of the gods. And they never lose their beauty or grow old," I told her.

I also said that a woman's breasts were born to live in the moonlight. I was really hamming it up until I had Anna blushing and laughing. I knew she wanted to do it.

"Just for a minute," she said.

So we did it. We took off our tops and settled down on the floor, on our backs. We made ourselves cozy in the little box of moonlight.

"I don't think the door's locked," Anna said. She started to get up but I grabbed her hand.

"Don't worry," I said, "no one can get in. And if they do," I said, "they'll be punished for looking at us."

"Only the animals can look at us," I said. And in fact Anna's cat was doing just that. Staring at us from the bed.

The moonlight was coming in the window and it was almost like something definite. It wasn't just empty air, it had fingers, it attached itself to our bodies. I noticed how Anna's skin was a lot whiter than mine but I tried not to look because I didn't want to make her nervous.

I told her how one day it wasn't going to be just moonlight all over us.

"I know," she said. "I think about it sometimes."

"I think about it almost as if they were already on top of me," she said.

Once I tried to get Luke to lie on my stomach to see what it would feel like. I don't mean sex. I wasn't naked or anything. I just wanted to understand the weight of another person. But it didn't work. Luke just put his head on my stomach and then I petted him until we fell asleep.

"It's going to hurt," Anna said.

"Probably," I said.

All of a sudden we burst out laughing. Then it was quiet for a while, except for my heart which was going about a mile a minute.

"What do you think of Kevin Ryder?" I said.

"Guukh," Anna said. "Horrible."

"Why?" I said.

She looked at me like I was off my rocker. "The clothes," she said. *"The hair."*

"Who does he think he is?" she said. "The devil?"

"He's pretty nice," I said.

Anna just shrugged and yawned. She was getting pretty comfortable on the floor, and so I peeked at her belly again. Boy, I couldn't get over the whiteness of it. It looked like it was dusted with powder. It really did.

The heat was blasting in the house but I could feel the chill of moonlight on my skin like the invisible fingers of aliens. Plus other things, also invisible, passed between Anna's body and mine. I bet I could have become pregnant with something that came off of her, some of that white powder. The alien fingers were moving it back and forth between us like bees.

If I could only put the white belly and the blue hair together, I'd have the most beautiful monster in the world.

Suddenly I noticed Anna was crying. It wasn't sobbing, it was just quiet lines down her face. I looked at her and she looked at me.

This is happening, I think. Anna is crying. For some reason it made me happy.

"I don't know," Anna says to herself.

"I'm bleeding," she says.

I don't understand, and then she touches her stomach. "It started this morning."

I ask her if it's her first time and she says, "yes."

She wipes her eyes.

"Maybe we should do some homework," she says. "I don't feel like sleeping yet."

She stands up and puts her shirt back on. She gets her books and brings them to the moonlight. It's the same world we've been living in, but different now. Everything starts to glow. The cat sees it. He sees the miracle. He comes over and rubs himself against Anna's leg. Anna opens a book and inside is a picture of a bird, as well as the bones of a bird.

Awful, I say to myself. *Lufwa*.

Anna puts the book between us and we begin to do our homework inside the miracle. We're in no rush. We have all the time in the world. We're like the secretaries of god.

The first time I bled I thought I was going to die. I also cried.

When I first found out about Helene I didn't cry right away. I was too busy noticing how many people were screaming in outer space and wondering why I had never heard them before.

There are a lot of worlds we don't even know about.

In the moonlight I remember thinking: Anna bleeds today. In four days H.S.S.H.

9

Today I tried all the planets. Plus I tried about a hundred new Spanish words because it's a language she studied in school. There's still a Spanish dictionary in her room. And the planets probably popped into my mind because of the play. *The Moons of Pluto*. Tonight's the big night, my big date with Ma and Da. Yesterday I had a terrific fit, with tears and everything, and Da called to get an extra ticket.

But as for the planets and the Spanish, nothing worked. Incorrect password, it said every time. After a while I started to feel like a criminal. Finally I moved on to the Bhagavad Gita for some inspiration. Do you know that book? I remember the day Helene bought it. We were coming out of Greenways Market with Ma, and a lady in colored sheets came up to us in the parking lot. I guess she was some sort of religious book dealer. Ma said no thank you but Helene wanted to take a look. Helene was pretty generous when it came to people in parking lots. Plus the book only cost five dollars and it had full-color illustrations. So I tried Krishna, Sanjaya, Arjuna, plus a bunch of other interesting names. Incorrect password, down the line.

Have you ever seen a picture of Krishna? He has blue skin and he was actually born that way, it's not a dye-job. Sometimes he has two arms, sometimes four. He wears a gold crown with a peacock feather at the top. He's fairly attractive, in a foreign sort of way. In the introduction to the Bhagavad Gita there's a whole history of his life. When he was young he hung out with the cows and the milkmaids and he was quite the prankster. Once he stole a bunch of cheese and stuffed it in his cheeks, but when his mother pried open his mouth she didn't see the cheese, she saw the whole universe. She nearly pooped her pants. That's not a verbatim quote, the poop part. I just thought to modernize it for you a little bit, give it a little more pep. I bet I could be an excellent translator if I wanted. The job is basically pretending you're a foreigner, but in your own language.

When Da saw me later with the book, he asked me what I was doing with it. I told him I was just looking at the pictures. Da's not too keen on religious books. Plus it probably reminds him of you-know-who. The day she bought it she had it with her at the dinner table and she read all of us a passage. I was able to find the sentence because it's one she underlined. *When Arjuna saw many of his friends and relatives in the opposing army, he became overwhelmed, confused, and filled with compassion.* The scraggly pencil line under the sentence is so pale it makes you want to cry. I've been carrying the little book around the house for hours, like it's an expensive purse that goes perfectly with my outfit. Ma hasn't noticed yet, or if she has she's biting her lip.

I don't know what I want exactly.

I guess in some ways I'd like to see her. A lot of people have seen the dead, it's pretty well documented. One of the main ways they come back is in dreams. For some reason people used to see them a lot more in the old days. Supposedly poor people see them more than rich people. And old people more than young. Dogs supposedly see them all the time. I read a whole bunch of information on the Internet.

Sometimes when you see dead people they'll want to give you something, but if it's a piece of food you're not supposed to eat it. Even if they try to give you money, don't take it is the general rule. Because stuff from the land of the dead can be poison or it can bring you bad luck. You might suddenly be sucked into another world and you'd never be able to come back. If Helene wanted to give me an apple or a dollar bill, I would definitely take it. I wouldn't hesitate.

But I've never seen Helene. She hasn't come in a dream, not once, not in the right way, in one piece. She hasn't ever stood under a tree in the backyard or under a streetlight at night. She hasn't appeared in the house, floating down the hallway and tempting me to follow her. The only person who ever comes in a dream is the man who pushed her, but he doesn't even have a face. Sometimes it's just dreams of trains.

One of the things I wonder is: Do the dead want us to be dead too, or do they want us to be alive? Sometimes I wonder if Helene is jealous of me. Is she mad at me, does she wish we could swap places? And then I wonder does she even have a mind to think of me at all. Is there anything left of her out there? I'm glad I have the letters and the e-mails and the drawings. But the password is the most important thing, it's like a locked door and behind it might be ghosts. Maybe it's just old-fashioned ghosts that try to give you apples. Modern ghosts probably have new ways of doing things. They wouldn't be against getting through to you electronically.

I also think Helene could be playing with me. The last year she was alive she ignored me all the time, so it could be the same game she's up to now. But after a person is dead they should be different. After a person is dead they should be full of love and compassion. They shouldn't be so cold.

Like for instance, Helene never let me wear her clothes. She had some pretty nice things. Tomorrow, I've decided, I'm going to wear one of her dresses. It's part of my plan. The dress probably won't fit perfectly but it doesn't matter. I could almost *be* Helene if I wanted to. It might take a bit of work but so what. It's an interesting idea. What would Ma think of that, if Helene suddenly showed up in the living room?

Tomorrow is the big day. One year exactly.

It's funny, in a few years I'll actually be older than Helene. Unless the dead grow old too. I don't know how that works exactly. I remember a long time ago Ma used to have an ATM card with a secret code. Sometimes she let Helene and me punch in the numbers when we were at the grocery store or the bank. Ma made us promise not to ever tell anyone the magic numbers. And she told us a clever way to remember them. When Helene is twenty-six, she said, I'll be forty-six.

2646

I wonder if Ma still has the card. If she does, she needs to change the code.

1646, for example. Ma could really put whatever age she wanted on her side and she'd never have to worry about doing the math for Helene. Even if the dead grow old in outer space, on Earth they stop where they stopped. Period, end of story. On Earth she'll always be sixteen.

————

Dear Helene,
Sunday would be good for me, after 4. I have something for
you, you'll laugh when you see it. Working on a new song,
I could use your help, it's a fucking mess ahhhhhh. Let me
know about Sunday.
Love, Louis

Helene had some ingenious hiding places for her letters and e-mails. I only found the ones from Louis a few months ago. Most of them were folded up and shoved inside a secret zipper compartment in the belly of a stuffed bear. I think I'm the only person who's ever seen them. Not even the police noticed them when they came to the house and rudely went through H's room like she was the criminal.

I keep the letters in the basement now, which is basically no-man's land since Helene died. Ma and Da never go down there. It's where Helene used to practice her singing when she didn't want to be disturbed. Sometimes, if she was singing loud and you were in the kitchen, you could hear her voice come right up through the floor.

And I guess she sang with Louis. Which sort of breaks your heart if you think about it too much. Which I don't!

———

I've been trying to call Anna for about an hour but there's no answer. I wanted her opinion on what to wear to the play tonight. In the end I just called Kevin Ryder because I had to call someone. My heart was racing for some reason. Reading the love letters always puts me in a funny mood.

Kevin and I didn't have much to say to each other. I asked him if he still had his hair.

"What do you mean?" he said.

"The blue," I said.

"Yes," he said, "it's permanent," and I asked him if his mother fainted.

"Practically," he said.

We both laughed a little, which was nice.

"I've been thinking of changing my hair too," I say.

"Maybe a different color," I tell him.

I ask him can he recommend a good hair colorer.

"You can do it yourself," he informs me.

I ask if maybe he can show me sometime, and he says, "sure."

"It's chemicals," he says.

"I'm not afraid of chemicals," I say.

"Don't go blue," he says.

"No," I say, "I wouldn't."

"That's your color," I tell him.

Sometimes I know just what to say to people.

"Blue wouldn't look good on me anyway," I say.

"You could go black," he says.

Black. Just the word gives me a heart attack.

"I'll have to think about it," I say.

And then that's pretty much the end of the conversation. "I have to go," I say.

I don't tell him I'm going to the theater with my parents. I don't want to give him the wrong impression. Like I'm some kind of baby afraid to be alone in the house.

I want him to think of me as the girl with black hair, even though that's not exactly the color I was thinking of. Red is more like it. But if I did red, I'd probably get struck by lightning. The watchers might not be too pleased. Or, who knows, maybe they'd be ecstatic. One thing I can tell you is they would definitely notice it, that's for sure. *Look at her, little miss redhead, we better keep our eye on that one.* I can practically hear them already.

10

The play had absolutely nothing to do with space, nothing to do with planets. It was all about Joe and Judy Moon and their mentally retarded daughter who live—guess where? Pluto, Missouri. Which is not even a real place.

The play was definitely not my cup of tea. You believed everything but it was boring. You kept hoping the mentally retarded girl could secretly fly or read people's minds, but this wasn't the case. She was just retarded, and she hardly had any lines. What a role for an actor, it was mostly about drooling.

Ma wore a black dress with silver flowers on it. I forgot what a wonder she can be when she tries. She put her hair up and let a few snakes of it fall down the back of her neck. Da wore a black suit that made him look like a millionaire. It could have been the two of them before I existed.

I just wore jeans and a sweater. I'm saving the fashion fireworks for tomorrow. I've already chosen Helene's dress. My dress. Hopefully I'll be feeling better by then. My stomach's still a little funny from everything that happened at that stupid play. My head's not too great either. What a night, I'm telling you. Odious. Odious with cherries on top.

Our seats were good but at a bad play good seats are the last thing you want. It's like death row. Da sat on the aisle and Ma sat next to him and then me. At one point Da took Ma's hand. It was the sad part of the play when Judy Moon is talking about her life before Joe, when she was a professional ice skater. The signs outside the theater said "funny and touching," but I didn't laugh once. Da laughed exactly three times but only through his nose.

What was interesting was thinking about how these people were not really Joe and Judy Moon. They weren't married in real life because in real life they were actors. In real life his name was William Miller and her name was Cynthia Callis. I kept feeling sorry for them except I didn't know who I was feeling sorry for, Joe and Judy or William and Cynthia.

At intermission Ma ran into the bathroom. Da and I waited in the lobby. He had a glass of wine and I had a juice and a cookie.

"What do you think?" Da said.

"I thought it was supposed to be funny," I said.

"It's a different kind of funny," Da said.

"What kind?" I asked him. But he didn't answer me. He sipped his wine and looked up at the paintings on the ceiling.

"How about that?" he said. He sort of got lost up there.

Lately I've noticed Da is starting to disappear. He's basically following Ma, but where is she even going?

"How's your cookie?" he said.

"Awful," I said.

I glanced around at the snazzy crowd in the lobby and I thought about the people who died at the opera last year. Drinking wine and eating cookies just like us. Da kept looking toward the bathroom. He looked nervous.

"She's been in there a long time, huh?" He said it like maybe he wanted help.

I asked him did he want me to go get her. And just then the lights went on and off a few times, which means get back to your seat.

"You go and sit down," Da said.

I just stood there. For some reason I felt like the three of us should stick together.

"Go on," Da said. "That way you can tell us what happened if we miss anything. You know where our seats are, right?"

I nodded and then I just left him standing there with the glass of wine glowing in his hand. I didn't look back. I'm superstitious about looking back at someone when you're walking away from them, on account of that story about the musician who messes everything up when he's walking out of the underworld. He gets the chance of a lifetime, but he's twitchy and he blows it.

In the theater the curtain was closed but you could feel people breathing behind it. When I got to my seat the woman next to me looked over and smiled. "Are you having a nice time, honey?"

She was old and smelled like potpourri.

"Yes," I said.

"I love that little girl," she said. "Breaks your heart."

"Do you think it's funny?" I said.

"Oh yes," she said. "The mother's a card."

I said to the old lady how I didn't hear her laughing and she said she was laughing inside. Which I thought was an interesting comment. She patted her chest to show me where the secret laughter was hiding. And then the lights went down and she said, "Shhh," as if I was the one who started the stupid conversation.

When the curtain parted it was a completely different world. The living room had vanished and the whole stage was white. You couldn't tell if it was supposed to be the North Pole or heaven or were they just trying to blind us. The light was crazy bright.

Lucy Moon was onstage all by herself. Lucy was the daughter. She just stood there and for a long time nothing happened. It was like a mistake. Then finally Lucy started to make sounds. Half animal and half baby. I thought maybe this was supposed to be the funny part. I looked at the old lady next to me and she had her hand over her mouth and her eyes were all buggy.

When I looked back at the stage it had started to snow. It was fake snow but somehow even better than real snow. It was pretty amazing actually. Lucy Moon looked to her right and then to her left and then all of a sudden she screamed. It was the cry of the wild.

When Lucy stopped screaming she looked out into the audience. She looked right at me. I was in the third row, pretty close. "Help me," she said. I didn't like the sound of that. I turned around but I couldn't see Ma or Da anywhere. When I looked back at the stage Lucy was still staring at me.

"I want to go home," she said. But retarded-like. She was practically crying.

I could feel the heat moving up my neck.

I turned to the old lady. She made a gesture like I should get up and do something.

"It's a play," I said.

I had no idea what the hell was happening, it was like I was dreaming.

The old lady put her mouth by my ear. "Audience participation," she said.

Lucy was holding out her hand toward me.

"I don't know the lines," I said. My neck was really burning. Even my throat was on fire.

"Be a good sport," the old lady said. And she pushed me a little.

I looked at Lucy and I shook my head. Everybody was staring at me. I could feel the cookie moving around in my stomach. Finally Lucy turned to someone else thank god, a man in a red shirt. He got up from his seat and climbed the stairs toward the stage. The old lady clicked her tongue at me. Fuck you, I said. Except I didn't say it for real. I said it inside ha ha like her stupid laughter.

And I don't even know what the man in the red shirt did for Lucy because I'd turned to look for Ma and Da again. But the next thing I knew the snow had stopped and Lucy was kissing the man's cheek. Thank you, she said. *Dank you*. I watched the man go back to his seat, smiling and brushing the fake snow from his shoulders like he was some kind of hero. And when I looked back at the stage all the furniture was there again, I don't know how they did it. And there was Lucy, safe and sound, smack in the middle of her living room. And then Joe and Judy entered like nothing had happened and the stupid chitchat started up again.

That's when I threw up on Ma's empty seat. I kept my head down in case it happened again. I felt a tap on my shoulder. But it wasn't them. It was the old lady.

"Here," she said. She was trying to pass me a hanky.

"Wipe the seat," she said.

When I sat back up I didn't watch any more of the play. I closed my eyes and counted. My face felt like it was melting. When it was finally over I ran down the aisle while everyone was clapping. I realized I still had the old lady's hanky and I threw it on the ground. Ma and Da were by the back door and I wanted to grab onto them but I just stormed past them.

"Hey hey," Da said, "slow down."

I ran outside. It had turned cold and the wind was snapping some flags.

"They wouldn't let us back in," Da said.

I looked at Ma.

"You didn't see it?" I said. It made me crazy that she might not have seen the snow or the screaming or how I got sick on her seat.

"We watched it from the back," Da said.

"You can't just disappear," I said.

"What are you talking about?" Ma said.

Da asked me what was wrong.

"I don't feel well," I said.

Ma touched my forehead but it didn't mean anything. She didn't keep her hand there for more than a second.

"You don't have a fever," she said.

"How would you know?" I shouted.

Da coughed. "I'll get the car," he said.

I stared at Ma as hard as I could.

"I thought it was going to be about space," I said.

Ma laughed. "Don't be ridiculous," she said.

My old feelings came back and I hated her stronger than ever.

"The acting was good," Ma said.

"Drool school," I said.

Ma was half-smiling but I could see how fake it was. Cynthia Callis would have done a much better job. Ma's dress was flapping in the wind and I thought, just fly away if that's what you want.

"What did you say?" Ma said.

"Nothing," I said. I felt like the streetlights were punching me in the face.

"Here," Ma said, and she put her sweater over my shoulders.

"I'm not cold," I said. But I was freezing.

I could see how scared Ma was that I might start screaming. The way I used to scream the first few months, when I woke up from the dreams. In some ways, I thought, I have Ma in the palm of my hand. I imagined breaking her in a million pieces. I wanted to put my fingers around her throat and make her start singing.

"Here comes your father," she said.

Da came around with the car and I ran over to it. I lay down on the back seat and wrapped Ma's sweater around my head, which meant, *Keep Out, Private Property.*

No one said anything the whole way home. Ma's sweater

had perfume on it, the kind I love that smells like powder, but tonight it just made me sicker. I thought I heard Ma and Da whispering at one point but when I poked my head out of the sweater I realized it was just the radio. Da had put it on real low. It was the voices of strangers.

I have to get out of here, I thought. I started crying but I swallowed it.

"What are you eating?" Ma said.

That's when I stopped breathing. I made myself into a dead person.

But then I had to breathe again, I couldn't help myself.

When we were pulling into the driveway I saw Da's eyes in the mirror. I guess he saw me as well. We looked at each other for a second, and with the mirror between us it was almost like the truth was coming out.

It was so big I bowed my head. I threw up in the car. Everything started to spin, and then time went funny again. A few years passed or maybe they went backwards because the next thing I knew, Da was carrying me into the house and putting me in bed. Which is something he used to do a million years ago when I was a baby. When I was the angel of the world. When we were the luckiest people ever to live on the face of the Earth.

11

Da said I was shouting. Delirious, he said.

"What did I say?" I asked him.

He said he couldn't make it out.

I asked him what time it was and he said it was three in the morning.

"Sleep," he said. His voice was good. He was absolutely my father.

I had kicked the covers off the bed and he put them back around me.

I asked him did I say anyone's name.

"No," he said. "Close your eyes."

And then he was gone. I don't even know how he disappeared from my room. All night he kept coming and going like dolphins at Sea World. Ma came in once. She didn't really come in, she just stood by the door.

But it was mostly Da. At one point he took a doll from

my shelf. He put her in bed with me. "Not too old for Polly, are you?"

"That's not Polly," I said. "That's Grace."

"Which one is Polly?" he said.

"Polly is dead," I say. "Polly died."

"Oh," he says. "Okay then, Grace."

When Da put her next to me, I just let her lie there. I didn't take her in my arms. I pretended she was a stranger, that I didn't love her. When I make up a story, I can pretty much stick to it. The Tree told me once I had a beautiful imagination. But you have to be careful, he said. You have to be careful not to take it too far.

How far is too far? I wonder. When there are men who push girls in front of trains, nothing seems too far.

The sun's not up yet but I can say it.

H.S.S.H.

I can see light just starting to come in the window, the first fingers of it.

Please help me, I say. And I don't even know who I'm talking to. Am I talking to her? Am I talking to you?

And the truth is I don't even know who you are.

Are you the watchers? I wonder.

Are you here?

12

For Helene's fourteenth birthday Ma took H and me to a farm where we could ride horses. Ma used to ride horses when she was a girl. It was a big part of her life apparently. I didn't want to go near them at first. Ma asked if I was scared and I said I was, and she told me not to be because they were the sweetest animals in the world. It was their long heads that worried me. Plus their chompers were also an issue. The way their mouths twitched and moved sideways when they ate, they seemed like maybe they had mental problems.

Ma pointed to a big brown horse and said he looked just about perfect for me. "Go ahead," she said, "you can pet him."

I looked up into his eyes, which did look fairly intelligent. When I touched him he moved his tail in a way that made me think of a queen. And then he tossed his head and air came out of his nose and I ran away from him and Ma laughed. "He's just excited," she said. "He likes you, Mathilda."

Ma was smiling and her cheeks were all red because of the cold air.

"Why don't you ride him first?" I said.

And that's what she did. She rode the brown horse and she waved at me from the top of him. I'd never seen Ma ride before, even though I'd heard a million stories. Jumping over fences and the blue ribbons and the trophies, which are in boxes down the basement now but used to line the walls of Ma's room in the house she grew up in. At least that's the story.

Helene also rode that day. She'd only done it once before but she was a natural. Her body knew exactly what to do. She came up to Ma on a gray horse and the two of them took off toward some trees in the distance that looked about five inches tall. The two of them could have been sisters and I could have been the mother I was so proud of them. It was pretty much a perfect day.

This is the sort of thing we should be sitting around the table talking about. Telling stories about Helene, the best days we can remember. It's supposedly one of the ways normal people grieve.

Instead I have to wake up one year after my sister ended and I have to put on her dress and march into the living room like a ghost. And even if it's awful it's the only way.

When I first got out of bed I felt a little woozy. Even now, if I move too fast, my breath goes funny, like a dog.

The dress is laid out on my bed. It's yellow. The color of butter. And there's some green stitching on the skirt. Ma will remember this dress. It's pretty amazing. The green stitching swirls all over the yellow almost like music. A boy gave it to Helene as a gift. She never said who. But when a boy gives you a dress for the first time, it means you're a woman. As soon as Helene came downstairs wearing it, we all knew she wasn't the same person.

Ma and Da probably think they're clever letting me sleep. Maybe their secret hope is I'll stay in bed sick all day and wake up tomorrow. I can hear the TV on downstairs. Which is strange because they usually don't watch TV in the morning. It's amazing that they haven't even come up to say good morning yet, or how are you feeling? They come and go all night like dolphins but in the morning it's humans again. Keep your distance!

I half put on the dress but then I have to take it off.

I lock my door.

The dress is crumpled up on the floor now, and I pick it up and smooth it out on the bed. I pull two hairs from the top of my head, just to take a break.

Then I take a deep breath and put on the dress. The sun is pouring in the window, which is just another slap in the face. I look at myself in the mirror and I almost lose my nerve. And not because I look terrible, but because I look good. The dress fits perfectly. I brush my hair. I pinch my cheeks to bring out the fire. I almost feel like a bride.

I'm pretty much ready. I'm going to go downstairs and I don't care if it's the last thing I ever do. I kiss myself in the mirror and it scares me, because my lips are cold. Or maybe it's the lips in the mirror that are cold. It's impossible to tell the difference.

13

I don't know any prayers. I wouldn't even know how to start. Someone should have taught me at least one, for situations like this.

I went downstairs, that's the first thing.

I went downstairs and the house smelled like cigarettes. Everything was quiet except for the TV and so I went toward that. Into the living room.

Ma was there. And Da too. He was standing and she was sitting but they were both watching the television. Ma's body was blocking the picture. She was wearing a bra, which isn't normally how she goes around the house. I could see the freckles on her back. Why are they watching a movie? I wondered. They were totally engrossed. It was infuriating.

Then I heard a voice on the TV say "unidentified" and I immediately thought of flying saucers. I made a cough to announce myself.

When Ma turned around she had tears in her eyes. She stared at me and I stood perfectly straight. I waited for her to say something. She opened her mouth but nothing came out, and then she just turned back to the TV.

Da was the same. Silent, with water in his eyes.

It's happening was my first thought. I've made it happen. Grief.

But the television was the confusing part.

Maybe they're trying to make me mad was my second thought. I moved around Ma so I could see what show they were watching. It was a movie about an earthquake or a fire. There were people screaming and some of them were running. It looked like a disaster movie, except it wasn't. It was the news.

Da came over and squeezed my shoulder.

"There's been another attack," he said.

I looked at the TV again but it didn't make much sense. There was a lot of smoke and rubble. There were also people lying on the ground and they weren't moving.

"Where is it?" I said. "What country?"

Then all of a sudden the picture on the TV changed. It was like a homemade video of the same place, but before the fire. You could see a big white building that was perfectly fine. Lots of people were walking into it, mostly men in dark suits. Whoever was filming it was standing about a block away, and they must have been shaking because the picture was jumping all over the place.

And then the explosion came. The building started to wobble like a mirage in the desert. And then there was an even louder sound and that's when the whole building shattered, with pieces of it flying everywhere.

"Oh my god," Ma said.

Some of the pieces fell on top of the people who were still outside. Everything turned to smoke. It was worse than the opera house. It was almost as bad as the planes from when I was little.

And then the picture changed again. The person who was holding the camera swung it around and pointed it at his own face. It was a blurry man with blue eyes and a beard.

"You will all die," he said.

And then he shot himself, and it all went dead.

"Oh my god," Ma said again.

That's when I remembered I was sick and I wanted someone to put a cool washcloth on my head.

"It's probably not real," I said.

Ma was sobbing now. But it was all wrong.

"Ma," I said, "it's a movie." I sat down next to her because I felt like maybe I was going to pass out. My whole body was burning.

What's going on? I thought. What's the big joke?

On the TV it was back to the scene of the smoke and the screaming.

"I have to go to school," I said. But the words sounded funny because my teeth were chattering.

"It's okay," Da said. And he came over and hugged me.

"She shouldn't be watching this," Ma said.

"Where is it?" I said. But they didn't answer me and so I got up to look out the window to make sure it wasn't happening around here.

When I looked back at the TV there was a black woman who had turned white. She couldn't catch her breath and a skinny white cop was helping her walk down the street. She was making sounds like Lucy Moon.

"Terrorist," a voice said on the television.

The yellow dress was dying all over me.

I marched across the room and turned off the TV.

"What are you doing?" Da said. "Turn it back on."

They both just stared at me like they were helpless, their faces just hanging there. They looked like somebody's children.

"Turn it back on," Da said again.

Ma was pointing her finger at the TV like an idiot.

"Mathilda," she said. "Don't."

She was blind at first but then she saw it. Her whole face changed color.

"What are you wearing?" she said. You could hardly hear her but then she said it again.

"What the hell are you wearing?"

Da came around me and turned the TV back on. "Move out of the way, baby," he said. "I know it's upsetting."

I kept looking at Ma. There were still tears in her eyes but there was no way of knowing which ones were for the building and which ones were for Helene.

"Go and change," she said without even looking at me.

I stood there. I didn't move. I could see that Ma was shaking.

"No," I said.

Ma got up off the couch and came over to me. She looked like she needed crutches.

"What do you think you're doing?" she says. She grabs me by the shoulders so fast it scares me.

"Do you think you're funny?" she says.

"Michele," Da says. And he tries to pull her away from me.

But Ma's stronger, she shakes him off.

Then it's just Ma and me, eye to eye, like the last two people in the world. I can see it coming, like an agreement Ma and I made a long time ago. Her hand swings out and slaps me. Someone else feels the pain.

Da has no part in this and he knows it. Ma is the only one. *"Go and change"* comes out of her mouth like a snake.

Suddenly Da comes between us and Ma lets him lead her over to the couch. He keeps her from falling. It's obvious Ma is his number one concern.

And now she's the one playing dead. She won't open her eyes. Da looks at me like I've broken his stupid heart. He shakes his head.

I'm sorry, I want to tell him. When I walk past him he doesn't touch me.

"Hundreds dead," the television says.

Da collapses next to Ma on the couch. I walk behind them but I don't leave. I stand in the doorway watching them. Ma in her underwear and Da in a pair of shorts and no shirt. On the television is still the movie of black smoke and rubble but I don't look at it. I look at the freckles on Ma's back dancing around like germs under a microscope. Da puts his arm around her shoulders like he's her boyfriend. His hair isn't even combed, it's sticking up all over the place. I don't love them. I don't.

I stand behind them like a ghost.

Ma and Da's bodies are moving up and down like they're laughing. Da's hand caresses Ma's gorgeous neck. They just sit there watching the end of the world like lovers at a drive-in movie. In their underwear like they've just had sex.

And my beautiful awful thought is, I haven't even been made yet. Ma and Da are young and the sex has just invented Helene.

You will all die.

No no no, I say, like I'm making a deal with someone. Let me go back to sleep, I say. I'm practically begging. Let me go back to sleep, and when I wake up I promise, *I promise*, not to remember.

PART TWO

14

We are a country at war, the President says. His lips are upside down. The enemy is invisible, he says. It doesn't make
sense but still it's terrifying. It's easy to picture everything
on fire, even your own house. Once on television I saw a lady
picking through a bunch of broken boards looking for her
belongings. It wasn't a war, it was a tornado, but the feeling
was the same. The broken boards were all that was left of her
house. Her dirty dress was flapping in the wind, it was like
the death of the pioneers. Where am I going to live? she kept
saying. She said it about ten times like she was drunk. Eventually she found a few plates but they were all in pieces.
Sometimes, after a war, it's even worse. Thousands of people
wandering around looking for water. Sometimes it happens
in winter, but what can you do? A house is a pretty flimsy thing
when you get down to it.

Sometimes I wonder about Eyad from my class, if he's

one of them. A terrorist, I mean. I know he's not but sometimes I still entertain the thought. Someone pushed Eyad's mother last week when she was shopping. They knocked her to the ground. I don't understand why she doesn't just start dressing like a normal person and take off the costume of the terrorists. Fit in is what people like that should try to do. Why ask for trouble? I notice Eyad keeps his head down most of the time, which I suppose is the best thing. He doesn't look like he wants to hurt anyone. And his name backwards is Daye, which is fairly positive.

But even if he's not a terrorist, he might be related to one. Yesterday he wore a T-shirt with a flag on it. Our flag, and I guess it's his too. But still, it was embarrassing in a way. Plus it's a little suspicious. It's like wearing a shirt with your name on it. If I saw a boy with JOE printed on his shirt and he came up to me and said, Hi I'm Joe, well I'd have to wonder if he was or he wasn't. I wouldn't just out-and-out believe him. Sometimes I watch Eyad and I try to read his mind but he's a tough nut to crack. Did I tell you about his white teeth? Amazing. Imagine if I fell in love with him. What would people think? He really is a sweet person but no matter how you look at it, the experts say, you can't trust him completely.

STAY ALERT, STAY SAFE. That's the expression now. It's up all over the school, in red letters. Whenever we have a terror drill, I always sneak a peak at Eyad to see his reaction. But pretty much he looks as scared as anyone.

Sometimes I think about the bombs strapped to the bodies of boys and girls. The suicide children who give themselves up for their cause. It's getting to be a big problem over there in one of those problematic countries. Just last week there was a fifteen-year-old girl who did it. She took twenty-eight people with her. I mentioned her to Anna and Anna said, "What a waste."

"A waste of what?" I said, and Anna said, "A waste of life."

"Whose life?" I asked her, and she said, "The girl's."

"What about the victims?" I said.

"Them too," Anna said.

"Why do they even do it?" she said. "It's senseless."

"You don't understand," I said. "They're zealots."

"What's zealots?" Anna said, and I told her people with passion.

"I don't like them," Anna said.

"Well, they don't like you either," I said. "They don't like any of us."

"What's not to like?" Anna said. "Do they want everyone to walk around with sheets over their heads?"

I laughed when Anna said this even though I knew she was confusing things. The suicide children are different from the people with sheets over their heads. There's more than one problematic country right now. Sometimes even I get confused.

"Sheets on your head is so attractive, don't you think?" Anna said.

"Definitely," I said. And then I grabbed my jacket and wrapped it around my head so that only my eyes peeked out.

"Like this?" I said, and I made jabbering noises like I was speaking a roostery foreign language. The two of us nearly peed our pants. Anna fell down on the bed where the cat was flagrantly giving himself a bath. He was licking right between his own legs. It sounded like someone going to town on a piece of fruit.

"Sometimes I worry about my brother," Anna said.

"He'll be okay," I said, even though I didn't really believe it. Soldiers are dying right and left, and sometimes they come back missing an arm or a leg.

Anna asked me if I would pray for him, and I said that I would. I didn't mention that I didn't know any prayers. I figured I could just look one up on the Internet.

Later I asked Anna if she would be willing to die for something she believed in.

She said no.

Then I asked her would she be willing to die to save someone else's life.

"Whose life?" she said.

Mine, I thought, but I didn't say it.

"Your mother's life," I said.

"I don't want to play this game," she said, and she got up from the bed and looked out the window.

I got up and stood next to her. We just stared outside and we were obviously waiting for something, but it wasn't something you could put your finger on exactly.

"You have to be strong," I said.

I put my hand on Anna's shoulder, which was the right thing to do. I could hear the cat on the bed still licking away. What a slobberpuss!

Have you noticed how everything in the end comes down to animals? It's the number one theme in my head lately. Not only cats and dogs, but terrorists and boys on top of girls and even a person's own mother on her hands and knees crawling around the kitchen. I couldn't believe it when I saw it, but there she was. Ever since H.S.S.H. she's been a real mess. When the people you love become animals it's awful. You're half afraid to even go near them.

15

I'm watching her but she doesn't even know I'm there. She always used to say she had eyes in the back of her head but I guess they've gone blind. She's on her knees in the kitchen, a total dog, huffing and puffing and pulling stuff out of the cabinets. I can hardly stand to look at her. The bottoms of her feet are black.

What are you looking for? I almost say, but then she finds it. A bottle. I jump out of the doorway and hide in the hall like a cop outside a room of potential danger. I can hear the vodka *slub-slub* into a glass. I can hear her drink. She makes a little sound in her throat. It would be a perfect moment to barge in and scare her.

But that's not what I do anymore. Now I just leave her alone. I watch her from a distance, I don't get right on top of her. I'd like to, but lately I worry I might kill her if I did something too shocking. Breaking plates isn't the way to get through to her anyway. You have to use psychology when you're dealing with a case like this.

Ma's always home now when she should be at school. She's taking some time off, Da said. Last week was the worst. I found her in her bedroom with the curtains closed and no lights on. Daytime but she'd made it dark. She was naked, that's the main thing. She was rolled up in a ball and her hand was between her legs. The sound is what I would call a whimper. I think maybe she was doing it to herself, like in Da's magazines. Either that or she was crying.

I've started to wonder about Ma's loneliness. I've never thought about it before because of my father. The meaning of marriage is the end of loneliness, but maybe not.

Now she's in the kitchen drinking again, and soon she'll sleep. That's pretty much her new regimen. And Da won't be home for hours because he has a lot of work at school, or so he says. Sometimes he gets home before I go to bed, and we have something to eat in the kitchen.

"How's your mother doing?" he always says.

"Headache," I say.

"Give her a few days," he says.

These are pretty much our standard lines now.

Sometimes I think I should go to her, I should climb into bed with her. But the thing is, after Helene died I cried for months and months but Ma was deaf. After Helene died I was basically alone. Da was there but that's not the issue. Da is Da, Da isn't my mother. A person's mother is a whole different story. A person's mother is supposedly a big part of a person's life.

"Why are you standing there?" Ma says, coming out of the kitchen.

The drink is still in her hand and the awful thing is when she comes toward me I can smell her. The awful thing is she kisses me. Her lips touch the top of my head but there's no passion in it, it's the kiss of a zombie. And then she disappears into the fog. Even though you can't see it, there's the feeling of smoke everywhere, in every room of the house.

It's been five weeks since the terror. Five weeks since H.S.S.H. The day after the anniversary, Da brought home some flowers. Stargazers, Helene's favorite. Ma put them in a vase and she still hasn't thrown them out. At this point they're not even flowers anymore, they're basically just crackers and crumbs. It's a mess, I'm telling you.

Luckily I have a bible now. Anna lent it to me. I keep it on my desk where the heathens can see it. Sometimes I put it right in the middle of the kitchen table.

In the beginning was the Word, and the Word was God.

But the truth is, the word is not god. The word is California. Which is the one place H always said she was going to live when she was older. When I typed it into the computer there was a pause and then I heard the music that plays when you open your mail. *Welcome HeyGirl!* appeared in beautiful blue letters on the screen. I don't know that I can describe to you the feeling. It was like a gift from god. I was finally inside H's e-mail. But then my joy was ripped out from under me. Because inside was just emptiness. *You have no messages*, the computer said. I almost started screaming.

There weren't even any old messages. Too much time had passed. Everything had disappeared. It was kind of the last straw. I wondered why god would unlock a door just to show you emptiness. It made me wonder if maybe he was in cahoots with infinity.

Anna says I have to love god no matter what. You can't question him, she says. And to tell you the truth, breaking into H's e-space did make me feel a little closer to heaven. The more I thought about it the more I didn't care that it was empty. Plus it made sense that no one was writing to her. Everyone knew she was dead.

But then I thought, what if I tell them otherwise? What if I send a message to someone from H's e-mail? Because maybe the dead can't do anything without the help of the living. Maybe ghosts don't just appear, maybe you have to invent them. And then once they're born, they can do whatever they want.

My first thought was, send a message to one of H's old boyfriends. And then I thought, no, send one to Ma. My heart pretty much stopped when the idea hit me. It's brilliant when you think about it. I went to sleep feeling like a terrorist. But I wasn't going to kill people, I was going to bring them back to life. That's a whole different kind of terror. It's the terror of god.

16

In school Mrs. Veasey makes us do a minute of silence. Every day at 8:48, which was the time of the bomb. It's always strange stopping in the middle of everything to go quiet, and then starting up again a minute later. It's like going under-water to see how long you can breathe for. When we do it I always feel like something is supposed to happen. But it doesn't. There's no thunder or lightning or even just some stupid bird flying into the room. You never get any sign that the silence is even listening. It's always disappointing. Also you feel embarrassed. Mrs. Veasey stands up and bows her head and everyone imitates her. A minute of silence is actu-ally a long time. A person could write a novel in a minute of silence.

"Don't look at the clock," Mrs. Veasey is always saying to someone.

Sometimes I listen to the ticking and I'm furious. I have to bite my cheek.

In some classes the teachers read long lists of the dead. These dead people get special treatment because they died in a national tragedy. But I don't see how they're any different from normal people who die. Sometimes in the silence it's hard to keep myself from shouting her name. In the silence I get mad that no one is thinking about me, about my family.

Today, during the minute, Bruce Sellars laughed. I was glad he did it. When he laughed, a few other people did too. It was like the devil flying across the room. Mrs. Veasey's face went completely red and she pointed her finger at Bruce Sellars like a gun, but she didn't budge from her silence. Bruce stopped laughing but when the minute was over Mrs. Veasey exploded. She was practically shaking. I wondered if maybe she knew someone inside the bombed building. She screamed for a good five minutes, going on about respect for the dead and the country. Afterwards we went back to math but it was basically incomprehensible. Even Mrs. Veasey didn't know what the hell she was talking about. She kept repeating herself and she made about three errors in her calculations. I almost corrected her but then I thought, just shut up Mathilda, leave the poor woman alone.

At lunch I saw Kevin outside on the lawn. I asked him did he do minutes of silence in his class and he said they did. He said two girls started crying today and they couldn't stop. I told him the same thing happened in my class. I told him I was one of the criers.

"Terrible," I said.

"Awful," he said. The exact word!

Kevin's hair was still blue, still beautiful. I looked around for Anna but didn't spot her. I wanted to see the two of them standing side by side. The blonde and the blue.

"I've been thinking," I said.

Kevin looked at me and he didn't seem the least bit impatient. We actually had pretty good eye contact. Suddenly it hit me that Kevin's hair wasn't just blue, but that it was angry as well, the way parts of it were sticking up like little knives.

"I've been thinking maybe we should test out my basement," I said.

"What do you mean?" he said.

"In case of a disaster," I said.

"Where would you go?" I asked him. "Do you have a place to hide?"

He said he had an attic but I told him attics weren't the ideal place in my opinion.

"It's not Nazis," I said, "it's bombs."

"A basement is better," I said.

"If it was biological weapons," he said, "it would still get down there."

"But slower," I said. "You'd at least have a chance."

He looked at me to see if I was playing, but I was dead serious. I knew all the potential dangers because we did FEMA in our class. I asked Kevin if he'd ever done "Today in Disaster History" at fema.gov.

"Sometimes," he said, "if I'm bored."

At fema.gov you can go to a calendar and you can basically click on any day to find out if there was ever a disaster on that day. And usually you find one. A fire or a flood or a tornado and sometimes terror. There hasn't been as much terror as floods and fires, of course. But plan on more, the website says.

I told Kevin how I've started bringing food and water into my basement.

"I'm going down there no matter what," I said. "It has to be tested."

"With your parents?" he said, and I said, "No, alone."

"I'm not even going to tell them," I said.

"They'll hear you," he said.

I just smiled like a genius. "We'll have to be quiet," I said.

I told him Anna was coming down the basement too, even though the truth is I haven't asked her yet.

"Anna McDougal?" he said. His tail practically went up in the air.

I better be careful, I thought.

"When are you doing it?" he said.

He leaned in a little closer to me. "We should have a meeting," he said.

Just then a bird flew over our heads. For a second I thought it was an enemy plane, I really did. My heart actually jumped. And the funny thing is, even though it wasn't a plane with a bomb in its belly, it practically was. The bird landed in a tree and then it shat on one of the lunch tables. *Shat* doesn't sound like a real word but it is. Shat!

"Oh my god," I said, "how rude."

Kevin clapped his hands. "Get the fuck out of here!" he said, and the bird did. It flew off and landed on the next tree, but it kept watching us out of the side of its head. In my mind I wondered who sent it. Whose bird was it?

"If you want to come to my house on Saturday," Kevin said, "my parents will be out."

"To make a plan," he said, just to let me know it wasn't a date or anything.

"Okay," I said, and then the embarrassment started up, I think for the both of us.

Kevin nodded and walked away looking at the ground. He put his hands in his pockets and then he turned his head and spit. It was disgusting and brilliant. The sun was shining in every direction. Suddenly I felt happy for the first time in ages. I tried to spit but I only dribbled.

"What are you looking at?" I said to the bird. I shook a fist at it but it didn't move. It didn't even blink.

———

There's a lot of ways to think about the terrorists. You have to ask yourself what their emotion is. Are they angry or sad or evil? It's the same question I asked about the man. The one who pushed Helene.

If they're angry you might be able to calm them down. All you have to do is give them what they want. Except what if they want everything, your whole way of life? If they're sad it's even worse. Their sadness is because of things that happened in the past, and it's been there so long that it's in their blood now. It's beyond logical, the sadness. It's almost biological.

Most likely the terrorists are evil, and if that's the case there isn't much you can do. Evil is beyond reason. Evil is the opposite of god and even if you don't believe in god you still have to believe in evil.

Some people say kill them. But good luck. Apparently the terrorists are smart, they know how to hide. They know how to live in caves. They might be geniuses for all we know. Maybe they've even read the Bhagavad Gita. I wonder if it's been translated into the language of terrorists. And do all of them even speak the same language? If it's Arabic then it looks like animals wrote it with their claws. I would love to be able to write like that, it's better than Chinese even.

What they did to us was a big success and who knows when they'll do it again. Right now they're just waiting. They have a lot of patience, these people. It's like the man at the train. Maybe he watched Helene for years before he finally put his hands on her. And now you have to always worry, who's next?

Kill them is my main thought. Other times I don't know. Sometimes I wonder if maybe the terrorists are sad because of something we did to them. But what? I know a lot of things are my fault, but not *everything*. The man with the beard and the blue eyes who shot himself, he comes into my head a lot. I don't know what he wants.

Helene told me once, "They're killing innocent people, Mathilda." And she wasn't talking about terrorists, she was talking about us. Meaning we were the killers. She had a funny way of looking at things sometimes. When she tried to explain this stuff to me, she would grab my hand, the way Anna does if we're watching a scary movie. Helene was very dramatic, but she wasn't a liar. If she could have adopted ten baby terrorists, she would have done it in a heartbeat. She had a real love for the downtrodden.

Mrs. Frisk across the street is just the opposite. She has about ten flags on her lawn. When terrorists see our flag blowing in the wind I wonder if it's like a red cape to a bull. I wonder if it makes them crazy. In the end someone dies. It's usually the bull. But not always. Sometimes the bullfighter dies. Sometimes the bull goes right through him. I've seen pictures on the Internet. You can even watch a bullfight live on the Internet if you want. But I don't recommend it. It's a lot more horrible than you think.

17

The basement was a pigsty before I started working on it. Thick dust on everything like velvet and boxes piled up on the floor. Old stuff we don't need but can't part with for some reason. Books and clothes and broken toys. Some of Helene's stuff is down there as well. Plus a Ping-Pong table, half a bicycle, and some old-fashioned furniture. A few boxes are filled with what Da calls memorabilia and Ma calls crap.

Before this house was our house it was the house of Da's parents. I didn't know them, they died before I was born. My grandfather supposedly died from falling off a dog. And then, after the mother died, Da got the house. My rotten inheritance he calls it because something is always falling apart. But at least it's in a good neighborhood.

The basement is basically one big room, but then there's a smaller room in the back. The small room has the water heater in it but also a bunch of shelves full of jars. The jars are stuffed with fruit mostly but also some vegetables. It's the work of Da's mother. All the jars are covered with dust and you can't even read what's written on the labels anymore, it's all faded. You can pretty much tell what's peaches and what's corn but some jars are a total mystery of blobs and slivers. In one there's something with seeds but the seeds look like teeth. It makes me think of baby alligators.

"Throw them out," Ma said once, but Da said no, he wanted to keep them. "They can't be any good," Ma said. And Da agreed we shouldn't eat them but he said to leave them anyway, they weren't bothering anyone.

The jars give you the feeling of Frankenstein's laboratory. There's also silver cans of who-knows-what. Fingers and toes and chopped-up brains. Who knows what the grandmother was up to down there. Maybe she was a maniac. Maybe she was the one who did in the old man. Falling off a dog is a pretty unlikely story.

I'm also loading up on water. I've got about ten gallons lined up against the wall, plus I've got a pretty good pile of food. Breakfast bars and nuts and juice boxes. Also pretzels, peanut butter, and a big jar of cherry-flavored vitamin C to prevent scurvy. Who knows how long we'll be down there.

I have a flashlight and extra batteries. I have blankets. I have a knife I found in one of the old boxes. It fits in a leather case that you can wear on your belt. Maybe it belonged to Da's father, or maybe it was the property of Mrs. Frankenstein. I just thought it might be a good thing to have around. In case of intruders.

Most of H's stuff I've put neatly to one side. I covered it with a sheet. If Kevin and Anna come, I don't want it to be right out in the open. It's not exactly a conversation starter.

Ma and Da have no idea I've been down here. I've tried to talk to them about the possibility of disaster, but they don't seem particularly interested. FEMA recommends talking to your parents about anxiety and other feelings, and also about your family's preparedness. But Ma and Da can't even hear me. It's like they're already in their own private bomb shelters inside their heads. Which is fine by me. If they don't want to share, then I won't either.

Anyway, the basement is starting to feel like a place I could live. When I used to go and visit the boys' fort in the woods, sometimes the boys weren't there and I'd go inside and lie on my back and I had the best thoughts I ever had in my life.

I let Luke come down here with me once in a while. He doesn't get in my way. He plops himself down on the cement because it's nice and cool, and he can probably smell the earth underneath, and possibly bones as well. Indian bones and whatever else is buried there, prehistoric cats and dogs, maybe even the bones of dinosaurs. Who knows what's under a house. The house you live in is only a recent development in the history of the world. Before it was a house it could have been a jungle or a desert. A million years ago it might have been the middle of the ocean. You don't know. You only know the here and now. The rest you have to imagine.

———

"I can't come," Anna says, "my mother won't let me."

"Why'd you even tell her?" I say. "It's supposed to be a secret."

"I had to tell her," Anna says.

"What do you expect me to do," she says, "just run away?"

"Yes," I say. "Exactly."

I sit on the couch and Anna sits next to me. "I'm sorry," she says.

"You're gonna make me stay down the basement by myself?" I ask her. I haven't told her yet about Kevin.

"What if something happens to me down there?" I say. "Can't you just come for one night?" I'm practically pleading. "Just one lousy night. You can tell your mother we're sleeping in my room."

"I don't know," Anna says.

"I need you," I say.

I look straight into her eyes.

I need you.

Magic words. They go straight to her heart. I can see the blood come to her cheeks.

"Maybe," she says. "Maybe for one night."

And then she smiles, it's small but I can see it. I know she wants what I want. Something new. Something different. Sometimes Anna seems like a doll, the way she tilts her head, but if you look closely into the eyes of the doll, you can tell she wants to be ripped apart. She wants, just like me, to be another person.

"We'll do it together," I say. "You and me."

"Okay?" I say.

The doll nods.

"Yes," she says. *Yes!*

———

Before going to bed I go into the kitchen and I get two pudding packs and a spoon. I'm not allowed to eat in my room but I do. And I'm only supposed to have one pudding pack a day, supposedly the sugar deranges me. And according to her I'm turning into a bubble. As I'm sneaking up the stairs Da sees me. His eyes come out of his book. I don't panic and I don't try to hide the pudding packs. I just stand there and wait for the verdict. All Da does is shake his head, not to say no to the food but rather to say, what in the world are we going to do with you Mathilda? Mathilda and her pudding packs.

Poor Da, I think, don't worry so much.

I suppose he should have stopped me but Da is the sort of man who would die if someone didn't think he was a good person. And that's exactly what he is. I've decided Da doesn't have a bad bone in his body. If I think about it I would have to say that Da is the father of Helene and Ma is the father of me. It disgusts me to admit it, but it's true. I'm just as willful as Ma, that's a big part of the problem. Even though Helene acted tough sometimes, she really was a gentle sort of person. She hated scary movies and loud noises. She was like a deer in a lot of ways. But the funny thing is, she trusted people. She definitely got that from Da. One time we were on our way to school and Helene walked right up to a crusty-footed homeless man that smelled like number two and she handed over her sandwich. He could have raped her and she was la-di-da, here's a nice fat ham and cheese. She gave more stuff to strangers than she ever gave to me, but still, you'd be a liar if you said she wasn't a good person. People fell in love with her right and left. Teachers, parents, boys of course, plus Ma and Da were pretty devoted to her. And even though it got on my nerves sometimes, I was probably her number-one fan. It's hard to even imagine why anyone would want to hurt a person like her. But I guess the world is full of hunters and men who want to do evil, and there's never a shortage of weak people they can pick on.

When I get to my room I pull out an old book of mine. *The Diary of Anne Frank*. I look through it while I eat my puddings. Have you ever read this book? It's sort of boring but on the other hand it's the saddest book in the world. Anne is always writing away about this and that, blah blah blah, food and clothes and her stupid family, but the whole time she has no idea she's going to die. But the person reading the book knows. The person reading the book is like god, he can see the past and the future. But the thing is, you can't do anything. It's like being god with none of the power. You can't stop what's going to happen. Even the simplest things, like Anne talking about the dress she's going to buy after the war, make you feel like someone's stuck a pin in your lungs. It really messes with your breathing. When I pulled out the book the main thought on my mind was the attic. The hiding place. It's an interesting concept. And the big question is, who are you going to let stay in there with you? You can't invite everyone. You have to be selective.

Anna and Kevin, of course. But is there anyone else? I wonder.

That's when Louis popped into my head. LDM@ blueforest.com. I could invite him, but really I don't even know who he is. Plus I've started to wonder where he was the day Helene died.

Did I tell you about Desmond?

When they collected Helene's body they found a few things in her pockets, including an unused ticket to Desmond. Which is about an hour away. It's sort of up in the mountains, and there's a lake up there Anna told me. Her brother went up there on a camping trip before he joined the army.

But of course Helene never got on the train. The train to Desmond was due ten minutes after she died. The train that got Helene was just a train passing through the station. It wasn't even her train.

When I think about the pusher, I'm glad I have the knife.

The truth is, there's too many men in my dreams right now. First it was just the one, and then Louis started to show up. But then sometimes it all gets mixed up. Sometimes Louis has a beard and blue eyes like the terrorist who shot himself. Sometimes he says he loves me. Sometimes he tells me the same things he used to tell Helene. I try not to listen, but then I do. He's very persuasive.

18

Dear Helene,
So many things are happening and so fast I can hardly
keep up. Last week was a terrible terrible time so if I seemed
weird on Friday I'm sorry. I know you're sad about things
in general and I want to talk about everything. Come up to
the house on Wednesday or I can meet you in Little Falls,
at the park. Tell me what you prefer. I keep looking at the
last picture we took of you, you look amazing. We
should do some more. I told the doctor that I'd been
spending time with a famous singer-songwriter ☺ and
he said you were a good thing but I already knew that.
Think about Wednesday.
Love, Louis

It's funny the way he writes his e-mails, formal like a
letter. He's probably an honor student doing college prep.

Maybe he's even in college by now, because time didn't stop when Helene died. *So many things are happening and so fast I can hardly keep up.* Which pretty much sums up my own feelings.

Plus it's interesting how he repeats the word terrible.

As for Helene's sadness, I know all about it. It's not breaking news or anything. Not that she was sad all the time but when she was it was like a force field no one could break through.

Helene was famous for days of crying and not leaving her room. Sometimes, if you were walking by, it sounded like someone was strangling her. I could tell she had her face in a pillow or pushed into one of her stuffed animals. She had a huge collection of bears and bunnies and lambs and she wasn't even embarrassed by them. They were very plush and I guess good for crying into. Maybe that's why she kept them. Every once in a while I would barge into her room, just to make sure she was okay. "Get out!" she'd scream, like I was the greatest enemy on the face of the Earth. Afterwards she'd lock the door and Ma would stand outside the room and try to reason with her. The whole time Ma was talking, her hand would be petting the stupid door like it was Helene's head.

And just when you thought you couldn't take it anymore, *snap!* Helene would turn into her old self again. She'd stroll into the kitchen with her hair brushed back, smiling and laughing and talking a mile a minute about her plans for the future. One time Ma and I were eating bowls of cereal and Helene walked in and announced she'd finished a new song and that maybe it was really good and would we please listen to it. And then she closed her eyes and sang it to us right there in the kitchen. Whenever she sang in front of people, which wasn't that often, she always closed her eyes. I don't even remember what the song was about. All I know is, when she was finished, Ma and I applauded and you couldn't wipe the smile off Helene's face. She really had two sides to her. Most people only saw the sunny side. The dark side pretty much stayed in the house. Though I guess Louis had a peek at it.

I can meet you in Little Falls, at the park.

Amazing because Little Falls is the town we live in. The park is a place I've known forever. Apparently Helene was conducting her secret affairs right under our noses.

Another e-mail from Louis a few weeks later says, *What do you want from me? What am I supposed to do? Please just go and talk to those people, I'm sure they can help.*

The date on this e-mail is only a week before the train.

His messages drive me crazy because I can't figure out what a lot of it means. Sometimes he's almost cold and it makes you wonder what's really in his heart. I decided I couldn't wait any longer. I decided to write him from H's e-mail. I wasn't sure how to imitate my sister exactly, so I thought it best to keep it simple.

Dear Louis, I miss you. Love H.

I haven't sent it yet. I put it in the "send later" file. I also wrote a second message.

Dear Ma, I can see you. Sometimes I'm right next to you. I can see you but I can't do anything. Do you think of me a lot? How is Da? How is Mathilda? Please send me a message. Love, Helene

I didn't send this one yet either.

If I did send the messages, what would they mean? And would it be a sin is my other question. I don't know how god feels about people imitating the dead, but my thought is he's probably not too keen on it. When I wrote the message to Louis, I was fine. But when I wrote the one to Ma, I sort of got dizzy. Afterwards I was almost sick again.

What I want to do is find the right words. To say exactly what Helene would say if she was here. Or what she would say from wherever she is. It's a lot of work trying to speak for a dead person. You have to find the perfect voice.

When I sent a message to Kevin, he replied immediately. *Ok*, he said, *c-u later.*

Come at 4, he wrote. *No one will be home.*

Of course when I wrote to Kevin I wrote it from my own e-mail, so it was a no-brainer.

———

The walls are painted black. It's crazy. It's like a bedroom stranded in deep space. Something impossible could happen there, that's the feeling. Like the laws could be different, the way they are in black holes. While I was getting my bearings I looked around at Kevin's posters. They were all music groups I'd never heard of. Human Oatmeal. Sado-Kitty. A.S.T.O. Which Kevin explained stands for Arnold Schwarzenegger is Technically Obese.

I asked Kevin how he got his mother to let him do black walls. Apparently they made some sort of deal. She said he could do whatever he wanted with his room provided he make good on his promise of "improved academic performance."

When he imitated his mother he gave her a British accent. It was pretty funny actually.

The only thing that didn't make sense in the black room was the aquarium. A huge tank with tropicals. It was sort of out of place, but still it was amazing. It was basically a whole city of fish. I couldn't stop staring at it. At the bottom of the tank there's a sunken treasure chest overflowing with gold coins. There's also a cave the fish can hide in, as well as a miniature car with a skeleton trapped inside. The ocean floor is made up of a million blue pebbles. Some of the fish looked hand-painted. Some were practically see-through. There's a light in the tank too, and when Kevin shut off the lights in the room the aquarium was like another world. In the dark I felt like I was the idiot and the fish were the geniuses.

"Remember the fort?" I say to Kevin. "In the woods?"

"That was a long time ago," he says.

He turns the lights back on and I can tell he doesn't want to talk about the fort. Why dwell in the past is probably his philosophy.

"It's probably in ruins now," I say.

"I bet there's skeletons inside," I say. But he doesn't laugh.

"Do you want to feed the fish?" he says. He was really into the fish. It was a little corny but it was sort of beautiful actually. It was the way a child loves things, like the way I used to love Luke.

"Sure," I say.

Kevin gives me the food and when I sprinkle the flakes in the water I feel like I'm making fish soup. I almost start laughing.

"Not too much," Kevin says. "If you give them too much you can kill them."

Kevin and I watch the fish swim to the surface. They vacuum up the flakes with their kissy little o-mouths.

"What's your brother been up to?" I say.

"I don't know," Kevin says.

"Is he planning on joining the army?" I ask him.

"No," Kevin says. "He's going to college next year."

"Oh," I say. "That's great."

Suddenly the picture that pops into my head is all of Helene's boyfriends sitting in the same class at the same stupid college. Helene was planning on college too, I feel like shouting at them.

"That's enough," Kevin says. He takes the fish food away from me.

"Why don't you sit down?" he says, pointing toward the bed.

"I'm fine," I say.

"Do you have any cigarettes?" he says.

"I don't smoke," I say. But then I remember the cigarette from the backyard, the day of the bulldozer.

"I quit," I tell him.

I look at Kevin and he looks at me. I think maybe there was some sexual tension between us. It felt like mud, like walking through a swamp. I wonder if Helene did more than flirt with boys, more than kissing and feeling up. I wonder if she actually had sex before she died.

"Why do you have that chain on your door?" I ask Kevin.

"Privacy," he says.

"My brother always used to barge in on me," he says.

"Your brother's pretty big," I say. "He's like an animal."

In my head I can picture him on top of Helene.

Kevin gets up and goes over to the fish. He taps on the glass. The fish dart away like they've been shocked by god.

"What about the basement?" Kevin says. "When are you going to do it?"

"Soon," I say.

"How about next weekend?" he says.

"Okay," I say. I look at the fish and not one of them is moving. It's like the water has suddenly turned to ice.

"I have food down the basement," I say.

Kevin and I stare at the frozen fish. We do a minute of silence, we can't help ourselves.

"Do you think we could all die?" Kevin says. "That everyone in the world could die?"

"Yes," I say.

"It could happen tomorrow," I say. "It could happen while we're sleeping."

"My father says they're not finished," Kevin says.

"Who?" I say.

"The terrorists," Kevin says.

He taps the glass and the fish come back to life.

"And who knows what they'll do next," I say. "You can't predict the behavior of people like that."

Kevin's face gets a little twisted watching the fish.

"Animals," he says.

Animals.

19

The phone rang four times before Ma picked it up. I was at a pay phone six blocks from the house.

"Hello?" she said.

I crunched up a piece of notebook paper by the mouthpiece to make it sound like static.

"Hello," she said again. "Is someone there?"

I put the paper over my mouth to disguise my voice.

"It's me," I said.

"I can't understand you," Ma said.

I made the paper crackle some more. I tried to say what I'd planned but I couldn't do it.

"Who is this?" Ma said.

Helene, I wanted to say.

Instead I just hung up.

I felt like punching myself. Sometimes I can't stand how weak I am. I have great ideas but then I hesitate. At least I'm doing the basement, I thought. In my mind I went through all my plans again. The basement, plus the e-mails, plus visiting Desmond on the train. For about five minutes I stood there by the phone mapping out my ideas. The thoughts were coming one on top of the other and everything was crystal clear. Plus the weather made me feel like I was in my own private world. It was afternoon but there wasn't a lot of light. The sun was so far away it was practically sending a letter.

That's when I noticed I was wearing the completely wrong shoes. Sandals. My toes were sticking out like it was summer. Good choice, Mathilda old buddy. Jesus. I really did have to laugh at myself. When I got home my feet were so cold I had to jump up and down to thaw them out. I thought maybe the noise would get Ma's attention, but she didn't come out of her cave.

I went into the living room and there was a white-haired man talking out of the television. On a screen above him was a picture of the terrorist who shot himself. I couldn't understand anything the white-haired man was saying. All I could see were the blue eyes of the terrorist. They were almost Anna's eyes. People from other countries shouldn't have blue eyes. Why make things more confusing?

"What are you watching?" Ma said.

Sometimes she does this, she just appears out of nowhere.

"Nothing," I said. And I shut off the TV.

Ma had a cleaning rag in her hand but I didn't believe it.

"Cleaning?" I said, and she grunted a little and went over to the cabinets and pretended to dust them. She was moving like a woolly mammoth trying to get out of a tar pit. I wanted to ask her if she had gotten any interesting phone calls today, but I just kept my mouth shut.

"Do you need some help?" I said.

She wouldn't even look me in the eye.

Sometimes the thought in my mind is two thoughts and they're the opposite of each other. *I wish my mother was dead* is the first thought. The second thought is *Everyone is dead except for her.*

"Let me help you," I say, and I try to take the rag out of her hand, but she says, "Don't touch it." She pulls it away like I'm trying to steal her diamond ring.

"Ma, I'll help you," I say. And I wasn't kidding. The place was a real mess, it was going to take teamwork to pull it together. But she just shakes her head and goes into her mumbling routine. That's her big new thing. That and the half-sentences. She'll start to say something but then she doesn't finish the thought.

"I'll put on some music," I say.

In the old days Ma and Helene and I would put on music and we'd work together to do the whole house. We'd dust the table legs and the scrolls on the chairs and the lampshade pleats. We'd even dust the chess pieces. The way Ma was cleaning now was completely wrong in my opinion. She was basically just pushing the dirt around. It made my blood boil just watching her. I tried to take the rag out of her hand again.

"Stop it," she says.

"For god's sake, stop it!"

That's when I ran upstairs and went into Ma's closet. I found the plastic bag hidden in the back. I pulled out one of the recordings Da had made a million years ago on his old tape recorder. Before I knew what I was doing I was back downstairs and I put the tape in the stereo and I pressed play. I turned the volume up as far as it would go.

When Helene's voice came out of the speakers I have to admit I wasn't sure I'd done the right thing. It was the voice of a child. Helene sounded about nine or ten. Ma stopped moving. I could picture how the woolly mammoths just sank in the tar once they stopped resisting. I kept my eyes on Ma's hands to see if they started shaking. But it was my hands that were shaking. I leaned against the stereo cabinet so that I wouldn't fall over.

Ma looked at me and she smiled in that strange way alcoholics have, like she had a toothache. Maybe it wasn't a smile at all. Anyway the look on her face sent me for a loop. I switched off the tape as fast as I could.

Ma came over to me with the smile or whatever it was stuck on her face. She's going to clobber me, I thought. I was ready for the explosion, for all the walls to come tumbling down around us. But then what happened was even worse. Ma picked up my hand and she kissed it. She pressed my hand to her face. It was horrifying. I wanted to fall through the floor.

"Don't be scared," she says. Her grip felt like it could crush my bones.

"I'm not scared," I say.

"It's all right to be scared," she says.

And I wonder, why is she saying this to me now? She should have said it to me a year ago in the time of the nightmares.

If I'm scared now, it's none of her business.

"No one's going to hurt you," Ma says. Her face with the

twisted smile was becoming something else. Water filled her eyes, but it didn't fall. It wasn't officially tears.

"I have to do my homework," I say, and I break away from her.

"Mathilda," she says.

"Mathilda."

Why does she have to say my name like that? Why does she have to say my name at all? I know she'd rather be saying someone else's name. I know she wishes it was another girl standing in the room. Instead it's me standing here, and I'll be standing here for as long as Ma lives. The wrong daughter forever. I know what's in Ma's heart. It's a black thing, worse than wolves. Inventing the ghost of Helene is just giving her what she wants. And if it sends her over the edge, what do I care? She's already leaning over the cliff. She's practically begging someone to push her.

When Da came into my room, I was already in bed. I was wearing my red pajamas, it was like a scene from a Christmas movie.

"Are you ready for Santa Claus?"

"Oh yes Da, I can hardly sleep."

Except that's not what we said, don't be stupid.

Da came in and he looked tired as usual. Tired isn't even the right word. He looked *exhausted.*

"Hi Da," I say.

He comes in and sits on my bed.

"I was reading," I say, even though I don't have a book anywhere near me.

I know he's wondering if I heard him and Ma arguing downstairs. He should be the first one to speak about it, so I wait. He's obviously got a lot on his mind. He just smoothes my hair, but he can't find the words.

"Ma," I finally say.

"I know," he says. "She's going through a rough patch. We have to make things easy for her."

"I'm not bothering her," I say.

"Listen to me," he says, and he forces my eyes to his like a magnet. "You have to stop your nonsense."

He takes my hand. "You don't want to lose her, do you?" What kind of question is that? I think.

"It's not my fault," I say. "I'm not doing anything."

"A lot of people are upset," I say. "It's an epidemic, it's the whole world."

"We're not talking about the whole world," he says. "We're talking about your mother."

"I know," I say. "But Helene . . ."

"What about her?" Da says. He looks at me like he's confused, like I've changed the subject. But in my mind it's the thing we've been talking about from the very beginning.

"We can't do anything about that," Da says. "We can't go through all that again."

But we haven't gone through it at all, I think. Have we?

"Baby, we all miss her, we all . . ." but he doesn't finish.

I could see Da was in pain and that it was different from my pain. You could feel the ocean between us, with dark water freezing cold. Did someone say grief is an island? If they didn't say it, then I said it. It's my invention. You can look it up one day in the book of quotable quotes.

Grief is an island. —*Mathilda Savitch*

Da looks at me and I would be lying to you if I said there wasn't love in his eyes.

"Can you be good?" he says. "Can you please be good?"

I don't know is the honest answer, but I tell him yes. It's not his heart I want to break. I'd like to ask Da a million questions but I don't want to hurt him with the thoughts in my head. I'd like to ask him what kind of mother lets her daughter leave the house with sandals on when it's freezing outside?

"Give me the tapes," he says.

"No," I say. "Please Da."

"Give me the tapes," and this time he closes his eyes when he says it.

I get them from under my bed. A plastic bag with Helene's voice inside. Why couldn't I have just left her quiet in Ma's closet? Now she's real again, and Ma won't be able to live with that. I know her. She's going to make Da throw the tapes away. She's going to make him destroy them. But still I hand him the bag. I don't stop it from happening. It's a strike against me in somebody's book. The watchers, god, Krishna. They all turn away from me in shame.

Oh Da, I want to tell you so many things. And not just about Helene. I'd like to tell him about the watchers and about Louis and also what I heard on TV, how they're still finding people in the rubble. Sometimes they only find shoes, sometimes just a ring or a tooth. The President narrows his eyes. We will not rest until every last murderer is punished, he says.

When Da leaves the room, I think about the island of grief. I wonder how large it is and how long it will take me to explore it. I wonder how long I've been here without even knowing it. And who knows, there might be another person hiding here. Maybe there are savages in the bushes. Maybe Louis is here. Maybe even the man who killed her. The truth is I'm ready if it comes to a battle. It's not over yet, Helene. Not by a long shot.

20

Sometimes I think I'd like to be a person with brain damage, with nothing but the whale of joy jumping around inside of me. They used to make people forget their bad thoughts by sticking ice picks in their heads. I saw a show all about it on the Science Channel. It was pretty popular once, but it's illegal now. Now it's all done with pills supposedly. But obviously the pills don't work too hot because if they did everyone would be walking around like zippity-doo-dah. I tried a couple of O's pills, the ones I stole from her medicine cabinet at school, and all they did was give me a cramp and a half.

The problem is, at a certain point you can't stop thinking even if you want to. I swear, sometimes you just wish you could go back into the dark like a primitive person. But you can't, that's the problem with evolution. Once you have a little bit of knowledge, more of it just keeps coming at you like birds around a bagel. Sometimes when I learn things, I wish I hadn't learned them. Like did I really need to know about Da's magazines or Ma's bottles or even the things I know about my own body?

Like for instance, my legs are crooked. My knees turn in toward the middle. It's almost a deformity. I never noticed until one day I compared them to Anna's legs and I almost had a heart attack. Honestly, sometimes I wish I had no legs at all and a silver wheelchair. That's a real attention-grabber. Wheelchairs are like thrones you never get off of except for bathroom and sleep. It's elevating in a way. In my opinion, people have it all wrong about the sadness of wheelchairs.

Of course, I'd like to have fake legs as well so that I could walk around sometimes. I would dance with a boy and then afterwards pull up my dress to show him my plastic legs, just to watch him fall over from the shock of it. I'd do that with a hundred boys until I found the one who got down on his knees and kissed my fake legs. That's how I would know I'd found the right person. I wonder if Kevin would do it.

Of course, I wouldn't be able to feel the kiss, on account of the fact that I'd have no sensation down there. Even if Kevin bit my leg I wouldn't feel it. I could pretend it felt amazing or I could pretend it was painful. What I felt or didn't feel would be completely up to me.

Kevin and Anna are meeting me tonight in the yard. The plan is to slip down the basement as quietly as possible, and then whatever happens happens. The basement is my only reality right now. That's where I'm putting all my attention. I told Da I'm sleeping at Anna's. And Anna got permission to sleep over here. I don't know what Kevin said to his mother, but I'm sure he's got it all worked out.

I really am excited. Even though the basement is about hiding from terror, it's also about the future. And in the future there are other people, not just Ma and Da. Ma and Da can just stay on their own planet. I'm pretty much done with them. The basement is phase one of my new life.

I'm fairly confident Kevin and I will have sex at some point. I saw Kevin's thighs once in gym class and even though they were skinny they were impressive. Looking at them made me feel like I had to pee, but the funny thing is, I didn't have to pee at all. Apparently that means you're attracted to someone. I was craving some advice on the subject and so yesterday I pulled out the whole collection of Helene's e-mails. I reread every single one. Not just the ones from the stuffed bear, but also the ones she'd hidden in books on her bookshelf and a few that I found inside the folded-up flaps of a Monopoly board at the back of her closet. When I first read these e-mails last year, my life was still a little blurry and I guess I didn't quite pick up all the details. But now that I'm in tip-top shape again I have a whole new view of things. And I can tell you, Helene definitely had sex before she died. The more I read the e-mails from her boyfriends, the more I think maybe she had a lot of it.

Before Louis there was jon@foozer.com, B2@fatcity .com, lastchance@bc.com, friendguy@greenstripe.net, billo@ msl.com, plus a whole bunch of others. Most of these boys were writing to her in the year before she died. In the last few months, it was just Louis. The thing is, I thought sex was supposed to make a person happy, but it didn't seem to have that effect on Helene. The last few months she hardly talked to any of us. Half the time she was in her room with the door locked and the other half she was running out of the house in some sexy get-up. I think maybe she had compulsions. But no one ever thought of sending her to the Tree. Apparently, beautiful people can do whatever they want and no one can stop them. Ma tried a couple of times. Sometimes she'd put both her hands on H's shoulders and say, *You be careful, okay? Promise me.* Ma wouldn't let her go until she did. When Helene left, Ma would step outside on the porch and smoke a hundred cigarettes.

I hope Helene did amazing things with her body before she died. Sometimes you hear about old ladies who are virgins. Imagine dying a virgin. Imagine dying without someone ever having touched your breasts. Dying without someone ever having put their finger inside you, or even more. Without ever having been kissed or thrown down on a bed, and not only kissing your lips but your thighs and your feet as well. And then you kiss the other person's thighs. A person should taste everything before he dies, even the things the priests would tell you, that's disgusting, spit it out. Eve ate the apple and I would have too. If I was one of those old ladies who'd never had sex, and I was in my hospital bed dying, I'd get one of the young doctors to come over and I'd say to him, excuse me but I have a last request, could you do me a favor? How could he refuse? He'd have to give me his thighs. If I managed to resist the apple my whole life, I'd eat it just before I croaked.

I hope Helene ate the apple.

I know she did.

I hope it tasted good in her mouth.

———

Heygirl,
Get your ass over here, I'm hard, r-u wet? B2

Hi H:
Yes! When?
Your "good" friend ☺ Jon

Dear Helene,
The poem about the mountain, the one in which "you" are
standing on the boulder, is amazing. I think it would make
a killer song. FYI, I can't find that Indian book you lent me,
did you take it home by accident? Mostly I just want to look
at the pictures ha ha, though if you say it's good I really do
want to read it. I woke up wanting to kiss you, and then how
about the way we did it last time? I'll call you tonight
around ten. Be in your room. Mom says hello.
Over and out, Louis

Obviously he's different. Obviously Louis is the boy Helene would have married. But sometimes I think he's trying too hard. Plus, you can't believe everything people write.
Some people exaggerate. Yesterday I composed about ten
e-mails to him, but none of them seemed exactly right. Then
I realized I could send an e-mail with no words. Just a blank
message from HeyGirl. Just to see how he'd react.

I sent it this afternoon! It took me about two hours to
press send. I felt like the man with his finger on the red
button that will release the nuclear missiles. Should I do it,
shouldn't I do it? When I finally hit the button, the watchers

perked up. I felt one just behind my shoulder. Which was nice because it made me feel like what I was doing was important. That I wasn't just playing games. The watchers don't watch you unless you're onto something.

Your mail has been successfully sent, the computer said.

Who knows, maybe Louis believes in ghosts. I like the way he writes "you" when he's talking about the girl standing on top of the boulder. He's smart enough to know that the girl in the poem may or may not be Helene. He understands that sometimes people pretend to be other people. "You" could mean "anyone." Just like when jon@foozer.com writes "good," he really means "bad."

21

Suddenly we're laughing and we can't stop. We cover our mouths but the sound sneaks out in jerks and squeaks. Kevin's rolling on the floor like a patient from the funny farm. When I told the story about my grandfather dying from falling off a dog it brought down the house. I even acted it out a little. I did the heart attack and everything. Help me, I said. Oh Lordy, help me! And then I just fell over, kicking my legs and letting out the final death rattle that went something like *kkha-kkha-kkhaaaaa-kkkkkh*. When we recovered we all had tears in our eyes.

"Do you think they heard us?" Anna whispers.

"No," I say.

"If they did," I say, "they'll probably just think it's mice."

"Are there mice?" Anna says, which starts Kevin laughing again.

Earlier, when Anna came into the backyard to meet me, Kevin was already there. She gave me a dirty look and pulled me aside to talk in private. She said she wasn't going down the basement with him, and so I just flat out told her she didn't have any choice, there was no turning back. I made my eyes into the eyes of the evil hypnotist, controller of wills.

Plus Kevin was clever. He could see there was a problem and he came over to Anna and me and asked Anna if she wanted him to leave. Which put Anna on the spot.

"I don't care," she said. She looked at me and then back at Kevin. I could tell she was trapped. She didn't want to suddenly be the only prude in the group.

"You can stay if you want," she said. Then she adjusted her jacket like she was Miss Casual America.

"I just didn't know," she said.

Besides, Kevin had combed down his hair and in the dark the blue wasn't so noticeable. Basically he just looked like a normal person. He smiled at Anna and it wasn't phony or anything. Plus he has great teeth, ting-a-ling white. It's like a little bell goes off every time he smiles.

When Kevin went to pick up his bag on the lawn, Anna looked at me like *you better know what you're doing.* And I looked back at her like I did, because I do. I know exactly what we're doing. We're doing the future. Part of which will be people living in basements hiding from bombs. And once the world ends, the only way it'll begin again is from the boys and girls underground. Eventually we'll crawl out into the sun, if there's still a sun, and we'll have to start from scratch. Nothing will exist. Everything in the world will have to be invented all over again.

————

After the laughing we're quiet for a while. I hand out the blankets and the pillows and we all make up our little areas. Anna and me close to each other, and Kevin at a respectable distance. Some of the sheets are old, from when I was little. One set has bunnies all over it. It's a little embarrassing but luckily no one mentions it. I give Kevin the solar system sheets, I give Anna the plain blue ones, and I keep the bunnies for myself. As we make up our beds I feel like the three of us are the stars of a movie about soldiers in a war. I'm also the director. It's actually not a frightening movie, it's more about the bonds between men. It's a feel-good flick basically.

"Is anyone hungry?" I say, and I push the goodies into the center of the room.

"I brought some stuff too," Kevin says. He gets his bag and pulls out three bottles of beer. Anna looks at me like the mother of god but I just ignore her.

"Only three?" I say.

"I have more," Kevin says.

"I don't drink," Anna chimes in.

"One beer won't hurt you," I say.

"Try it," Kevin says. He opens the bottle and holds it out toward Anna. He gives her his best smile. "It's from Holland," he says.

Anna takes it.

"You don't have to finish it," Kevin says.

The beer doesn't taste good exactly but I suppose that's not the point. After a while it does make you float above your humdrum concerns. The basement starts to sparkle like a little piece of heaven. Everything is a little better than you thought. Even the bunny sheets are suddenly a stroke of genius. The beer is almost like gratitude in a bottle. I wonder why vodka doesn't do the same thing for Ma.

I look at Anna and she's sipping hers like a man condemned to death. I make mock pout-lips at her but she doesn't react, she just tosses her hair. Suddenly Kevin starts laughing again.

"What?" I say, and then for no reason my own laughter leaks out as well.

"You look funny," he says.

"You do," Anna says. "You look like a fish."

"She does," Kevin says, and he imitates me with my mouth open.

Anna does the fish-mouth too and it's amazing I don't want to kill the two of them. Even though they're making fun of me I sort of feel honored. I feel like they know me. Maybe they can even see the gold locket and the bird feathers in my stomach. Maybe they know all my deadly secrets. So I just make the fish-mouth back at them. I make the fish-mouth back at them in all its fishy glory and then I look around for the spy cameras. I sort of hoped the watchers were seeing this. I hoped they were taking notes. The three of us together, happy in the midst of the war. It's important that moments like this get preserved. One day if there's nothing left of us, whoever comes next will be able to look at the recordings and say, *Oh, so that's what they were like.* It's not real immortality, but at least it's a scrap.

"There's a lot of stuff down here," Kevin says.

"Junk," I say.

"Can I look around?" he says, popping open a second beer. He doesn't wait for my permission. He gets up and moves toward some boxes.

"*Shit,*" he says, jumping back, "*mouse!*"

Anna snaps to her feet and Kevin snorts.

"I'm kidding," he says.

"Maybe it was a ghost," I say.

"Maybe," Kevin says, and then he starts to make the sound of a horror movie. The music right before the moment of terror. My stomach does a little turn. This is the wrong direction, I think. We don't want to get started on ghosts. I want to punch myself for bringing it up.

"Shut up," I say to Kevin, "they'll hear us."

I notice Anna squinting at me, surprised, sniffing at my fear.

"Give me another beer," I say.

"Say please," Kevin says, and I do.

Anna looks at Kevin and I can tell she sees his power. She brushes her hair behind her ear. "I'll have one too," she says, and Kevin turns to her. He just stares at her, waiting.

"Please," she finally says. *Please.*

———

"I don't like the test sirens," Anna says. "Sometimes they keep me up at night."

The three of us are sitting in a circle with our beer bottles in front of us like microphones. We're slouching over them like the men at the UN on television.

"Why do we even have sirens?" Anna says. "The terror didn't happen here."

"It's stupid" is her grand summation.

130

The beer is making her more talkative than usual, it's fascinating.

Kevin asks did we see the pictures of the attack in Russia. The bomb at the school. I tell him I did, that I saw it on the computer.

"Did you see the way the mothers were crying?" I say.

I tell Anna and Kevin how I clicked on the video clip, "Howls of Grief as Town Buries Children." It was amazing. People don't cry like that around here. Around here people cry like a drip in a sink. The old women in Russia were down on their knees with their hands up in the air like Jesus freaks. I also saw a picture of a girl in a white coffin with white fabric inside bunched up to make a nest for her. She had on a pink dress and there were roses all around her and on top of her. She looked like Snow White. The pink dress had ruffles on it. You wouldn't want to wear it to school or even in real life but it was the perfect dress for someone who's dead. Especially a child.

"Was it terror there too?" Anna asks.

"Of course it was terror," I say. "That's all it is anymore."

"Did you see the picture of the boy with the black hair and the red lips?" Kevin says.

"The pale one?" I say, and Kevin says, "Yeah, the one in the tiny wooden coffin."

"He looked like a baby vampire," I say.

"He was beautiful," I say, and Kevin nods his head, sadly, like the baby vampire was his own son. And then we all look down and I guess it was some sort of prayer because I could feel my heart swelling.

I didn't tell Kevin and Anna how, after I played "Howls of

Grief as Town Buries Children," I couldn't turn it off. In my head, I mean. The Howls of Grief got into everything. For a few days even Luke's barking sounded like the Howls of Grief. Even laughter on the television.

After we talked about Russia we just drank our beers in silence. That's when the spider appeared. It dropped down from the ceiling on its invisible wire and hung in the air a few inches from the floor. When the spider finally landed he crawled over to the cuff of Kevin's jeans. None of us were moving and I suppose the spider just assumed we were pieces of furniture. Then Kevin lifted his hand to crush it but I said, "No, leave it alone." Not that I thought this spider was suddenly a guardian angel or something, but it did have the feeling of another miracle, the way it came out of nowhere, almost like we'd invented it. It was one of those spiders that have little legs thin as eyelashes. How did we ever hurt things like that? Back in the old days, in the fort. I wondered about the blindness of us, and the blue Krishna came to mind, with his stupendous love for all beings.

"Kill it," Anna said, "what are you waiting for?" And Kevin's hand slammed down and then the spider was nothing more than a little smear of ash on Kevin's pants. I thought of the black end of a match after the flame goes out. In my mind it was like Kevin had just put out a fire. That's what death is.

"I can't sleep on the floor if there's bugs," Anna says.

"I'll sleep with you," I say. I don't mean it sexual but Kevin makes a pigeony sound of lovemaking.

"You didn't have to kill it," I say to him.

"It could have been poisonous," Anna says.

And she's right. I mean, why should I even care about a lousy spider? Not all of us have blue skin and a crown of peacock feathers. Not all of us can be love love love all the time. Not in this day and age anyway.

———

"What are you doing with that?" I say to Anna. She has a bottle of nail polish in her hand.

"I need to finish my nails," she says. "I always do them on Friday."

I look at Kevin and shake my head. "Nail polish in a bomb shelter," I say.

But Kevin doesn't react. He's poking around the basement again. I watch him out of the corner of my eye, just to make sure he doesn't disturb Helene's stuff.

Anna is already putting the pink on her nails. "I can't believe you brought that stuff to a bomb shelter," I say.

"Stop saying that Mattie," she says. "It's not real."

"I wouldn't bring it if it was real," she says.

I hate it when she gets like this. *If it was real.* I suppose she'll want to roast marshmallows next. Not that there's anything wrong with having a little fun, you just don't want to forget the big picture. Even when Anne Frank was laughing about the beans and all the farting going on in the attic, or joking about the cat peeing on the potatoes, I bet she never completely forgot about the Nazis. But, who knows, maybe she did. It was a more innocent time. Children didn't think so much about their own deaths back then.

"What are you doing in there?" I say to Kevin. He's in the back room now, with my grandmother's fruit. I can hear him moving around the glass jars, making sounds of disgust.

Anna doing her nails and Kevin in the fruit closet, what does it mean? I drink my beer and watch the two of them, and suddenly the movie jumps into the future, when we've all drifted apart. Anna is on the street wheeling a baby carriage, and we bump into each other. She doesn't recognize me but I recognize her.

"Anna McDougal?" I say.

"Yes," she says.

And then she remembers. "Oh my god, Mathilda?" she says, and she starts to cry.

"I didn't know what happened to you," she says. "In all the confusion of the terror, I thought I lost you."

"Oh Mathilda."

We do a minute of silence. Neither of us looks at the clock. We just stare into each other's eyes.

"You look good," I tell her. Which is what you tell people you haven't seen in a while.

"You look good too," she says. You have to say it even if it's a lie. But I probably will look good. I put myself in an expensive suit. Black.

"How are your parents?" Anna says.

"They're dead," I say. "They died."

"I'm so sorry," Anna says, reaching for my hand.

"What is all this crap?" Kevin says, breaking into my movie. In his hand is a jar of brown slivers.

"*Unnnnhhh,*" he says, straining to turn the lid.

"Don't open it," I say, but then I hear the pop of the seal and the ancient air slipping out.

Kevin finds a pail in the corner and he plops the brown slivers into it.

"Gross," Anna says. "Is that food?"

Kevin brings the pail over and we all look inside.

"It's my grandmother's," I say.

"Your grandmother's what?" Kevin says.

And even though I feel nauseous again, I start to laugh. I let the laugh take over my body until every part of me is shaking. I even stick my hand in the pail of fruit, just to prove how brave I am. I pull out a sliver and wiggle it.

"It's her toes," I say.

Anna squeals and Kevin groans.

Then I drop the sliver back in the pail, and suddenly the room is like a hundred degrees. My breath goes funny.

"What's the matter?" Anna says.

"Nothing," I say. "I just have to wash my hands," I tell her.

I go and get a bottle of water and pour some over my fingers. I pour too much and make a stupid puddle. All of a sudden I wish I was upstairs in my bed with Luke. I wish I'd never come down here.

But it's too late. There's no turning back. On the floor is a face looking up at me. My own face in the puddle of water. Hypnotist, controller of wills.

Stay where you are, you stupid girl.

Don't you fucking move.

22

The most important event in my life and I wasn't even there. That doesn't mean I don't see it. I do. I see it all the time. I always see Helene's hair blowing in the wind. Sometimes it blows in front of her face and I can't make out her expression. I know she's wearing her blue coat. I know she's got her brown boots on. I know she has on the earrings with the green stones the color of seaweed. These are just facts, it doesn't take any imagination to see them. What I don't see is the exact moment. Everything stops the second the hands touch her shoulders.

What happened to her body was pretty awful. I never saw it, I only heard rumors. Ma and Da saw it, and that's why you have to have some sympathy for them sometimes. All I ever saw was the locked box. The coffin. Were they even able to put her in a dress? I wonder. And what shoes was she wearing? The day of the funeral I looked in her closet to see what dress was missing, what shoes. But all her clothes were still there, as far as I could tell. Maybe she was barefoot inside the box. Maybe she was naked. But Ma would never have allowed it. Ma would have covered her.

When I'm watching the movie in my head, just after the hands on her shoulders, that's usually the end. Everything goes black. But then sometimes the movie starts up again, except it's not a movie anymore, it's a photograph. A picture of her body. The picture happens later, separately. It's her body after the accident. But it doesn't even look real, it always looks fake. It never looks like real blood. In my mind it's just red paint someone's poured over her.

Kevin is still fussing with the pail of slivers, squatting over it like a caveman. I keep my distance so I don't get sick again. Anna has a big black book in front of her. She's pulled out one of Ma's photo albums. Luckily it's an ancient one, before any of us were born. Ma showed it to me once a long time ago. Inside there's lots of women with long faces and names like Rose and Violet and Daisy. Ma doesn't even know who some of them are. We only know the names because someone wrote them down on the back of the pictures. *Violet in the garden, 1925. Rose in Joe Farrow's car, 1936.* I swear, sometimes I almost wish there was a big fire down here to burn everything up.

"Did you pee on the floor?" Kevin says.

"No," I say, but my heart jumps because it's my big fear.

"It's just water," I say. I'm still standing next to the puddle from when I washed my hands.

"Oh my god," Anna says.

"What?" I say.

"Where *do* we go to the bathroom?" she says.

137

"That's why I brought down the pail," I say.

Kevin laughs. With a stick he stirs the slop of dead fruit.

"Oh my god," Anna says again.

"Why," I ask her, "do you have to go?"

"No," she says. "I'm not going in a bucket."

I look at her and in my heart is suddenly the thought, I want to be strong. I want to be stronger than the pioneers, stronger than the Indians. I want to get through the whole winter with nothing but a blanket and a box of matches. I don't think Anna is up for the job. The picture comes back of Anna standing on the street corner with the baby carriage. It doesn't feel very far away.

I bet Rose and Violet and Daisy would have peed in a bucket. They probably had to in those days. I bet they could have taught us a few tricks about how to live in hard times. They would have tied Helene to a chair and wiped every bit of lipstick from her mouth. Maybe they could have saved her somehow. Ma and Da are too smart to save anyone. Smart people always turn out to be weaklings. Smart people are not going to be the ones to help you when you have to move a piano out of the house. When Ma and Da got rid of Helene's piano it had to be taken out by professionals. I bet Rose and Violet and Daisy would have moved it themselves. Rose and Violet and Daisy probably wouldn't even have gotten rid of it in the first place. I don't want to be weak when I grow up and I don't want to be surrounded by weaklings.

In his blue hair and his chains maybe Kevin could be a pioneer. I bet he'd pee in a bucket without blinking an eye.

"How's the soup coming?" I say.

He stirs the slop pot and shoots me a demented smile. "I need another beer," he says. And he hops to his feet and does a running glide across the cement floor in his socks, like he's been living here in the basement for a thousand years. He's perfectly at home.

"Anyone else?" Kevin says, but Anna and I are still working on our second bottle.

I go over and sit next to my darling. Her eyes are still in the photo album.

"Who are all these people?" she says.

"They're ugly," she says. "Are they your family?"

"No," I say. "I don't know them."

Anna closes the book and tosses it aside. She hugs herself like she's cold.

"I'm bored," she says. "I wish you had a TV down here."

I try to give her a hug but she squirms out of it.

"Stop," she whispers, like she's ashamed of our love now that you-know-who is in the room. She reaches into the goodie pile and takes a granola bar. She breaks it in half. Anna never eats the whole of anything. Half is her limit.

Kevin is looking through a pile of old board games. Parcheesi and Operation and Mousetrap, which used to be my favorite. Anna nibbles at her granola bar like she's queen of the rabbits. Upstairs it's quiet. Upstairs is a million miles away.

"If there was a bomb," I say, "it might be silent."

Anna looks at me, chewing, but her eyes are listening.

"You'd hear *something*," she says.

"Maybe not," Kevin says.

"A flash of light," he says.

"But we wouldn't even see that from down here," he adds.

A wave of joy comes over me, that Kevin is on my side.

"Your parents could already be dead," I say to Anna.

"No they're not," she says.

"You don't know," I say. "You won't know until you go home."

"Why are you being mean?" Anna says.

"I'm not," I say. "I'm just being honest."

"They're not dead," Anna insists.

"I only said *could*. I didn't say they *were*."

"Not everyone dies," Anna says.

What's that supposed to mean?

"Everyone does die," I say.

"Girls, girls," Kevin says. "Do I have to separate you?" His voice is the exact voice of Mrs. Thorsland the gym teacher. Even Anna smiles. She gets up and moves toward Helene's stuff.

"So your brother's killing the terrorists, huh?" Kevin draws himself closer to Anna.

"I don't know what he's doing," Anna says.

"But he's over there, right?"

"Yes," she tells him. Her voice cracks a little.

"That's good," Kevin says.

"It is good," I shout over to them, "I agree." But neither of them looks at me.

"I would go," Kevin says, "if I could."

"I would definitely go," he says.

And maybe one day he will, I think. And then it hits me that maybe it's Kevin's baby in Anna's baby carriage. Maybe Kevin is over there fighting and Anna is on the street corner waiting for him. The truth is I should never have put the two of them together.

Upstairs, Luke barks. It's almost a cry of pain. Everyone looks up toward the ceiling. There are voices too, human voices. An argument. And then the word comes out. *Mathilda*. It comes out of the woman.

"Is that your mother?" Kevin says.

Mathilda!

"Doesn't she know you're at my house?" Anna says.

A door slams and then my name falls down from another part of the house. I get up and stir the pot of slivers to distract myself.

"Are you going to answer her?" Anna says.

"She sounds mad," Kevin says.

"So what?" I say.

Anna starts to say something else but I tell her to shut up. The way I say it shuts up Kevin too. They both look at me like they've just remembered whose house this is, whose basement they're in. Luke makes another sound and then another door slams and then that's it, it's the end of the show. Ma and Da are silent again. Anna's hand is resting on the white sheet covering Helene's stuff like she's about to do a magic trick. Like she's about to pull the sheet and make everything disappear.

"Cut my hair," I say.

Anna and Kevin look at me like they don't even speak my language.

"I want someone to cut my hair," I say.

Poor Anna stands there baffled but Kevin, good old pioneer that he is, comes to my rescue. "I'll do it," he says, and his smile sneaks out, crooked like the devil's.

"Where are the scissors?" he says.

23

I'm sipping another beer as Kevin's hands move through my hair. Sometimes his fingers brush against my neck and the feeling goes right down to my stomach. I wonder if this is why Da gets his hair cut every few weeks. It's almost like going to a prostitute. The fingers of electricity on the back of your neck. Ma has always been the one who's cut my hair. In the summer, in the old days, she used to do it outside on the lawn. Helene always went first. My first victim, Ma would say as she wrapped the sheet around Helene's neck. Ma did a pretty good mad scientist back then.

But it's different when a stranger does it. It's more dangerous. Not that Kevin's a stranger exactly. It's his fingers I don't know too well.

"How short do you want it?" he says.

"Short," I say. "But not too short."

Kevin starts slowly and my hair makes a crackly sound

against the scissors. Anna watches us like we're committing the crime of the century.

"Why are you doing this?" she says. "Your hair was just getting long again."

"I'll do you next if you want." Kevin smirks in her direction.

"Do you even know what you're doing?" she asks him. "You're supposed to wet it first."

"I'll get yours wet I promise," Kevin says.

I can see the red come to Anna's cheeks.

"We'll tie her down," I say. "Tie her down and cut her till she's bald."

Anna rolls her eyes but I can tell she's worried we might be half serious. Kevin's snipping away now like king of the lobsters.

"Carol Benton got a new haircut," Anna says.

"Who?" I say. The name must be a mistake, I think.

"She got some red highlights put in it too," Anna says.

"Who are you talking about?" I say.

"Carol Benton," Anna says again, but louder.

It was almost like Carol Benton was hiding in the basement behind some boxes. It had the feeling of a trick, like there were hidden cameras somewhere. Do you ever get the feeling people are trying to film your reactions to things? Will she get upset, will she start crying? That sort of thing.

"Drink your beer," I say, keeping my face as normal as possible.

"You didn't notice Carol's hair?" Anna says with the gleam of evil in her eye. "I thought it looked nice."

"As nice as your mother's?" I ask her.

"What's that supposed to mean?" she says.

"Nothing," I say. "It's just interesting. The way her hair is shaped like a helmet."

"That's an expensive haircut," Anna says.

A picture of Mrs. McDougal flashes through my mind.

"Painter of blobs," I say.

"What?" Anna says. She doesn't get the reference and I don't explain.

What are we fighting about? I wonder. Is it Kevin? Maybe it's just the boredom of captivity. When you put animals in cages, sometimes they turn against each other. I saw an experiment all about it on the Nature Channel. Kevin is lost in my hair and says nothing. In the silence it's just the *click click click* of his claws.

"That's enough," Anna says.

"Mattie," she says, "it's short enough."

I tell her to roll over the mirror. I point to the big old dressing mirror on wheels shoved in the corner.

"Don't look until I'm finished," Kevin says.

"She has to look," Anna says. She pushes some boxes out of the way and then rolls the big dusty mirror across the room. It's taller than she is and she pushes it from behind. Which makes the mirror look like it's magically moving on its own.

When I see myself it doesn't completely make sense. The mirror is on hinges and it's swaying a little. I can see my face moving up and down like I'm on a seesaw. Kevin's in the mirror too, with the glinty scissors still in his hand. I almost don't recognize myself.

"It's lopsided," Anna says. Which is the understatement of the year. On one side my hair is hanging down in choppy strands that barely reach my cheek. On the other side the hair is so short it looks like fur.

"It's all crooked," Anna blurts out again.

"It's supposed to be like that," Kevin says.

"What do you think?" he asks me.

"It's a mutilation," Anna insists. That's her verdict, pure and simple. If she had a gavel, she'd probably slam it down on Kevin's head.

I look in the mirror and try to concentrate. For some reason I picture Ma falling to her knees. I picture her begging me for forgiveness. When you cut off your hair, if it's done right, it can mean a whole new life. I look at Kevin's eyes in the mirror but I can't make out his secret desire. Is it to mutilate me? Or is it to make me his bride? Maybe, for him, it's the same thing.

"Do it shorter," I say.

Monster is the thought in my mind. I want to be a monster.

"Do the whole thing like the left side," I say. Which is the furry side.

"Mattie," Anna says, "are you crazy?" Suddenly she's moving toward Kevin.

"No," she says with a voice I've never heard before. She actually tries to pull the scissors out of Kevin's hand. Anna the hero leaping to my rescue. But Kevin's too quick. He backs away laughing.

"It's okay," I say to her. "It'll be like Phunka's hair."

"I hate Phunka," Anna says.

"Phunka's great," Kevin says.

Phunka, if you don't know, is a woman who plays the electric violin and has the voice of cats and dogs. She's an

African. She has a new song against the war but they won't play it on the radio. Kevin discovered it on the Internet and made me a copy.

"Do you really want me to keep going?" he says.

I nod my head at him in the mirror. And I take off my sweater because I'm sweating. I'm wearing a tank top underneath. As Kevin starts to cut again, I watch the hair fall onto my body. Some of it sticks to my arms and my shoulders and the top of my chest, like I'm a man or an animal. Anna loses all her power. She just sits on the floor watching it happen. It was as if the cutting of my hair was killing her. I took it as a sign of her love for me. There were even tears in her eyes and I wanted to say, don't worry my darling. I wanted to remind her of the story from the bible about Samson and Delilah, except how this was the opposite. Because the truth is I was getting stronger and stronger the more Kevin cut.

In the mirror I was becoming someone else. A person in prison or a Japanese nun, and then suddenly I was Anne in the concentration camp, because a person can't always control her thoughts. My heart was banging itself against the wall. I felt a weird rush of power.

"I'm going to kill him," I whisper.

All of my hair is gone. It's just fur now.

Funny sounds were coming from somewhere, maybe my throat.

"I'm going to kill him," I say to myself. Kevin's eyes meet me in the mirror.

"Who?" he says.

"The man who pushed Helene," I say.

Then I look up and see Anna's eyes and I know I've said

the wrong thing out of my happiness. She turns away from me, embarrassed.

"No," I say, "I'm just kidding."

It was as if I'd just woken up and I was standing there naked.

"What are you talking about?" Kevin says. "Didn't she jump?"

"Anna," I say, trying to get her on my side, but she just shakes her head.

"You have to stop saying that," she says. She looks at me with her beautiful blue eyes.

"Don't," I say, reading her mind.

But then it happens. Her face turns horrible.

"She killed herself, Mattie. Everyone knows she killed herself."

Her voice is the voice of the Tree.

Nobody pushed her, the Tree said. *Suicide*, he said, as if he were talking to a retarded person, as if I didn't know what the stupid word means. Suddenly the big knife goes through my chest all over again, like it did when we first found out.

"I never knew anyone who killed themselves," Kevin says, but I can't even see him anymore. All I can see is my hair. All over me and all over the floor. Some of it is dancing in the draft that falls from the top of the stairs.

"What are you doing?" Anna says.

I'm on my knees trying to gather up the hair. But every time I try to pick it up it goes right through my fingers.

"I'll clean it," Kevin says. "Let me sweep it."

"No," I say, "leave it alone."

"Don't touch it," I say.

"It's just hair," Anna says. "Why are you crying?"

But I wasn't crying, I was doing something else. Something an animal does. I was trying to protect myself. Plus I couldn't look up again. It was better just to stay on my hands and knees like a dog. If I scream, I thought, everything will disappear. If I bark like a dog.

"Mathilda?" Anna says. And her brave hand touches my hairy back.

24

All people are children when they sleep. I saw Ma once, with
her mouth open and her head tilted up. She looked like a baby
bird begging for worms. It made me wonder how I look when
I'm off in dreamland. I wonder if I look better or worse than
I do in real life. And who knows if I'll ever sleep again anyway. I'm not planning on it.

Anna looks different with her eyes closed. Perfect but flat.
Clearly it's her eyes that give Anna her advantage. Without
them she's just some half-baked idea. Across the room Kevin
is sleeping deep deep, I can tell from the way he's breathing.
The few long pieces of his hair hang in front of his face like
vines. Above and below, the world is sleeping. I can hear the
wind outside the house, it's driving me crazy. *Shee shee sheee.*
She's a liar.

Fuck you, I say, to whoever wants to listen.

Sometimes I reach up to touch my head. The bristles of it

make me feel closer to god. The closer you are to god the farther away you are from other people. It's cold down here too. When I touch the back of my neck it's an ice cube. Without its blanket of hair it's completely naked. Do you ever have those moments when you don't know where you are? The middle of the night is like being on the moon sometimes. The night comes after the day is what most people will tell you. But sometimes I don't fall asleep and then it's the opposite.

I didn't hear the sirens tonight but I thought about them. The baby vampire was also on my mind, plus the people in England who died from a disease put inside a letter. It's some new disease that turns people into puddles.

Mostly I'm not sleeping because of Helene. The stupid truth of how she died. It happened over a year ago so get over it, I tell myself. I would, thank you very much, if her stupid body wasn't standing in the way, and what am I supposed to do, step on it? Ignore it? STAY ALERT, the signs say, but I guess not when it comes to dead people. When it comes to dead people you can just put a bag over your head, that's the Emily Post of it in my family.

But how is what happened to Helene any different from the war? People dying, and the horrible mystery of why. War is all there's ever been from the time I was born, and I can tell you one thing. There's always an enemy. And if you don't fight, they'll take everything away from you, even your own sister. The truth is, even if no one was standing behind her, somebody still pushed her.

Suddenly Kevin turns on a little flashlight and my heart stops. I wonder if I've been talking to myself and he's heard me. I almost say his name. Instead, I close my eyes and make my breathing more like the breathing of a sleeping person. If you want to make a documentary about animals, you have to become a stone among them. You have to pretend you're not interested.

Kevin's moving ever so slightly and I wonder if it has to do with masturbation. Which is pretty common among boys of a certain age. With my eyes closed I can hear every creak and crack. I can hear the soft sounds of the sheets. Upstairs there's sounds too, little heartbeat sounds of someone padding across the floor. I can't tell if it's the woman or the dog.

Kevin stands up, I can hear him. He moves in my direction one burglar step at a time. Even in socks he sounds like a giant. He's so close I start to worry. How well do I really know him? It's been years since the fort. And back then we practically had the same body. I can feel him standing over me. I can feel the blue shadow of him. And even though I'm afraid, I decide it's time. I have to do it. I have to open my eyes to him. I have to say, *yes, if you want to, I will.* Give myself away, which is what Ma said we should never do. I take a deep breath and start to ease open my legs.

But then Kevin moves past me and when I crack open my eyes he's facing away. He's headed toward Anna. His little penlight is aimed at the floor. In the darkness the beam looks like the walking stick of a wizard.

Sometimes things happen and they surprise you. But what happens most of the time is exactly what you expect, straight out of some stupid movie. This one will fall in love with that one, it's obvious from the beginning. The more different they are, the more they hate each other, the better.

Kevin sits down next to Anna. He watches her. He rubs his hands like they're cold and she's a fire. I suppose he's in love. Or worse. Possibly it's just biological. But he doesn't climb on top of her, he only touches her shoulder and when her eyes snap open he says, "Shhh." The first move Anna makes is to look over in my direction. "Mattie," I expect her to call out. But she doesn't. I wonder if she can see my eyes looking right at her.

"She's sleeping," Kevin whispers.

Anna turns to him. From the look in her eye, I think maybe it's a different movie than what I thought. If there's any music it should be the horror movie music again. The moment right before the terror. I wait for Anna to scream. I can feel her heart beating inside mine. Her mouth opens and a puff of scared air comes out. I can tell Kevin is scared too. His hand isn't a hundred percent certain as it moves from her shoulder and glides down her body. He does it slowly, like a doctor. Anna keeps breathing in bits and pieces, waiting for him to find where it hurts. When he touches her stomach, her eyes shoot over again in my direction. I don't understand. Does she want help or is she just making sure I'm asleep?

She can't see me, I decide, as Kevin's hand slips under the sheets. Anna sends her own hand fast in the same direction, I suppose to cover herself. She shakes her head no as Kevin leans over her. His hair touches her first. The blue hair on the white neck. He hangs over her like a bird floating on some secret river of air. His nostrils open and close like flowers. Anna's lips stay shut. It's amazing what you can see by the light of a measly penlight.

I'm not afraid of the kiss. A kiss is nothing. But Kevin's hand under the covers is a different story. That's more complicated. I wonder if Kevin's fingers are trying to make their way inside.

Help her, I think. But I couldn't. For some reason my

arms and legs weren't taking orders from me. My voice wasn't working either. Even the tears on my face aren't mine. Once or twice I know Helene came down here with a boy. To show him a song on the piano, she always said. But it wasn't non-stop music. There were plenty of pauses. Suddenly it was as if the living and the dead were both having sex down here and I didn't like it.

Kevin's hand is a funny puppet now, a mouse under the blanket. I feel a fist in my stomach. Who do they think they are? Do they think they can just go into the future without me? I'm so mad I don't even notice the voices upstairs. Kevin looks toward the ceiling and that's when I hear the commotion in the kitchen. But Kevin doesn't stop. His hand keeps moving and Anna takes a deep breath as the knife of his finger goes in. I can feel it. Why doesn't she stop him? Why doesn't she scratch his face? Is she secretly a whore?

Whoever's talking upstairs is practically yelling now. It isn't Ma or Da. *Your daughter* are the only words I hear. *Your daughter.* It's the police talking about Helene. Everything lights up, a flash inside my head. The police have found the killer and my perfect lie comes back to me in one piece. Why won't Kevin stop his nonsense? Anna looks up now with her stupid mute mouth crying to heaven. And just as she starts to say something, Kevin puts his hand over her lips to silence her. Anna's eyes go wild. The voice in the kitchen is unmistakable.

"*Mom,*" Anna shouts, pulling away from Kevin. She's crying now, but who cares. Kevin clicks off his stupid little penlight.

"Be quiet," he whispers, but it's too late for that.

"What the fuck do you think you're doing?" I say. I turn

on my own flashlight and shine it right into the lovers' faces. Disgusting is what they are, having sex in a graveyard almost.

"Are you down there?" the Nazis shout. They're coming for us at last. One of them is banging on the door so hard I think he'll break it.

"*Mathilda!*" They know my name. I pull the knife out of my belt.

"Anna?" another voice says.

"Open this door right now," the banger says.

"No," I scream.

Anna leaps up in her stupid pajamas. She shakes her hands like she's drying her nail polish. She moves a little bit toward the stairs.

"Don't you dare," I say.

"I'm sorry," she says with the ugliest face of tears you ever saw.

Kevin is walking in circles and won't look at me. The Nazis bang and shout and suddenly Anna runs toward the stairs. I follow her but she's too fast.

"I'll break the door," Da says.

"Break it," I say. "Go ahead!"

"I'd like to see you do it," I say.

I try to grab Anna on the steps but I trip. My mouth smacks against the floor. Anna's halfway up when the door breaks open and the light pours in. The Nazis are black blurs without faces. Anna runs into the arms of one of them. Kevin and I watch from below as Anna buries her head in her mother's breast.

"Disgusting," I shout.

I turn to Kevin but he still won't look at me.

"You won't say anything?" he says, his voice so small it's worthless.

Anna and her mother are still standing at the top of the stairs all blobbed together, the big blob stroking the little blob's hair. Why doesn't she slap her? I wonder.

"Mathilda?" Da says. He starts to make his way down the stairs. I back away from him and stand next to Kevin. I can see Anna and her mother disappear from the doorway, into the house. When Da gets to the bottom, when he sees me, I don't understand the look on his face. Then I remember my hair. Da shakes his head, and once he starts he doesn't stop.

"Give me that," he says, and he takes the knife out of my hand. I let him do it for some reason.

"You should go home," Da says, turning to Kevin. His voice is buried beneath a thousand pounds of sand.

"Mr. Savitch," Kevin starts, but Da cuts him off. "Go home," he says again and this time it's not a suggestion.

Kevin grabs his things and rushes up the stairs. I can hear the front door slam. Da looks at me with the knife in his hand and I wonder if he would ever kill me.

"Where's Ma?" I say. I look up the stairs for another blur in the doorway.

"Da," I say. "Where is she?"

But he doesn't answer, he just closes his eyes. Something in me says take his hand, and so I do. I grab the hand that's not holding the knife, and we just stand there like that for a long time. I look up the stairs again and I don't even see a dog. What's going on? I wonder.

"Da?" I pull at his arm but he doesn't open his eyes.

"Da?"

155

PART THREE

25

When Ma met Da she was sixteen, can you believe it? Da says she was so shy she couldn't even look him in the eye, she was always looking down. According to Da, a person had to duck below her to catch her eye and if you did that she would laugh and then you had her.

Da smoked cigarettes in those days. He was eighteen. Their love was instantaneous. Supposedly Da stole some money from his father one day and he bought Ma a fur coat which turned out to be a fake and it didn't even fit her. Plus she thought it was vulgar. Even back then Ma had very particular tastes. She made Da take back the engagement ring he bought her and then they went together to a special store two hundred miles away so Ma could get the ring she wanted in the blue box.

I used to get all the stories. Like their honeymoon in the hotel up on a hill and it was all lit up at night like heaven Ma said. Oh, and their first night in the restaurant with the gold ceiling. There was champagne and a chocolate cake that came to the table all in flames. Da got up and sang a song and everyone thought this is the life. People talking in a language they didn't understand but that night, Da said, he and Ma understood everything.

There are beautiful things in the world and there are sad things and when they come together they make a star. The light is far away and the strangest part is that the light is inside you. But no matter how hard you look you can never see the star itself, you only see the reflection of it on a lake, which is also inside you. When I told the Tree this he looked at me like I was quite the specimen. Round and round she goes and where she stops nobody knows. Which is what they say in the casino, where the lovers won—can you believe it?—three thousand dollars. I wonder if Ma got naked in the hotel bathtub and Da poured in the buckets of money. I can just picture it. A five-star honeymoon if ever there was one.

Back then I would have agreed with Da that she was the one to marry. But if I knew what I know now, I would have convinced him to marry someone else, a dancer or a singer, a policewoman maybe. Someone solid. Not a reader of books, not someone who just disappears. From now on, if anyone asks me what my mother does, I'll just say she's a female Houdini. Wouldn't that be a great person to have as a mother? Can you imagine it? I'd come home from school and she'd be upside down in a tank of water, practicing. I'd want to help her but I'd have to have faith. Helping her would defeat the whole purpose. I'd just have to wait and then, afterwards, when she was out of the tank, I'd pour her a drink. She'd sit in a chair and I'd dry her hair with a towel. That was close, I'd say. You had me worried, Ma.

The thing is, though, when a female Houdini disappears in a puff of smoke, the trick isn't finished until she comes back. If you keep people waiting too long, they get angry. And if you never come back, then you're a failure at magic as far as I'm concerned.

When Da and I came upstairs from the basement we sat in the kitchen and Da made a bunch of telephone calls about the situation. He called everyone he knew but Ma wasn't there.

"Did you try the pound?" I said, but so low Da didn't hear me. I don't know why I said it because to tell you the truth I was sort of scared. You never know if certain things run in the family. Depression and whatnot and where it leads.

"She just drove away? Where do you think she went?"

"I don't know," Da said, and I could tell he didn't. I could tell the question was eating him up.

"Do you think she did it because of me?" I said. I couldn't remember the last thing I'd said to her. I could hardly even picture her face. I kept trying but my brain kept screwing it up.

"Why didn't you follow her?" I said, and that's when Da gave me his full attention.

"Because I had to look for you," he said. The way he said it you would have thought looking for me was the worst punishment in hell.

"Lying to everyone like that," he said. I knew he was talking about the basement and the lie of sleeping over at Anna's, but I worried that somehow he knew what I'd said about Helene. I could tell he was mad at me for a lot of things, more than just the basement. The funny thing is, he still made me a sandwich.

Everything would have been fine if Anna's mother hadn't called to check up on her precious daughter. We could have disappeared forever down there. Now I'm back where I started, upstairs again, with Ma having the last word like always. Ma's not even here and still she's everywhere. Mothers are like that. When it comes to biology, mothers are a real problem. They stick to you because you have a lot of their cells and everything. It's worse than a monster movie.

"She probably just went for a drive," I say. When Helene and I were little, Ma wouldn't think twice about driving for two hours just to take us to a zoo or a museum or even that fancy shoe store she was crazy about. "You know how she likes to drive," I say.

"What were you doing down there?" Da says, changing the subject.

"Nothing," I say. I don't want to start talking about terrorism with everything else going on. I try to eat the sandwich but I can't. The kitchen still smells like Luke's poop.

"He's been shitting all night," Da says. And I'm surprised to hear Da talk like that because it isn't his normal language. I look at Luke in the corner, shamefaced on his special bed of newspaper and plastic garbage bags. I forget sometimes that he's old.

"How long do dogs live?" I ask Da.

"He'll be fine," Da says.

I bring him over half my sandwich.

"Don't feed him that," Da snaps. "For christ's sake Mathilda."

In some ways it's a whole new Da. With his messed-up

hair and the black shadow of his beard he's like a movie star on a bad day. Even after Helene, he still combed and shaved every morning and put on his perfect face. Tonight he looks like the kind of person who could throw a beer bottle from the back of a bus. I keep waiting for him to tell me to go to bed, but he hasn't yet. Maybe secretly he wants my company.

Now he's on the phone again and Luke is whining for something. Maybe he just wants a pet, a good old rub on the back. Usually he'll just walk over and push his head into you if he wants that, but maybe he's too sick. Either that or he's too scared to get off his plastic bag, for fear of shaming himself again.

"Luke," I say. "Lukey-boy." It wakes up a tiny wag in his tail. The clock says 2:15. The kitchen isn't even a kitchen anymore, it's a waiting room.

"Did you call the hospitals?" I ask Da.

Watching him on the phone, his back curved into a question mark, I think about the last two kisses Ma gave me. The one when she was drunk and the one after I played Helene's tape. Even though they were awful, I wonder if maybe I reacted in the wrong way. The meaning of a kiss isn't always a hundred percent clear. A kiss is a complicated thing. I wonder when was the last time Ma kissed Da.

A picture of her finally comes into my head, but it's the wrong one. It's a picture from a photo album, when Ma was a girl. She has green shorts on and a yellow shirt. And then out of nowhere I remember the story Ma told me once about the time she tried to scare a bird out of a grapefruit tree. This was back when she was a kid. The bird was making a lot of noise and it was driving her crazy because she was trying to read. She ended up throwing a rock at it and the rock actually hit the bird in the head, which wasn't her intention at all. The bird fell out of the tree and plopped into the dirt like a piece of fruit. Ma ran inside to tell her mother and when the two of them came out, the bird was gone. Apparently my grandmother laughed and said you can't kill a bird with a rock. Ma was furious, and even though she never wanted to kill birds with rocks she spent the next few weeks trying to do it, just so she could bring one inside and drop it in her mother's lap like the happy hunter. I asked Ma did she think the bird had brain damage afterwards and she said, I don't know, I hope not. And then we both started laughing. I used to love when Ma would tell me about her life when she was my age. It made me feel like we were best friends, or that we could have been if I had known her back then. She would have been just my type. A girl who's too shy to look you in the eye but still knows how to throw a rock. It's perfect. But thinking about the stupid story now just made me madder.

"Did you call the police?" I say. Da is still standing by the phone, pretty much asleep on his feet. His eyes are closed. Does he even hear me? It's obvious he's thinking about Ma the same way Kevin is probably thinking about Anna right now. *Will she ever come back to me? Will she ever love me again?* If I want him to hear me I'll have to shout. Because when two people are in love you basically have to become an intruder if you want their attention.

"The way she drinks," I say, "she'll probably have an accident."

"It'll be her own fault," I say.

Da opens his eyes and for the first time in my life I'm scared of him. He looks like a terrorist with nothing to lose. Under his eyes the color is almost like someone had punched him.

"What do you need?" he says. Like I'm a stranger begging on the sidewalk. "What do you need, Mathilda?" He points the question at me like a stick.

"Nothing," I say. "Nothing Da."

Bzzzz, wrong answer. Da keeps staring at me.

"You have to go," he says, quiet and terrible, and I don't even know who he's talking to.

Go where? I think. What does he mean? I think maybe he means kicking me out of the house and suddenly a big rush of heat shoots up my neck.

"I'm not going," I say. Luke lifts his head when I say it.

"Sit down," Da says. "You don't even know what I'm talking about."

"I don't care," I say.

"Sit down," Da says, "and stop shouting."

"Your mother and I think you should talk with Dr. Milles again," he says. He means the Tree.

"No," I say, and Luke barks.

"Just to talk," Da says. "It helped you last time."

"Ma is the one who needs him," I say.

"Maybe she's with him right now," I say. "Maybe they're lovers."

Da sits at the table and pretends he has a headache.

"He's perfect for her," I say.

Da's hands are on his face. Suddenly I realize he's about to disappear too. The hair on his knuckles grows longer and longer the more I look at it.

"I'm just kidding, Da,"

"She'll be okay," I say. Sometimes you have to lie to people. I breathe like the Tree taught me. His one good bit of advice.

"I'm breathing," I say to Da.

"That's good," he says. "You do that."

But he's still in outer space, inside his hands. A slow sigh comes out of him like he's a tire losing air.

"We didn't know where you were," he says, half to himself. "You can't do that to her, baby. You can't . . ." but it's another drift-off.

Something like ice is all over the windows. I can't tell if Da is crying or not.

"Maybe I should go to bed," I say. "Da?"

His hairy hands are cold when I touch them.

"Yes," he says. "Okay."

Luke tries to follow me out of the kitchen but I tell him, "No, stay."

"Good night Da."

"Sweet dreams," he says, and I don't think he's trying to be funny.

"No!" I say to Luke, who's trying to follow me again, the stupid musher.

26

I lock the door of H's room and turn on the computer. While it warms itself up I look out the window. Through the trees I can see the lights on in Kevin's house. I wonder what he's told his parents, what story he's concocted to explain coming home in the middle of the night. He'll probably get off easy. When boys lie, nobody thinks it's such a big deal. But when a girl does it, she's lucky if she doesn't get thrown in a padded cell.

Walking back to the desk I catch myself in the mirror. It's still a bit of a shock. Without my hair, my eyes are about ten times bigger. I look like something out of the jungle. I think of warriors with bones through their noses playing drums. I can still feel the *pum-pum-pum* in my stomach as I type CALIFORNIA. The computer's brain clicks and twitters and then it happens.

Welcome Heygirl! You have three new messages!

When I see who they're from the drums stop. Everything goes quiet. Three messages from LDM@blueforest.com. Three messages from the murderer. Even after ten deep breaths I still can't read them. I get up and have another look around. Kevin's lights are out now. I wonder if the fish have gone inside the plastic cave to sleep. If fish even sleep, that is. I don't know too much about their nocturnal habits.

Tap tap tap. I think someone's coming for me but when I look down it's my own fingers on the windowsill. They're going a mile a minute like I'm typing an S.O.S. to Kevin across the darkness. It's not something I mean to do, my fingers are just doing it on their own. I command them to stop, and then I open the first message.

Helene is that you? What's going on? Did you get the hundred fucking messages I sent you? I've been out of my mind. Your cell phone, nothing worked. I gave up over the summer. Would you please please write me, you can't just send a blank message after all this time what the fuck does that mean? Don't play games with me. I love you, my god, it's been hell around here. Everything is a mess but it's getting better I mean. Please please write to me or call. I know you're probably pissed from when I took off, but I just needed to get away for a little while, my mother was on me about everything. I told her about the problem. Are you trying to get back at me? I love you so fucking much you have to believe me. I came to Little Falls the first couple of months you stopped writing and walked around for like ten hours each time. I don't even know where your house is, there's no listing for Savage in the phone book. I went to our park and sat there until it was dark. I'm sorry, if that's what you want to hear. I can drive to you, come to you whenever, this weekend or any day after four. Or you can take the train to me. Are you still in school? Talk to me. Fuck Helene I can hardly type my fingers are shaking so much.

A car starts up and I jump. But it's just Da. I suppose he's off to find her. He'll probably drive up and down the main roads where the restaurants are, and the bars. And if that doesn't work, he'll take the dark roads up into the hills, maybe even all the way to the falls.

Suddenly all I can think of is the curse of the Savitches, and Ma or Da driving straight off a cliff. In my head I try to drive for them and keep them safe but I'm so tired I end up losing control.

Even though it's late I call Anna. Her mother answers and I hang up. I just wish I could sleep in her bed with the sheets that smell like milk. Even just for five minutes. Forty winks is all I need.

I can't sleep. I'd just walked in when I got your "message." I was a little drunk so I'm sorry if I went on and on but you can understand. Not sleeping, thinking of you. Please write.

That was Louis's second message. The third one is only four words.

Please. I love you.

What does he want? It doesn't make any sense. If he's the one who pushed her, then wouldn't he know she was dead? It makes me a little dizzy. Is *Helene Savage* a different girl? How can he not even know my sister's name? I go over to the mirror again and study myself. I really wouldn't be so good at playing Helene, I decide. I'm ugly. I don't know why I lie to myself. A couple of tears drip down my face but they're nothing special. Maybe it wouldn't be the worst thing in the world to talk to the Tree again.

I wish Da was here. I even wish she was here.

Dear Ma, I can see you. Sometimes I'm right next to you. I can see you but I can't do anything. Do you think about me a lot? How is Da? How is Mathilda? Please send a message. Love, Helene

This is the message I composed a few days ago, but never sent. After I read it, I pull three hairs from the top of my head. I make the sign of the cross like Anna showed me, and then I do it. I press send.

And then I write to him.

Dear Louis, I'll come to your house, remind me where it is again. H.

And then I turn off the computer.

I have to figure out who he is. How he did it. There's all sorts of ways to kill someone. You don't need a gun or a knife or even your hands. Some people can do it with their minds alone. Sometimes you just have to wish someone was dead and then it happens for real. What I want is justice. Because no matter how you look at it, there's been a crime.

I can't just sit around and do nothing. Someone's got to finish the story.

When god appeared to Joan of Arc he came as an angel of light. After that, she did everything he told her. Once you agree to be the secretary of god, you can't just quit. When you have a job to do you just do it. So what if you're scared, get over it. *Go to the end*, Phunka says, *where the fire is, where the griffins live. Put on your goddamned boots!*

27

Supposedly everyone has someone who looks exactly like them. But isn't that person supposed to live on the opposite side of the world? Can the two of one person live in the same town, go to the same school? Anna's double is talking to Carol Benton in the cafeteria. It's strange. The lights in there are so bright you almost have to blink. Anna's leaning against the far wall and one foot is out of her shoe. She's tracing her toe against her leg. It's almost sexual.

Carol Benton is holding her books to her chest with her arms crossed like some phony Egyptian statue. I can't tell what they're saying to each other. Carol Benton is doing most of the talking, big surprise. Anna keeps pushing her stupid hair behind her ear, even when there's no hair to push. I'm saying Anna but I might be talking about her double. And besides, Anna backwards is Anna, so I can say Anna and mean the opposite, according to my rules.

Carol Benton says something with her eyes going wide and Anna smiles and covers her mouth. I'm watching them from outside the cafeteria, which has big glass walls like a huge aquarium. People keep walking past me, brushing against me, but I'm a stone in a river. I don't budge. I shouldn't even be at school today but Da didn't bother to keep me home. We're both upset about Ma, but we pretend everything's normal. Don't worry, he said, she probably got lost. You know your mother, he said, and I said yes, I did. Carol Benton turns her head and possibly sees me. She stops talking for a second and then she's right back at Anna with her lips flapping again.

I haven't had a chance to talk to Anna yet, about the basement. When I called her house this morning it was Mrs. Mc-Dougal who answered again and I lost my nerve. And then I was late getting to school. By the time I got here Anna had already been kidnapped. One of the problems is Carol Benton's head is too big for her body. The same with her breasts, which are wrong for her age. Who needs breasts that size anyway? I'm happy with bumps. Big breasts are a deformity almost.

Suddenly there's a giant wave and I go flying against the glass wall. I knock my head pretty hard. You know how they say you see stars? Well, I actually do. When I turn around to see who the pusher is, all I can make out is a blur of people hurrying to get to class. I feel something wet on my face and I touch it. Blood. There are already drops on the floor coming out of my nose. I scream at the pusher whoever he is and I can feel the blood in my throat. Some of it drips onto my shirt.

And then who shows up but Ms. Olivera. She's hopping

toward me, making clicking sounds like it's time to feed the chickens. She pulls a tissue from her pocket and tries to put it on my face.

"No," I say, "I don't need it." She's not my mother. I put my hand over my nose.

"Take it," she says, holding out the tissue. It's obviously been used and I want to throw up.

O pulls my hand away from my face and forces the tissue under my nose. I let her do it. I let her hold a used tissue to my face in front of everyone. The blood keeps coming, red as anything. The tissue is soaked. It's a rose in O's hand and she's holding it to my nose, forcing me to smell it. It smells like money, like coins.

Why is O here? I wonder. Why is she part of my life? I wouldn't choose her as the person to save me. With her free hand she touches my head with butterfly fingers. "Why are you wearing a hat?" she says. I wonder why she's touching me. I wonder if she's the kind of woman who's never known love. Possibly she's a lesbian. When the bell rings I jump. Anna is still there across the glass room and when our eyes meet she looks down. I want to run to her but I stay put.

"I didn't do anything," I say.

"I know," O says. "I saw what happened."

But what does she know, what did she see? Nothing if you ask me. She can't see my thoughts. All of a sudden she pulls the rose from my face and hides it in her fist. What does she think she is, a magician?

"Did you see who pushed me?" I ask her.

"Don't worry about it," she says.

"Was it Michael Flatmore?"

"Nobody pushed you," O says, "you just got caught in the rush."

"Come with me," she says with her fingers fluttering again.

"I'm fine," I say.

"Just to clean you up," she says.

I tell her I can do it myself, thank you.

"How's that nose?" she says. She gently lifts my chin to inspect the damage. I wonder why O never had any children. I wonder if she wanted them. Maybe there was something wrong with her insides.

"Come to my office anytime," she says. "If you want to rest."

"And take off that hat before you get to your next class."

"Okay," I say, and I back away from her. I can see the rose peeking out between her fingers.

"Can I have the tissue?" I say. I don't want O having any more power over me than she already has. Blood is even worse than hair when it comes to magic. When she drops the rose into my hand it's heavy, limp. It's worse than you think. I dash off down the hallway with the stupid thing, holding it in the palm of my hand like an egg.

———

I don't even go to my locker first. I go outside without my coat. I can't stay here at school covered in blood. I know Kevin's in woodworking at this hour and so I sneak around to the north side of the building where the shop rooms are. I don't see him at first because it's not woodworking, it's boys in helmets with blowtorches. It must be welding or something.

Which I didn't even know was an option around here or I would have signed up for it. With all the fire and metal it's like looking into a medieval castle, the secret room where the knights practice their crimes.

I recognize Kevin by the back of his neck. Plus I can see his black boots with the chains on them. A burst of fire shoots from his gun. Sparks dance around him like lightning bugs. Whatever it is he's making I can't figure out. It's a tilty tower of rusty metal scraps. It looks more like a disaster than a work of art.

Looking at people through glass is as real as anything. It's no different from how I normally feel with people. You can see them, but you can't touch them. I knock at the window but Kevin can't hear me through his helmet. When I knock again, a fat man appears out of nowhere. I suppose he's the teacher though I've never seen him before. His face is blimped up from hair. A beard, plus he practically has an afro. He's shouting something at me through the window but I can't understand him. The humongous hair blots out everything. He's like Sasquatch.

Running up the hill I almost start laughing. Up the hill into the trees spilling their colored leaves. It really is a beautiful school. You'd be lucky to go here if you had the chance. I'm half sorry to be saying goodbye. I'm practically flying. My feet make an amazing sound against the crispy carpet of red and orange. I can hear myself breathing like the chase scene in the woods. Better not trip, I think. Tripping is always the problem in a slasher film. Once you trip you're pretty much doomed. The evil overtakes you in about two seconds.

When the trees open up I'm in town. But I keep running. My plan is to go straight to the train station but somehow I end up standing in front of a church. Our Lady of Perpetual Something or Other. The stonework is practically a thousand years old. It looks like the sort of building that could fall down on top of you. It really does. But I knock on the door anyway. I was getting pretty cold without my coat. After a few minutes of waiting I just push open the big wooden creaker of a door and walk inside. You don't need an invitation to go into a church is what I've heard. Anyone is welcome apparently. Which means the place is probably full of criminals and prostitutes and homeless people. But what the hell, I think, it's better than freezing to death.

"Hello?" I say. But nobody answers.

28

The world beyond the world they call it. It's a real place but supposedly you're also in the presence of god. You're safe here is what I've heard. But to tell you the truth, the first thing I noticed was it wasn't too cozy, temperature-wise. Someone was really stingeing it up on the heat. But maybe that's part of the mood. The coldness of god. Which makes sense. Cold would be the opposite of hell. According to the Christians, it's quite stuffy down there.

The place smelled a little bit like a library. Up front, a man on a ladder was fixing a light. He wasn't a priest, or if he was he wasn't dressed for duty. Jesus on the Cross was the main attraction. It was a church for Catholics. This town is lousy with churches. There's one on almost every hill, but the Catholic ones are few and far between. It's mostly Protestants around here, plus a few fanatics who go to the church with the neon lights of SAVE YOUR SOUL out front.

I walk down the center aisle to get a better view of Jesus. His eyes are closed, but he isn't dead. I don't think that's the message they're trying to convey. He's suffering. That's his main job according to Anna. When I get close I think maybe his eyes aren't shut all the way. Please don't look at me, I think. I saw that in a movie once, a statue opening its eyes, Anna and I both screamed. The funny thing is, as I'm thinking please don't look at me, part of me was wishing that he would. It was two thoughts for the price of one.

I give Jesus the up down, since he's basically flaunting himself. He doesn't have a bad body. Skinny but there's muscles. You could imagine his routine was jogging or swimming. He's dressed pretty skimpily in like baggy speedos. It's not a great look, it's a little diapery. There's the blood and the crown of thorns, which is pretty shocking when you see it in person. I take off my hat and stand before him. The man on the ladder ignores me, like I have every right to be here.

The candlelight was really doing a number on the place. The light and shadows jumping on Jesus' body made it look like he was twitching. Plus it felt like people were lurking about in the corners. I wondered if the dead hang around in churches.

I kneel down on a little padded area from where you can look up at the altar.

"Jesus," I say. First I just wanted to get his attention. And then I said a couple of other things to him about my life and my situation. I tried not to lie but I might have exaggerated a little. I didn't think he could punish me for that because I didn't belong to him. I actually felt pretty open with him, to tell you the truth.

"Can I help you son?" someone says.

I turn around and there's a lady there. She must have snuck in while I was gabbing.

"Oh excuse me," she says.

"Miss," she says, correcting herself. I suppose she's a nun. She's got everything on but the pelican hat.

"I couldn't tell from behind," she says.

I slip my cap back on my head. "Was I talking too loud?" I ask her. I tell her I was praying.

"Oh that's fine," she says. But she offers the advice to maybe whisper the next time.

I tell her I just wanted to make sure he heard me.

"Oh he can hear you," she says. "He can hear your thoughts." I wonder if maybe she's a lunatic. I notice her outfit isn't in the best condition. It was a little frayed around the collar.

"I'm not from this church," I say. "I'm just visiting."

Half of her thinks this is fine and half of her doesn't.

"Are you cold?" she says.

"Not really," I say.

"Don't you have a coat?" She smiles.

"Yes," I say, "but not with me."

"Oh," she says, nodding her head.

"I have tons of coats," I say.

She keeps smiling at me. "Because we have some in the back," she says. "If you decide you're cold. You just need to ask."

I wonder if she thinks I'm homeless. It's hysterical. I ask her if she knows any prayers. Which makes her laugh for some reason.

"Oh yes," she says. She says she knows quite a few. She walks over to one of the rows and picks up a red book in a little book-holder built right into the bench. She opens the red book to a particular page and points to something. "This is a good one," she says.

I move a little closer to her. She hands me the book, but I'm not about to audition for her.

"Do you ever say something that's not from the book?" I ask her.

"Like what?" she says.

"Just something you made up," I say. "Your own thing. Like stories."

"No," she says. "What kind of stories?"

"I don't know," I say. "About whatever's bothering you."

"If you say the words of the prayer," she says, "things won't bother you so much. That's why you say them."

"But they're not my words," I say.

"Yes they are," she says, "they're everyone's words."

She was a lunatic, I decided. You'd almost have to be in her profession.

"Do you make wishes?" I say. I could tell she was getting to the end of her rope with me. You'd think a nun's rope would be longer than most people's, but I guess not.

"Some people make wishes I suppose," she says. "I don't." Suddenly she got a little tight-lipped. Do you ever notice how people can get like that when you ask them certain questions? You ask them a simple question and they act like you're moving into their house or something.

"Why don't we get you a coat?" she says.

I don't even bother to argue with her. "Sure," I say. I kind of liked her. The black costume was pretty charming. And her hair was white, short but not as short as mine. It was an interesting white, it had shadows in it. It was like the white of a storm cloud.

————

In the back of the church there were rooms with wooden walls and benches and bookcases. It was like a mansion back there. I half expected to see fat men smoking cigars. But it was pretty much deserted, there weren't even any priests around. Maybe it was their day off. Maybe they were still sleeping. Apart from Sundays it's probably a life of leisure for them.

I followed the white head down a hall that connected the church to another building. The place was like a maze, I'm telling you. I wasn't sure what I was getting myself into. I just hoped I could remember my way out again. When we got to the famous coat room, it was a pile of junk, worse than our basement. We stood in the doorway staring at the crap. Whitey smiled at the stuff like it was pirates' gold.

"You can have whatever you want," she says. She points to a rack against the wall. "We have some children's coats over there."

"I'm not homeless," I say.

"How about this one?" she says, going for a felty orange number. "Or this. Oh this one would be good and warm." She pulls a second coat off the rack. It looked like it was made from guinea pigs.

"No," I say, but she hands it to me anyway. It was three different colors, black, brown, and white. It was disgustingly soft.

"Oh I think that's the one," she says.

"Whose coat is it?" I ask her.

"It's a donation," she tells me.

"Is it from someone who died?" I say.

"Oh I don't know about that," she says. "I don't think so."

"It's clean," she says, "if that's what you're worried about."

"It's a good coat," she says. She was really pushing the damn thing on me.

"How much?" I say.

"Oh no," she says, "you just take it."

It was oh before everything with her. Oh this oh that. It was sort of funny in a way. It added to her charm.

"Try it on," she says.

"When I get outside," I say. I wasn't about to put on a coat of hair.

"That'll make you look nice," she says. Like she'd have any idea about the art of looking good.

But she really did have a smile that got under your skin.

"Can I ask you a question?" I say. She seemed like the right person to ask, being she was professionally religious and all. And even though she says "yes, of course," suddenly I can't do it. It was like I had locks inside me. I'd heard suicide was a sin, but I still wanted to ask more about it. I wanted to know if arguing with someone before they killed themselves would make you half responsible. It's a question that's been on my mind for a long time actually.

I wanted to ask if someone could kill herself and be killed by someone else at the same time. Whether it was Louis or whether it was me. Because the thing is, Helene and I had a big fight that morning. Did I tell you that? The Tree doesn't even know about it. How can I help you if you won't talk to me? he used to say. But not everything in your heart makes it to your mouth. A lot of it gets lost on the way.

The nun was waiting for my question and I had to say something. Her smile was hanging over me like a threat.

"Will the terrorists burn in hell?" I ask her.

"What terrorists?" she says.

"The bombers," I say, "and their people. From the desert."

"Oh right," she says. "I don't keep up on those things too much."

I wondered where these nuns slept. Underground? Maybe they don't do newspapers and television. Maybe it's against the rules.

"It's a big deal," I say. "My friend Anna's brother is over there."

"Oh my," she says. "It's terrible out there."

"We'll pray for them," she says. I didn't know if she meant the soldiers or the terrorists, but I didn't bother asking. It probably would have been better to talk with a Krishna person, they're usually younger, but I don't know where they stay around here, other than outside supermarkets every now and then. I've heard they have a shack up in the woods somewhere. Supposedly they keep peacocks there.

"Do you want to call your mother?" she suddenly asks me. I wonder if my face is doing something funny.

"No," I say, but she doesn't give up.

"You do have a mother?" Whitey says.

What kind of question is that?

"Oh yes," I say. "She's up for the Pulitzer."

Whitey looks at me like she's confused.

"Thanks for the coat," I say. I make a smile for her.

"You're welcome, child," she says. And before I can run, a bolt of lightning shoots straight out of her heart and hits me square in the chest. *Jesus*. It nearly knocks me to the ground.

29

It's a fairly far walk to the station and I had no choice but to put on the guinea pig coat. Something was really blowing in. The last of the leaves were coming down in droves. Have you noticed how everything is fake, even the trees? Once you pick up on it, it hardly ever goes back to being real. Even the woman on George Stanton Avenue taking out her garbage is acting. Her perfect costume is a pink bathrobe with big fat yellow daisies on it. A live television audience should be laughing at her. Either that or the Howls of Grief. Her quilty robe is blowing around her legs like the Liberty Bell.

"Good morning," I say.

"Good morning," she says, and the audience goes wild with our routine. The perfect way we deliver our lines. A few blocks later a man is raking up leaves but the wind keeps stealing from his pile. It never gets any bigger, but he just keeps raking away like he's got all the time in the world. I don't bother to inform him otherwise. When I get to the shacky neighborhood around Monroe, two little kids, babies really, are playing with a beaten-up dollhouse in their yard. Part of me wants to clap my hands and chase them away like stray cats. After that, I sort of start running again for some reason.

The station is an old building with two ticket windows and a couple of snack machines. There's a waiting room with wooden benches and a flipper-board timetable. When the times change it's like an expert shuffling a deck of cards. I see there's a train to Desmond in one hour.

"How much to Desmond?" I ask at the window.

"One way?" the man says, and I tell him no, that I want to come back as well.

"Fourteen-eighty," he says without looking it up. He's probably told a million people fourteen-eighty from here to Desmond and back. Obviously it's not something he finds terribly interesting.

"My mother lives in Desmond," I tell him.

"Nice town," he says, and I say, "Yes it is, it really is." Even though the truth is I've never been there. The glass the ticket man's standing behind is a little streaky. Not exactly filthy but, still, you have an impulse to wipe it off. Nothing's more depressing than a dirty window.

"Do you want a ticket?" he says.

"No thank you," I say. I only had about five dollars in my pocket.

I ask him is there a train to Desmond every day.

"Every day, Missy," he says. Old people call you that sometimes. Mool calls me that every now and then when he's in one of his winky moods. Old Mool king of the curly fries.

I make a mental note to go visit him. Suddenly I was missing him like you wouldn't believe.

There's no other customers on line and so I just stand there. More than anything I want to tell the ticket man who I am. I want to tell him the truth about going to Desmond. My sister was going there, I want to tell him.

Oh yes, the redhead. I can just about hear him saying those exact words. He looks like the kind of person that would have an excellent memory.

Did I tell you Helene's ticket to Desmond, the one they found in her pocket, was one way? Apparently she had it in her mind not to come back, no matter what happened. Maybe she wasn't a hundred percent sure she'd do it. Jump, I mean. I don't even like that word. Maybe the other plan was getting on the train to Desmond and starting a whole new life. But this is the kind of thought that doesn't get you anywhere. Because the truth is, for dead people, the future is pretty hopeless.

Except you also wonder about the theory that when people die, the last thought in their heads is where they go. So if Helene was thinking about a life in Desmond, then maybe that's exactly what she's doing. She might not even know she's dead. I saw a show on television once where this guy died and he just kept going to work every day and then home to his wife. The wife of the man wasn't too thrilled about the ghost of her husband sitting at the table every night expecting dinner, but the man was supposedly happy as a clam. When the psychic finally got through to the man and told him he was dead, he was pretty surprised. It was a rude awakening, that's for sure. All I'm saying is, if Helene doesn't know she's dead, I hope no one ever tells her.

After I say goodbye to the ticket man I get two bags of chips and I plop myself down in the waiting room. Even though I'm not taking the train, I just feel like sitting there. Every now and then an express train rushes by outside and the wind of the train pushes at the glass doors that lead out to the platforms. The doors open a little without anyone touching them. The pressure in the room changes and there's a sucking noise, like an asthma attack. It's a fairly unpleasant sound and I'm not the only one who thinks so. Every time it happens the other people in the waiting room look up and adjust their coats or pull their suitcases closer to their feet.

Through the glass doors I can see people waiting on the platforms. I don't see a girl in a blue coat, with red hair. Not that I expect to. I'm just saying I don't. The train to Desmond always stops at platform number two. But to get there, you have to go underground, through a tunnel. Ma and Da used to take the train to work but now they drive. If a train even shows up on television, Ma leaves the room.

I make myself go into the tunnel. My breath goes funny but I don't bother to do my exercises. I just go down the stairs with my stupid breath heh-heh-hehing like a sweaty dog. The tunnel smells like pee and bleach and there's a *plink-plink* drip of something from the ceiling. I can hear a train roar past overhead, and then another train, quieter, pulling in and stopping. My plan is to cross all the way and come out again on the other side. But then a man comes down the stairs at the far end of the tunnel. He probably just got off the train. All I can see is a coat, a hat. I can't see his face in the light down here. I can't see if he's young or old and I don't wait to find out. I turn and run back the other way before he gets anywhere near me.

Walking home I could feel him following me. The truth is, with the wind in my face and the dancing trees, I felt more like I was swimming than walking. I tried to swim faster but I couldn't. I was sort of exhausted. When I got closer to my house I finally looked behind me but the man was gone. Either that or he was hiding behind a tree.

The rest of the way home I took my time and walked on lawns so I could sneak peeks in people's windows. Which is a good way to get your mind off things. What happens in other people's houses is a big question for me. I know everything probably happens from sex crimes to Christmas carols, but sometimes it would be nice to have the evidence.

I walk past Anna's house, which is white and has a fake turret. It's practically a castle. The outside is quite shrubby. Manicured you could say. It's the kind of place that looks excellent when it snows. It really does. Sometimes when I'm at Anna's house and her parents are home I try to become invisible for a few seconds so I can watch them, to see what other families are like. If I go to the bathroom I stay in there and listen to what they say to each other. What's obvious is Mr. and Mrs. McDougal love Anna. They adore her. She's what you would call their pride and joy. Mr. McDougal still picks Anna up sometimes. He spins her and then puts her down in another spot like he's playing chess with her. I guess it's some sort of game they have, probably something they used to do when she was little. And even though Anna's too big for it now, she doesn't seem to mind. She even laughs sometimes.

When I look at Anna's house I can't imagine it on fire or all broken in pieces. I can't imagine the three of them looking through the debris for an old photograph or a silver baby spoon. No matter how hard I try to break the house apart, the whole thing sticks together. And I guess it can hear my thoughts, because as I'm standing there staring at the perfect white house, it practically growls at me like a polar bear.

30

Luke is by the back door like the saddest thing ever invented. He lifts his eyes up to me like the painting of a saint. I wonder if he thinks about a different life sometimes. The possible lives he could have had. Running around on a farm, chasing chickens. A wild dog in the woods or living on a cliff where he'd be closer to the moon, which all dogs have a special relationship to. It's like their master in a horror movie, but it's only scary from the point of view of a human being. To a dog it's a love story. I wonder how happy he's been all these years locked in a house with humans and endless biscuits.

Lucky for Luke he has me to remind him he's a lion. I remember, not too long ago, Da and I were coming back from taking him for a walk and Ma stepped out of the house to greet us. She was wearing her apron with the cherries on it. Her hands were wet and she was drying them against the cherries. She looked common and beautiful. She looked like she could have been anyone's mother, even mine. When I saw her my heart sped up, I got excited. I unclipped the leash from around Luke's neck and I ran across the lawn, clapping my hands. Luke jumped up after me and practically knocked me to the ground. Help, I screamed, like I was being attacked by a lion. But nobody laughed, which has always been the standard reaction to my routine of Luke the Lion Attacks Mathilda in the Jungle. It's an old routine, but still funny in my opinion. Luke was slobbering all over me. Help! I screamed. Save me! Maybe I made the attack too violent or something, because Ma went back in the house and Da followed her. Luke and I just kept going on with the show. This was only a couple of weeks after H.S.S.H. and I guess no one was in the mood. Maybe I should have just walked up to her and taken her hand, instead of acting like an idiot.

"Don't die," I say to him when I see him by the back door. "Okay Lukey?" I was sort of pleading. I get down on the floor where he's lying and I give him a good pet, even though he still doesn't smell too hot. I wonder what dogs eat in the wild. I think maybe rabbits. On cliffs they probably eat the eggs of birds if they can find them. In France they eat mushrooms. Luke is black, if I never told you, but in certain light he almost looks silver.

I'm petting him when it happens. The feeling starts in my stomach, and it always surprises me. It's only my fifth time and so at first I'm never sure what it is, and then I remember it's blood. It still comes as a shock to be bleeding between the legs. It means we're fertile, Anna and me. You almost feel like you don't even want a raindrop getting in there, even though supposedly it's only sperm that could cause you a problem. *Fertile* is a fairly disgusting word to have put on you. It's sort of demeaning. It's like factories. When I was little, I used to ask Ma if she was going to have any more babies and she always said two was enough. More than enough, she said a couple of times. Probably it wasn't easy going to school with Helene strapped to her back, but maybe that's why they got so close. I give Luke a little kiss and then I take care of myself in the bathroom like she showed me. It's really not a big deal, but it's not nothing either.

Once I'm fixed up I think to check the doors and windows, to make sure they're all locked. Alone in a house, bleeding, and a man possibly following me. It's a dangerous situation when you think about it. I call Da's office at the college but he's not there. Then I call Ma's office and it's sort of a relief to hear her voice, even if it's only a recording. I half mumble a message. Not an apology exactly. I sounded like a retarded person, I really did. It was almost funny.

I bring Luke some fresh water and then I go upstairs. Louis is waiting for me. When I read his message it's almost too much, I can feel my blood come faster. Guess where he lives? *Desmond.* He gives me his address. *28 Larson Court.*

How could you forget? he writes. He says again how much he loves me. That he'll take care of me. *I promise*, he says. *I'll take care of everything.*

Can he really not know she's dead? It feels like a game, but I don't know who's making up the rules, me or Louis. Who's trying to trick who? My brain goes back and forth. I feel awful and famous at the same time. But I don't forget who I am. I know I'm Mathilda. It's not like I think I'm Helene. Not really. If there's a blur it's just a tiny one.

It's like I'm a character and a real person at the same time. The whole thing feels suspiciously like a story. I wish I could talk to Ma about it, she's really good at plot and everything. She used to explain the greatness of Jane Austen to us, blow by blow. She was good at helping you understand how one thing led to another, and all the psychological complexities and everything. It always amazed me that you could be in so many people's heads at the same time. You float from one to the other, even though there's usually one person who's the most important. When you read a book like that, you really get a feeling of the watchers. And what's funny is how they love everyone, even the terrible people, even the fools. You can hardly understand how they do it. It's a kind of magic almost. Helene and I read all the great books when we were little. They were sort of forced on us, but it wasn't torture exactly. Ma and Da have an excellent library. They really do. And Ma supposedly wrote some stories when she was younger. Did I ever tell you that? She published them in magazines before she married Da and then for a little bit when they were newlyweds. I asked to see them once but she said she didn't have any copies. She said they weren't much of anything. Juvenilia, she said. Which means things you made when you were a child, and unless you're a genius they usually end up in the garbage.

I'll come, I say to him. *I'll come to your house*. I just pretend it's a story. *Tomorrow*, I write, and I sign it, *Love H*. I can't help myself.

———

Other than Louis, there's no other messages. Ma hasn't answered the e-mail I sent to her. The one from Helene. I only sent it yesterday, so she probably hasn't even read it yet. She's probably still driving. She has a sister not too far away but

I'm sure Da's already called her. We're not exactly a close-knit family or anything but a person's sister might be the one you'd go to if you were in trouble. Marie is her name. A long time ago she brought us hats back from somewhere, I think Peru. They were striped, lots of colors, and about a mile long. Elf hats, Helene said. They had white pom-poms at the end of them. Whenever we put them on, we used to speak in squeaky voices like Alvin and the Chipmunks. I don't know why no one ever took a photo of the two of us in those stupid hats. They really were pretty great. The photo would have been hysterical. I wonder if Anna and Carol Benton are sitting at school somewhere having another one of their famous conversations. Laughing about my bloody nose, which I'm sure is big news by now.

I go downstairs and get myself a glass of milk. I turn on the TV and it's some stupid daytime thing with ladies complaining about life. My husband does this, my son does that, blah blah blah. If you hate your families so much, why don't you just jump off a bridge, I feel like shouting at them. But I don't even waste my breath. I click until I come to some news about the war and the terror. Another man's been caught. He's involved somehow with one of the tragedies. I can't figure out if it's the first bombed building or the second or if it has to do with the poison letters or the opera house or the subway. In my mind it's all confused. A voice on the TV says something about an execution. Ma and Da don't want me watching stuff like this anymore. Ever since H.S.S.H. Da's been a madman about my viewing habits. Does he really think television is the problem? What I see on television is nothing compared to what I see in my head. Yes, sometimes it's horrible what they show. But the truth is I can handle it. I've grown up in a time of terror. You get used to it. They're always telling us at school to let them know, or to let our parents know, if we're having trouble sleeping or fear or nightmares. Which of course I have, but I have them for my own reasons. Not because of some stupid war. Anyway I would never go to the school nurse. Mrs. Melfino is Italian and she's an over-reactor. If you had a paper cut she'd probably say amputate.

Even though the last terror was pretty bad, there were other worse ones in the past. I remember bits and pieces from when I was little. The planes, for instance. Plus there's been quite a few wars in my lifetime, I've sort of lost count. It's sort of the same war, just different versions. A lot of it happens in deserts. A lot of it happens with beards and families in little cement houses and men kneeling in towers and women who beat their heads with their fists, and of course a big problem is the maniac children who get guns practically shoved into their cribs. Ma and Da used to be great crusaders against the whole thing. In the old days they went to protests and everything. But the truth is, Ma and Da don't care about the world anymore. After Helene, they basically gave up.

But for a while they were real peaceniks. My sister too. I guess you could say Helene had a big heart. She cared about a lot of things, and not just peace. Animals and Africans and virgin forests. She had signs up in her room that she made herself with colored magic markers and she went to marches even after Da said maybe it wasn't such a good idea because they were starting to put people on lists. And there was even a teacher from my parents' college who got arrested because of his radio show. But my sister had a mind of her own. She was very big on Petronella Peacock, the singer. Personally I don't like her, her voice is too whiny. She's on a hunger strike right now on account of the war. I can picture Helene doing the same thing, locked in her room starving and the tears falling down her cheeks. Sometimes it was hard to tell if she was weak or if she was strong. It still confuses me.

The truth is, I prefer the old times. Before all the stupid politics and Helene getting so serious. Because in the beginning, when we were both little, it was nonstop laughter. We'd walk around with our butts sticking out and our eyes crossed. I used to do some really great faces. My faces used to kill Helene. She'd hold her gut laughing like she was going to explode. When you can make people laugh it's really the best feeling. You feel like a magician. When I try to make people laugh now, it doesn't feel inspired anymore. These days if I try the old trick of sticking out my butt and crossing my eyes, half the time I feel like crying.

31

"Feel my head," I say. "Da, feel my head." I pull his hand to my forehead. "I think maybe I have a fever," I tell him.

He's barely walked in the door and I'm all over him.

"What are you doing home?" he says. "It's not even two o'clock."

"The nurse sent me."

"Don't lie," he says.

"I'm not." I tell him to sit down and I ask him does he want something to drink. I can be the perfect hostess when I make an effort. I'm just glad he's here.

"Where'd you get that coat?" he says.

I look down and realize I still have on the guinea pig. My hat's still on my head too. "That's probably why I was so hot," I say. I try to make it like a joke but it doesn't work. I don't have complete control of my face.

I take off my coat and Da takes off his. We both sit on the couch. It's like we're on a first date. There's not a lot of eye contact.

"I've spoken with her," he says.

"Who?" I say.

"Who the hell do you think?"

I ask if she's at her sister's but Da just looks at me like he's confused.

"With Aunt Marie," I say.

"No," Da says. "What are you talking about?"

"The one who gave us the hats," I say.

"Marie's dead," he says. "You know that."

"I didn't know she was dead," I say.

"Five, six years ago," Da says.

"Nobody told me." I can feel the heat shooting up my neck. I know Aunt Marie's not the issue but, still, somebody should have told me.

"You hardly knew her," Da says, as if that's any consolation. "Why are you getting so upset?"

"Did I go to the funeral?" I say.

"I don't remember," he says. "You were a baby, Mathilda."

"I wasn't a baby five, six years ago," I say. I do the math in his face with my fingers.

"Okay," Da says. "Okay."

"So where is she then?"

"Don't shout," he says, even though I'm not shouting. I'm just enunciating. Da touches his own forehead now like he's the one with the fever. His face actually changes color.

"She's at a hotel," he says.

"Where?"

"North of here," he says.

"In the mountains?"

"I don't know the town," he says.

"Desmond?" I say.

"No," he says. "God Mathilda." And he turns away from me in disgust. For a second, his face is the face of a murderer. I guess violence is everywhere, under everything. Even fathers.

"You're so much like her," he says, shaking his head. And I don't know if it's a compliment or an insult. I don't even know which *her* he's talking about.

"I'll go with you," I say. "Da, I'll go with you."

"Where are we going?" he says.

"To the hotel," I say.

Da looks at me and brushes the tears from my face. He can't help himself.

"It's going to be fine," he says.

"Don't lie," I say. "What if she won't come back?"

"She won't even let you touch her anymore," I say.

It's like I've shot an arrow into his heart. His face swallows the pain but I can still see it. My thought is to somehow pull out the arrow, to say something to reverse what I just said. But the truth is, when you try to pull out an arrow you just make things worse. Often you end up killing the person. I've seen it happen to a million cowboys.

"Your mother has her moods," he says quietly. "You all do." He breathes out of his nose like he's just heard the saddest joke in the world. Poor Da. I wonder what it's been like for him all these years, living in a house with girls. I wonder if he ever felt like running away and leaving all the femme fatales behind.

"When are you going?" I ask him.

"I'm just going to drive up and talk to her," he says.

"Not tonight," I say, but he says, "Yes, tonight."

"It's going to rain," I say.

"What's that got to do with anything?" Da says.

"You can't just leave me here."

He says he'll call Mrs. Frisk and I tell him I don't need a babysitter. I remind him about all the stupid flags on Mrs. F's lawn.

"One night," he says. That's what people always say, and then it turns into infinity. I wonder if he's going to disappear too, Ma and Da into the mountains. He reaches out his hand and he takes the hat off my head. He touches my face, even though I stopped crying ages ago.

"Your birthday's coming up," he says. It's a confusing comment, but when I think about it it's true.

"What do you want?" he says. For some reason it makes me nervous, talking about birthdays. But Da keeps his eyes pinned on me. Suddenly he's got 20/20 vision and I almost wish he'd go blind again. "Come on," he says. "What do you want?"

"I don't know," I say. "Nothing."

I wanted to say a gas mask. Because that's what Kevin told me he was going to ask for for his next birthday.

"I don't need anything," I say.

Then it's quiet. Da looks at the floor and smiles. It's the smile of an astronaut looking down at the blue Earth where he used to live. It's sad, because he doesn't know if he'll ever come back.

"What about a Bashful Baby?" he says.

"No," I say. "I don't collect dolls anymore. That was a million years ago."

"Besides, I have them all," I tell him.

"You never got the Japanese one," he says. "What was her name?"

I can't believe he remembers. Because the stupid truth is I never did get the Japanese one, she was always sold out. The Bashful Babies were quite a collector's item a few years ago, everybody was crazy for them.

"I'm not too big on them anymore," I say.

But Da keeps waiting.

"Maybe some fish," I tell him. "An aquarium."

"You two never did have fish," he says. He means Helene and me. And it's true. We had everything but fish. We had a ton of creatures over the years. When it came to pets we were fairly spoiled. We really were. Rabbits and birds and a frog and turtles and hamsters. We had newts. We even had a Venus fly trap. And of course Luke. The one and only.

"Tinka," I say.

"What's that?" Da says.

"That's her name," I say. "The Japanese one."

"But fish would be better," I say.

"Too old for dolls," Da says, "huh?"

And I shrug even though I mean yes.

Da suddenly picks up my hat and plants it back on my head.

"Do you hate my hair?" I say.

"What hair?" he says. And we both sort of laugh. We really do, just a little.

32

There are horses running across the land. There's a lot of dust, and no humans. It's pretty much a desert. The horses are running toward the horizon, but really it's a cliff. One horse goes over and then the others follow. For a second they're running into the air, for a second you think they can fly. But then they fall. They plummet. There are a hundred horses at least, maybe a thousand.

I don't know where I saw this movie or if I ever saw it. I woke up thinking it was a dream, but it's not the sort of thing I normally dream about. And I don't think it was a movie because who would do that to horses just to make a movie? In my mind it's not a special effect, it's completely real. It's probably the scariest thing I've ever seen. If I ever did see it, that is. I *feel* like I saw it, I just don't know *where*.

When Da's car pulled away I was standing outside on the steps. Da lifted his hand from the wheel and waved at me. I could have started screaming but instead I just swallowed it. Ma is Da's wife and that means more than being someone's mother. A mother is just the beginning but a wife is closer to the end. You're eventually done with a mother, but a wife is different. Especially if she's the love of your life and you promised to stay with her forever, which I suppose he did. If I could have one magical power it would be to get inside someone else's head, even just for a second, so that I could know what's important to other people, who they love and who they hate. You might treat certain people differently if you knew what was really in their heart.

The last time I saw Ma she sort of waved at me too. The morning before the basement, Anna and I were sitting in the backyard on the yellow lawn chairs. I noticed Ma was watching us from inside the house. She was upstairs, behind a window. It was fairly creepy. She looked like a retarded person who was locked in a prison. She didn't have any expression on her face. She lifted up her hand, but I didn't bother to wave back. I didn't want Anna to see her.

The thing is I want her to go away, but then I don't. It's the double thoughts again, which are getting to be a big problem. What is it about things and their opposites? Love and hate, for instance. Sometimes they get so twisted up in each other it's like they're having sex practically. It's sickening. The truth is I'm ashamed of her. So much that I don't want to be seen with her out in public. And I worry whenever I bring Anna inside the house. I always imagine Ma walking into the living room with her stupid Chinese robe on, which if I didn't mention it is way too short. And then what if she's drunk or doing her zombie routine? I'm afraid she'll touch Anna's head the way she touches mine. With that strange look on her face. Or she'll say things no one wants to hear. Like once, Anna was at the house and Ma smiled at her and told her how beautiful she looked. What a face, Ma said. *What a face.* How can she say these things in front of me? Say it to one person and not to the other one? It's like she's talking to you-know-who all over again. Even mothers play games. Don't think they don't.

Sometimes I think she should be locked up, and not just in a room with the Tree, but with straps and chains and something to cover her mouth. You don't want your mother walking around the house in a slutty robe or touching your friend's head or staring at you from a window with no expression on her face. It's unnatural.

What makes it even worse is how in the old days you would almost be proud to claim her as yours, especially when she came to pick you up at school in her old blue car. She'd put the roof down if it was warm and we'd pick up Helene next and then the three of us would drive home with our hair flying like mermaids. Sometimes I think of things like this and I love her so much I want to pull every last hair from my head just to prove it. But really the only way to grow up is to not look back. You have to stick to your guns. And my guns are goodbye and good riddance.

"Come sit down," Mrs. Frisk says. "What are you staring at with those eyes of yours?"

I turn away from the window and Mrs. Frisk is sitting in the big chair with a book. Da's chair. Luke is lying at her feet. She looks harmless enough but the truth is she's a retired teacher, so I'm always a little suspicious. This town is lousy with teachers. Next to churches, it's schools as the main at-

traction. Every little town around here has a little college or
a boarding school. There's a school for priests over in Lack-
ton. There's even a special needs place not too far away, a
sort of farm for deaf people.

"Why don't you do your homework?" Mrs. Frisk says.
She says we can do it together if I want. I'm sure she'd love
that. Homework's right up her alley. She's probably got a red
pen stuck in her bra. I wouldn't put it past her. That's what
these people are like. Their big mission in life is to find out all
your mistakes, especially your grammar. They want everyone to sound like a robot. And all they ever want to talk
about is school. It's their only point of reference. What are
you up to in school? is always the big question. What are you
studying? What are you reading? They're very narrow-
minded, teachers. It's almost like they're retarded in a way. If
I had to give it a name I wouldn't call it Academia, I'd call it
Retardia. I really would. It's not eating fruit and gabbing
naked on a hillside like back in the days of Ancient Greece.
It's stuffy rooms and boring books that smell like they were
fished out of the ocean. What are you smelling your book
for? Mrs. LaSalle said once. I had just gotten a brand-new
science book and I swear to god it smelled like a tuna sandwich. I nearly puked.

And I remember one time when old Joycie Andrews
babysat for Helene and me, and she told us she was going on
a boat trip. I was pretty surprised to hear of an eighty-year-
old retired professor going on an adventure like that, but
then she told us that the boat was a school. Can you believe
it? With classes and everything, seven days a week. What are
you going to eat on the boat? Helene asked her. Books? No,

old Joycie said, they have food. She really had no sense of humor. Helene and I nearly peed our pants though and old Joycie looked at us like we were the retarded ones. But we liked Mrs. Andrews, don't get me wrong. She always said, Call me Joycie, and so we did. She was a pretty modern type. And she had a good face for an old lady. Not too pruney like some of them get. You just wish she could have taken a boat to France or to the Bahamas or something. Some last bang before she died.

Sometimes I just wish a person could learn something. Something real. Something to help you talk to other people. Most of the stuff you get from books is garbage in my opinion. A person like Jane Austen tells you a little something, but novels are a different story. Besides, novels aren't what they shove down your throat in school. In school it's more about information. Math and dates and the names of ships. And who cares about Eli Whitney inventor of the cotton gin? You don't learn anything about how to make sense of your secret thoughts. Write them down, one teacher said. Which wasn't a bad idea. I think it was Ms. Massitelli, a couple of years ago. Write your thoughts down, she said, make a story. It's a good exercise but my problem is tenses. The present, the past, in my mind it keeps going back and forth. Was or Is? I never know which one to use. In my head it's a war. The war between Is and Was. When you have a sister who died, it screws up all your tenses. Plus you can't really make a life out of writing down your secret thoughts. Ma obviously couldn't do it.

"I'll make some hot chocolate," Mrs. Frisk says.

"We don't have any marshmallows," I say.

"We'll survive," she says.

Luke follows her into the kitchen. She's not a bad person.

She actually brought over a plate of cookies, I don't think homemade but it was a nice gesture. And Luke seems to like her, which is a good sign. Dogs can tell the real people from the impostors. I bend down to give him his rub. "He's been sick," I say. "But he's better now."

"You used to have a dog," I say.

"Yes," Mrs. Frisk says. But it's obviously not something she wants to talk about. I guess it's a sensitive subject.

"Rusty," I say. I tell her I remember old Rusty. How he used to get excited and slobber all over the front window when he saw someone walking up to the house.

"He was a good dog," she says, putting an end to the conversation. You can practically feel the period at the end of her sentence. Old women with dogs and no husbands is a pretty serious business when you think about it. Mrs. Frisk is a widow. Widows are like queens when it comes to death. They really don't have anything left to lose. I watch her as she does the hot chocolate. She doesn't use the mix, she does it the old-fashioned way with the can of cocoa, the sugar, the milk, and the salt. She's got a lot of makeup on just to baby-sit. It was really piled on. She looked like she was ready for something, I don't know what. The opera maybe. I had a thought to hit the high note right there in the kitchen. My heart was starting to race again for some reason.

"Do you remember my parents?" I say. "From when they were younger?"

"Yes," she says, "of course."

"Before you girls were born," she says. And then I see her face twitch. She knows she's said the wrong thing. I can feel the way the electricity drains from her body and shoots into mine. Suddenly I'm the one with all the power.

"You have a lot of flags on your lawn," I say, and she smiles and pours out the hot chocolate into two white mugs.

"Shall we sit at the table?" she says. "Watch you don't spill it." She gives me another little smile and I think maybe her teeth are fake. They actually look dangerous.

"With all your flags," I say, "I bet your view on the terrorists is kill them."

"Well, I don't know about that," she says.

"How many flags do you have?" I say. "At least five, right?"

"Your father wants you in bed early," she says.

"In school," I tell her, "we went to BetsyRoss.com and in terms of displaying flags, you shouldn't be doing it twenty-four hours a day. According to BetsyRoss.com," I say, "it's illegal."

"I didn't know that," she says, smiling.

"If you show them during the hours of darkness," I explain, "then they have to be properly illuminated."

She nods her head, still hanging on to her smile.

I also tell her the flag napkins people use on the Fourth of July are technically illegal too. Because you wipe food on them with your mouth and then you throw them in the garbage.

"I don't use flag napkins," she says.

"No, I'm just saying though. It's considered desecration." My heart was really going a mile a minute.

"Drink your cocoa," she says. "While it's hot."

I take a sip but then I get up. I really do have ants in my pants sometimes.

"Where are you going?" she says, and I tell her, "I forgot, I have to go to my friend Anna's house."

"No," she says. "Your father said you're not to leave the house."

210

"I have to see my boyfriend," I say. "He's waiting for me." I try to move around her and I can see she's getting a little nervous.

"Please sit down," she says. "I'm too old for this."

"Would you please sit down?" She's almost begging now.

"Mathilda," she says, shaking her head.

It's funny, sometimes when people say your name it's like they put you in a spell.

"Come sit down and we'll finish our drinks." She puts her hand on the outside of the white mug. "It's still warm," she says. "Come on."

And before I know it I'm sitting at the table drinking the hot chocolate.

I'll just sneak out later, I decide, after she falls asleep.

"You poor child," Mrs. Frisk says. Which I don't mind one bit, to tell you the truth. And plus, coming from a widow, it's practically a compliment.

33

I climbed into my bed early, around eight o'clock, and I must have fallen asleep. It wasn't my plan but then there I was smack in the middle of morning. The sun was out and the wind had stopped. It was a little strange to have slept through the whole night and I wondered if maybe Mrs. Frisk had put something in the hot chocolate.

I had a strong feeling Ma and Da were back in the house. In their bathrobes watching cartoons. That was the picture in my head. Feet up on the coffee table and between them a pecan ring from Kroner's. But I knew the real picture was probably the two of them waiting for me in the kitchen with their arms crossed. I stick my head into the hallway and I can practically smell her. I look in the mirror to check myself. I look at my whole body. There's definitely things happening. I look thinner. I'm not saying sexy. And, anyway, that's for other people to decide. Ma hasn't even seen my hair yet, I realize. I fuss with it in the mirror to make it stand up in little grassy tufts.

When I traipse into the kitchen she's there making breakfast, humming to herself la-di-da. She's wearing my mother's apron with the cherries on it.

"Are you hungry?" Mrs. Frisk says. "I'm making eggs."

"They're not back?" I say. "Did my father call?"

"Yes," she says. "Don't worry, they're fine."

I ask her when, when did he call, and she says just now, not five minutes ago.

"Why didn't you come get me?" I say.

"I thought you were sleeping" is her excuse.

"Everything's fine," she says. As if it's up to her to decide.

"Their friend is feeling much better," she says.

"What friend?" I say, and then I remember the lie. Da told Mrs. Frisk that Ma was visiting a sick friend and that that's where he was off to as well. Plus before Mrs. F came over, Da made me promise not to say anything to her. It's our business, he said. Da's not normally a liar and it makes me wonder how serious this whole business is, Ma driving to a hotel up north, who knows where.

"Did they say when they were coming back?" I ask her.

"I can stay as long as you need," she says. Teachers are always doing that, turning things around, answering your question with some suspicious switcheroo. Just once I'd love to hear a teacher say, I don't know. I don't fucking know when they're coming back. And just leave it at that.

"Come sit down," she says.

The table's set with plates and napkins and juice glasses. She tells me to make myself comfortable. It's hysterical. Make myself comfortable in my own house. I can smell the toast burning but when it comes out it's perfect. The eggs slide onto the plates with no argument. It's a real con job.

"Not so fast," she says. I'm already shoveling the stuff into my mouth.

"I'm in a bit of a hurry," I say. "A lot to do in school," I tell her. Which draws her right in.

"What are you working on?" she says and I tell her fall projects. I tell her I'm doing the skeleton of a bird. With toothpicks.

"That sounds hard," she says.

"It is," I say. "It really is."

People pretty much believe whatever you tell them, if you say it in the right way. It's amazing. People want to believe you, especially if you're a child. They sort of have to.

"I need to get to my friend Anna's house," I tell Mrs. Frisk. "We're doing the project together."

"Anna McDougal," I say, just in case she thinks I'm talking about some other Anna. "We're best friends," I say.

Mrs. Frisk sits with me at the table and eats her egg in the smallest bites I've ever seen. Which is surprising for someone with such big teeth. You'd expect her to be more of a chomper.

"How is it?" she says, and I have to admit it's a pretty good egg. I can't remember the last time I had an egg for breakfast. Lately it's just been cold cereal or breakfast bars, but I don't tell her that. I just shrug like it's no big deal, like a steamy hot breakfast is sliding onto my plate every day of the week.

"You cut your hair," she says.

I was wondering when that was going to come up. She's been staring at it since she got here. "Short, huh? But I guess that's the style now," she says.

"Not really," I say.

"I had my hair in a pixie once," she says. I don't know what the hell she's talking about.

"Besides," I tell her, "it wasn't my choice to cut it. My mother did it."

"Against my will," I say.

"It'll grow back," Mrs. Frisk says. But I can tell she's a little surprised by my mother's act of savagery.

"She slapped me too," I say. It just jumps out of my mouth. It's not even a lie. She did slap me, the day of the yellow dress. H.S.S.H., if you don't remember.

"She slaps me all the time," I say, a little louder, because Mrs. Frisk looks like she didn't hear me.

"Well," Mrs. Frisk says, "it's . . ." but she can't finish her sentence. She turns her head to look at the ghost of no one in the doorway. "Well, I'm sure you can be a handful," she says.

I almost want to tell her more, tell her he's done it too. And not just slap me but hit me with sticks and belts and burned my hand on the stove even. I'd pull up my shirt to show Mrs. Frisk the bruises and marks, if only I had them. I want to make things up, because the real things they've done to me I can't explain. How do you talk about zombies? How do you talk about the way they locked her in a box so no one could see her, not even her own sister?

"I know you've all been through a lot," Mrs. Frisk says. She picks up the teapot to pour herself some more. Her hand's a little unsteady and the tea makes a tidal wave in the cup.

"Oops," she says.

Oops, can you believe it? Is that the best she can do?

I put my napkin over the spilled tea. I don't mean to help, it's just a stupid reflex.

"Thank you," she says.

"She really only slapped me once," I say, just to set the record straight. I don't want Mrs. Frisk reporting Ma to the authorities. We have enough trouble as it is.

"Can I have some tea?" I say.

"Yes, of course," she says. "You like tea?" She pours some into my cup. The red liquid makes a bridge between the two of us.

"You will all die," I say. I say it tiny, like a prayer.

"What's that?" Mrs. Frisk says. But I know she's heard me. Everyone knows the words of the blue-eyed terrorist.

"You have to forget about all that," she says. She puts another piece of buttered toast on my plate. "Do you want some jam?" she says.

I ask her does she remember my sister.

"Of course," she says.

"Listen," she says. "In a few years you won't . . ." It's another broken-off sentence. "There's nothing you can do about it now," she says. Then suddenly her hand flies out toward me and starts patting my fingers. Her voice gets louder like it's story time for children. "When you were a baby," she says, "I remember how you used to go on walks with your parents, do you remember that?" I know she's trying to distract me by changing the subject. "All you wanted to do was walk," she says. "As soon as you were up on two feet no one could stop you. If Donald and I were in front of the house, you'd march by with your mom and dad following you. The little marcher, Don called you."

Part of me wanted to make her stop, but to tell you the truth I was sort of mesmerized. Plus I probably couldn't shut her up anyway, she was really on a roll, talking about what a great walker I was and my little voice and the way I wobbled and Oh what determination you had, she says, you were a right little soldier.

"Where did I go?" I ask her. "Where did I want to go?"

"It didn't matter," she says. "To the corner and back. Even the rain didn't stop you. You had your own little umbrella and everything."

It made me feel sleepy, listening to her. I wondered if Mrs. F was secretly a hypnotist. I had to make an effort to tear myself away.

"Thank you for breakfast," I say.

Mrs. Frisk gets up and follows me to the door. Before I leave she kisses me on the forehead. It's not a big deal. It's the equivalent of sticking a stamp on a letter. It's basically a shove-off. And it's not even from the right person. The kiss I want is Kevin's. And maybe Anna is still in the running. Or maybe I'll have to go all the way to Desmond to get it. Only fourteen-eighty, there and back.

"Can I borrow twenty dollars?" I say. "My Da was supposed to give it to me." I tell her there's a book sale at school today, and I want to get a few things to read over Thanksgiving break.

"Sure," Mrs. Frisk says. "Let me get my purse."

34

As I'm walking away I can't help myself. I turn back and look at the house. The face of it. The eyes and the mouth of it. Sometimes I feel bad for the house as much as anything. Standing there completely stuck and having to put up with all of us. Do you ever think about the lives of houses? I mean the walls and the doors themselves, not the people inside. I know it's just wood and bricks and metal but it doesn't seem dead. It has a kind of personality. I even wonder sometimes about the lives of chairs. Chairs and shoes and even forks and spoons if they're lying a certain way in a drawer. Sometimes I look at two spoons together and they seem like the perfect couple.

The thing is, I don't want to end up like Ma and Da. In a house with books and dust and all the love gone out of it. Plus the creaking stairs and the sad musher of a dog that walks in circles looking for the invisible door that'll take him who knows where. I want something else, but the words for it haven't been invented yet. At this point it's just a bunch of mumbling in my stomach. When I take off down the street, I imagine Mrs. Frisk's dead husband peeking out from behind his living room curtains. The little marcher, he says, look at her now.

When I get close to Anna's house I check my watch. It's early enough that I know she hasn't left yet. I stand two houses away, behind a tree. The little lamps on the McDougals' lawn are dark, and there's a pigeon on the roof. Maybe it's a dove. It's funny, as I'm watching Anna's house, I realize the watchers are watching me. And they weren't just above me, they were all around me. I could practically hear their thoughts. *Is she going to do it? Is she going to accomplish her mission?* Today felt like the day. I sort of felt guided. I almost felt like I'd be famous by the end of the day. I had Louis's address in my pocket. Maybe Anna will come with me, I thought. I wasn't too keen on taking the train by myself. In fact every time I think about it my teeth start to chatter.

And then who comes out of the house but Anna's mother. I duck behind the tree before she sees me. She's wearing a white coat and white gloves and guess what color the hat is. I could picture her waving from a float in the Christmas parade. She was pretty dolled up just to sell houses, which is what her job is. I wonder if she only sells white houses. I wouldn't be surprised.

She gets inside the car that's already parked in the driveway. She starts it up but she doesn't pull away. It's a little suspicious. I can see her looking through some papers. I know for a fact Mrs. McDougal doesn't like me, even though I've always been super nice to her. Whenever I talk to her, it's funny, I sound like a bird. I sort of chirp. For some reason she makes me nervous. The first time I knew she hated me was when she walked in on Anna and me playing Creeps. Creeps is a game I made up. We don't play it anymore but the summer we met we played it all the time. It was pretty much inspired by Michael Flatmore. The rules are simple. One of us pretends to be a boy and the other one is the girl. The boy says stuff to try to seduce the girl but she won't have anything to do with him. Sometimes the boy has to be very persistent. Sometimes he almost has to threaten the girl. I'm much better at it than Anna. Playing the boy, I mean.

In fact the time Anna's mother walked in, I was playing the creep. I was trying to get Anna's attention because she was ignoring me, which is part of the game. Hey, I said, come on, you've got a hot body. Get away, Anna said. You've got a nice ass, I said. Anna looked at me and tossed her hair and started to walk away but I didn't let her. What the fuck, I said, you think you're too good for me? Look at me, I said, and I grabbed her arm. *Look at me.* I was pretty threatening and just then Mrs. McDougal walked in. Anna ran over to the couch to get away from me. Her cheeks went completely red. You would have thought somebody had splashed paint on them. We're just fooling around, I chirped, but Mrs. McDougal wouldn't take her eyes off me. Really, the way she looked at me was incorrect. Plus her body got all stiff. Anna told me she lifts weights. I tried to picture Ma doing that and it made me want to roll on the floor. Ma and her dumbbells. It's hysterical just thinking about it.

Beeeep! The sound's enough to wake the dead. Mrs. McDougal is holding her hand down on the horn, and right on cue Anna comes running out of the house. That's when I move away from the tree. I lift my hand up and I make a smile as best I can. She sees me, and at first there's nothing. But then she moves her hand too. Just a little. I know she can't do more on account of her mother in the car. I start to walk toward her and she sort of shakes her head to warn me. I'm right behind the car when I catch Mrs. McDougal's eyes in the mirror.

"What are you doing here?" she says. She's jumped out of the car and she's standing exactly between me and Anna.

"I want to talk to Anna," I say. "Just for a second." I try not to chirp.

"I told your father I don't want you coming around here," she says.

"I'm sorry about the basement," I say. "Please Mrs. McDougal. Can Anna and I just have two seconds?" I have to pinch myself not to cry in front of her.

She looks at her watch. "I'm already late," she says. She tells Anna to get in the car. When Anna moves past me, her hand touches mine. I don't know if it's on purpose or not. Both of them shut their doors. The car starts to pull away. But then it stops. Slowly the front window comes down. Mrs. McDougal's face hangs there like the moon. "Are you going to school?" she says. "Do you need a ride?" I guess she doesn't want to be responsible for leaving a child out in the cold. She has manners but the thing is, you can tell they're a strain on her. She looks at her watch again. "Yes or no?" she says.

I don't even know what's happening. I get in the car, in the back. The air feels thick. Anna's in the front. She glances at me for a second and then turns away. I wouldn't be surprised if they were taking me to the cops. No one talks as we drive. A piece of Anna's hair hangs over the back of the seat and I keep my attention on that. Luckily I have a hat on to cover my own hair and I'm not wearing the guinea pig coat. I'm wearing my navy blue pea and I even have stockings on. It's a good outfit but still I don't feel presentable. The car glides through outer space. It's like driving to a funeral. I want to say something, but I couldn't think of anything. Everything outside was getting small, dollhousey, and I was the giant in the back seat, horrible, with horns growing out of my head.

As we turn down the street the school is on, Mrs. McDougal slows down because of all the children. I see people I know, but really I don't know them at all. I'm glad the windows of the car are dark. When we stop by the curb, nobody moves. Anna keeps her head forward. Finally Mrs. McDougal turns around to face me in the back seat. She looks at me good and hard, but it doesn't feel completely wrong.

"I started going to church," I blurt out.

Mrs. McDougal nods at me, and at the same time Anna shoots me a suspicious look.

"I'm not lying," I say. I know Mrs. McDougal believes in Jesus. I know he's a big part of her life. And I know she's planted him inside of Anna as well.

"You shouldn't make up stories about your sister," Mrs. McDougal says. When she says that, Anna looks down, ashamed. I guess she tells her mother everything. I'd like to bring up Kevin right there in the car, because I bet that's one thing she forgot to mention.

"I know I have to care about my soul," I say. I say it mainly for Anna's sake.

"Yes, you do," Mrs. McDougal says.

"I know I do," I say. And then it's Mrs. M that looks like the one who better pinch herself to stop the shame of waterworks.

"Okay," she says. "You don't want to be late." She turns to Anna and gives her a kiss. "I love you," she says. *I love you.* It sounds funny. But I guess that's how some people say goodbye.

35

"My brother's coming home" is the first thing she says. We've been standing on the sidewalk in front of the school, silent, with our hands in our pockets.

What do I care? I want to say. For some reason her brother coming home makes me furious.

"When?" I ask her. "When's the big day?"

"In two weeks," she says.

"Is he okay?" I say. "Is he all in one piece?"

She narrows her eyes at me. Blue ice cubes. "I thought you'd be happy," she says, and I ask her, "Why? Why should I be happy?"

Stay calm, I say to myself, don't mess things up.

"What are you looking at?" Anna says.

"Nothing," I say. But the truth is, I was adding up the numbers on a license plate. It's just something I do sometimes, to check my luck.

"What are you mad at *me* for?" Anna says. "I didn't *do* anything down there." The way she says it, in a whisper, I know she's talking about Kevin.

"Do you love him?" I say.

"What?" she says. "Are you crazy?"

I tell her I saw her talking to Carol Benton.

"Are you planning on turning into a whore?" I say.

She starts to walk away but I grab her arm like I'm playing Creeps. "What the fuck?" I say. "You think you're too good for me?"

"Mattie," she says. "Stop. What are you doing?" She thinks it's me, Mathilda, grabbing her. She doesn't remember the game.

"Creeps," I say.

She breaks free and straightens herself up to her full size. So what if she's getting taller than me. I'm still the giant around here.

"I saw you," I say. "I saw you in the dark fucking him."

"You're a liar," she barks right to my face. For some reason it makes me happy, to hear someone say it.

"What did you see?" she says. "You didn't see anything." I wonder when she got so strong. I wonder if maybe Kevin's finger did it. Planted some confidence inside her. When a boy's finger goes inside you, you're a different person.

"I'm not interested in him," she says. "And if you saw him, why didn't you stop him? You could have stopped him. You could have helped me, Mattie."

I have to swallow when she says it. And right on cue a tear slides down Anna's cheek.

"I'm sorry," I say. And that's when the second tear comes.

Anna is my sister as much as anyone, it all comes flooding back. It's obvious we still love each other.

"Will you come with me?" I say.

"Where?"

But I'm afraid to tell her.

"Let's go to Mool's," I say. If I can get her to Mool's, I think, I can get her to the train.

"Take off your hat," she says.

"Why?" I ask her.

"Let me see it," she says. I wonder if it's some kind of trick again, with Carol Benton waiting in the bushes. But I don't care. I take it off anyway.

"Oh my god," Anna says. "We really did it."

"You didn't do it," I say.

"I should have stopped him," she says.

"You tried," I tell her.

I touch my hair and feel the fur of it. "It's like he raped me," I say.

And then the silence falls on us like it does sometimes.

"I have to finish English," Anna says.

"I'll help you," I say. "What was the assignment?"

"An essay," she says. "On that stupid story."

"What story?"

"The one with the man in the bathtub. Put your hat back on," she says.

"I have tons of thoughts about that story," I tell her. "I can help you."

She shakes her head and starts to walk toward the school. I follow her.

"No," she says. "I'm serious." She keeps her distance. "My mother doesn't want me to."

"To *what?*" I say. I try not to shout.

"Don't walk with me," she says. "Please," she says. "I'll see you later."

"Wait," I say. I run up behind her. "Take this." And I hand her the paper in my pocket. I've already memorized the address.

"If I don't call you tonight," I say, "give it to my father."

"What is it?" she says. "Where are you going?"

But I don't answer her, I just march away. I cross the street, and when I look back I see Anna do the most amazing thing. She drops the paper with Louis's address into a garbage can. At first I feel sick, but then I realize what she's doing. She's memorized the address too and now she's discarding the evidence. Good girl, I think. Good girl.

36

Do you know those girls who made up the fairies? The ones who cut out pictures and pinned them to flowers and everyone believed them. This was a while back, in England I think. Back in the days of Sherlock Holmes. Sometimes the girls put the fairies on their own shoulders and then someone took a photograph. If you look at them now, the photos, they look completely fake. But so what? It was a good try in my opinion. And how terrible is it anyway, lying about fairies? It's the sort of thing you *want* to believe in. People still believe in those fake fairies, even now that the girls are dead and buried with the word phony carved on their tombstones.

The thing is, I saw two little girls on my way to the station. They were holding hands and racing to school and they got me thinking about things. They were pretty cute, wearing that sparkly lip gloss that little kids wear. I bet it tasted like strawberries. And they were giggling up a storm and they even had on mittens. It's not easy to hold hands in mittens but they were doing it. Watching them, I sort of felt like their mother, like they'd popped right out of my stomach. I sort of felt split open, and the whole world was spilling out of me. I almost wanted to follow them, to see if they could take me backwards, to the place where it's just two girls laughing like idiots and not a care in the world. I wonder if the fairy girls stayed friends their whole lives. I bet they did. I bet they're even buried in the same grave.

"To Desmond?" the man says, smiling at me. It's the same ticket man in the same vest. I almost want to kiss him for remembering.

"Round trip," I tell him. I give him the money.

"Twenty minutes," he says. "Platform two."

Now would be the time to ask him about Helene.

"Do you need something else?" he says.

"No," I say.

"You're all set then."

He winks at me. He knows.

In the waiting room there's a lot of men in black coats hunched over newspapers. They really did have terrible posture. It was sort of depressing and so I just decided to make a run for it. I ran down the stairs and went straight through the tunnel. When I came up on the other side I was completely out of breath. I almost felt like I was going to pass out and so I just concentrated on my *in through the nose, out through the mouth*.

I couldn't believe I was finally there. Right where she was standing. It was like walking into a movie. The funny thing is, just as I got my breathing under control, the sun slipped behind a cloud and the movie went from color to black and

white. There were a few people on the platform but I didn't
feel like looking at them. I saw a pay phone and I decided to
call Ma's cell. I used to have a cell too, but Da took it away
from me after I told him I was expecting a call from Helene.
For the first few months I slept with the little phone in my
hand because I was worried she might call after I fell asleep.
The dead do most of their business at night. They don't have
bedtimes like the rest of us.

I wonder if maybe Ma went away because she couldn't
deal with me disappearing too. I want to leave her a real message, a real apology. Plus, to tell you the truth, part of me
was hoping she'd stop me from going to Desmond. I wasn't
exactly gung-ho about getting on a train and going up into
the mountains of blueforest.com. I take a deep breath so that
I don't end up mumbling like a retarded person. When Ma's
phone starts to ring I almost hang up, but I decide to wait for
the voice mail.

"Hello," she says. It catches me off guard, because it's not
voice mail, it's really her. For a second I don't know what to
say. My teeth go clacky again.

"Are you home?" I ask her.

"Mathilda?" she says. The way she says it you'd almost
think she'd been waiting for my call her whole life.

"Where are you?" I say.

"Listen," she says. "Stop shouting."

"Is Da with you?"

"Will you stop shouting?" she says. "Sweetie, will you
listen to me?"

But before I can answer, the worst thing happens. A train
whistle screams and an express comes roaring through the station. I know Ma can hear it. She makes an awful sound, like

she's just come up from holding her breath underwater. I don't know what to do and so I just hang up. I close my eyes until the train passes.

"Are you all right?"

It's a woman in a green suit, carrying a briefcase.

"I'm fine," I say, even though I'm barely breathing. I walk toward the tracks because I can see another train coming around the bend. Mine. It's exactly on time. It's not just my teeth shaking now.

On the morning of the day it happened, Helene was crying in her room and I barged in and told her to shut up. I was sick and tired of her getting all the attention. She tried to take my hand but I wouldn't let her. When she said she wanted to kill herself I practically laughed in her face. Why don't you? I said. *Why don't you just do it?*

I think of running back into the tunnel but it's too late. I close my eyes. Maybe I'm dead already, I think. Maybe it's me who's dead. Maybe I confused everything and I'm talking to you from inside my own coffin. I take two steps forward, right toward the train, but I don't feel anything. No one puts his hands on me. No one pulls me back and no one pushes me. I'm on my own. Right there on the edge. I can feel the wind of the train against my face. It's warm, like a person.

When I open my eyes I'm standing right in front of the door. It whooshes open like a spaceship. But no one comes out. *I'm sorry*, I say.

"What are you waiting for?" someone barks behind me. "Get in!"

PART FOUR

37

"Do you have a pen?" I say to the man.

Actually he was more of a boy, but he had a baby with him, which made him seem older. The baby was swaddled in about twenty layers of fluff and she was chewing on the boy's sleeve.

He looks at me like I'm not speaking English. "What?" he says.

"I could use a pen," I say. "If you have one."

I tell him I usually have a load of pens but I guess forgot to put some in my bag this morning.

"I don't got one," he says. And he turns back to watch the world racing by outside the window. It was a real rush job. The train must have been going about two hundred miles an hour.

I don't even know why I asked the boy in the first place. He had a crew cut and a big nose. He was sort of a brute, not the pen sort at all. And you could tell he was poor, from the clothes and his manner of speech and just his air in general.

"Maybe she's hungry," I say.

"What?" the boy says. That really was his favorite word.

"I have crackers," I tell him.

"What do I want with crackers?" the boy says just like a boy.

"For the baby," I say. "If she's hungry."

"She's not hungry," he says. Some mother he was going to make. A real nurturer. I suppose he thought the baby was chewing on his sleeve for exercise.

"I have some chocolate too," I say, and I pull a half-eaten Star Bar from my pocket.

"You can't give a baby chocolate," he says.

"I didn't know that," I say. "Is it like dogs?"

"Is what like dogs?" he says.

"You can kill them," I say. "With chocolate."

"They can't tolerate it," I explain to him. "And even if they don't die, they get pretty sick."

"Uh huh," he says.

And since we were starting to have a real conversation I ask him if it's his baby and he nods and I tell him how pretty she is. And she was sort of, even if she didn't take your breath away like some babies. She had a nice easygoing face. It was hard to believe the baby had come from the boy. The baby was about ten times more special than he was. For a second I almost felt like it should be my baby. Also the boy had this nervous habit of moving his leg up and down. I don't think he even knew he was doing it, but the problem was it was sort of shaking the baby.

"She's not crying," I tell him.

He looks at me and I point at the baby. "You don't need to shake her," I say.

"Fuck you," he says, and he gets up and grabs his things and moves to another seat.

I could feel my face go hot. I wanted to apologize even though I wasn't even sure what I'd done wrong. I almost wanted to marry the stupid boy and help him take care of the stupid baby, that's how bad I felt.

Plus the *fuck you* was a shocker. I've said it a few times myself but I didn't grow up around that kind of language. Ma and Da never use it. But I know there's a whole world of angry poor people out there and they use that language quite a bit. A lot of them live out on the edge of town and up here in these hills. Whole communities of them. Whole tribes of people living on food stamps and tiny vegetable gardens. Sometimes they stay up all night breaking beer bottles out of despair.

I finally get a pen off the conductor and I settle in to my notebook. I decide to try the English essay, the one Anna said we had to do. Our feelings about the story of the man in the bathtub and the boy on the bicycle. I dig through my backpack but I don't have a copy with me. All of a sudden I was dying to read it again. "The First and the Last" it's called. The story keeps moving between the old man and the boy and you keep wondering how they're connected. The boy has a message, a letter, and you think maybe he's going to deliver it to the old man, but my theory is they're the same person. The old man is falling asleep in a bathtub, or maybe he's drowning. The whole set-up is a little confusing, but on purpose. It's possible the old guy is drunk as well.

When I read the story I sort of felt like the drowning

man's memories were my memories, even though I don't remember a house on a hill surrounded by purple flowers or gray stones the color of ashes. Still, when I read the story, I felt like I'd written half of it myself, and the author guy was responsible for the other half. And when the two halves came together it was like the end of amnesia and all the memories came flooding back. The best stories are like that. They're like spaceships. They take you somewhere far away and you think, oh, what a weird place. But then you think, wait, maybe I've been here before. Maybe I was even born here.

My hand was flying across the page to keep up with my thoughts. Plus the train was flying too and where was I even going? Louis, yes. But who is he? I thought. I really had no idea who this Louis character was, and was he really that important? Plus, where was Helene in all of this? More than anything in the world I wanted her to see me on this train. But did she even want me to go to Desmond, or was she thinking, butt out, mind your own business? Maybe the whole trip was a big waste of time and getting back home was the main thing. Maybe Ma and Da and Anna and Kevin are the main characters. But I couldn't just turn the train around. It wasn't a book I could just stop reading. I had to finish what I started. That's just how I am. Most people start something but then they flop. Ma's a great example. I wonder if she really destroyed all her stories, the ones she wrote when she was young. It's like when they burned the library in Egypt. When Mrs. Veasey told us about the burning down of Cleopatra's library her glasses got all foggy. A lot of important things were lost apparently. A whole bunch of Greek tragedies plus a hodgepodge of other stuff. And when Ma dies I guess that'll be the end as well. Whatever stories are left inside her will just disappear. But I guess that happens to everyone. Why should I even care about Helene's story? Would she have taken the time to tell mine, if I was the one who'd gone away?

When I take a breath and look up, everything is different. Out the window it was getting treeier and treeier. The train was going over a bridge and there was water below. I didn't know if that was good luck or bad luck. But there was no turning back, that's for sure. It was sort of written in stone now. *She's crossed the bridge*, I scribble in my notebook. *She's in the trees.* Part of me felt like maybe I wasn't among the living anymore, that I had crossed over to another place. The place where the watchers live, and all the people they've carried away.

We were pretty high up in the hills. The window was moving a little too fast and the land outside was a total blur-fest. I was the tiniest bit nervous and so I decided to get up and stretch my legs. I move between the cars even though there's a sign that says not to. I pass through about five cars and then I see her. A woman with a sheet over her head. Not a ghost, a foreigner. She's leaning down and talking to some-one. When I get close I see it's kids, a boy and a girl. I think to back away but then she looks up. It's Eyad Tayssir's mother. I can tell she recognizes me because she smiles.

"Aren't you in my son's class?" She has a funny kind of accent. She sort of over-pronounces everything. Close up, I can see the black fabric over her head has shiny threads run-ning through it. It reminds me of Ma's dress with the silver flowers.

"Would you like to have something to eat with us?" Mrs.

Tayssir says. She's arranging little packages of tinfoil on the fold-out table. I wonder if she's planning to blow up the train.

"No," I say. I tell her I just had some chocolate.

The kids are already going for the food. They both have dark eyes and beautiful bird-wing eyebrows. They're eating with their hands, something stringy.

"What is it?" I say.

"Try some," she says.

I don't want to be rude and so I have a taste, but as soon as I swallow it I feel funny. Poison, I think. It was some kind of spicy meat.

"I thought you were all vegetarians," I say. I was nearly choking.

"Who?" she says.

"I don't know," I say. In my mind I think I'm confusing her with the Hare Krishnas. There's too many types of sheet-wearers and they all have different rules.

Luckily Mrs. Tayssir doesn't ask me why I'm not in school today. She just keeps smiling at me. We both smile at the kids eating, except I'm only pretending. I don't know how much she knows about me. I don't even know if she knows my name.

"I'm Mathilda," I say for some reason.

"I'm Aneesh," she says. Her smile is beautiful, like Eyad's.

"It means *friend*," she says. It's a suspicious thing to tell me.

"And this is Azhar and Perizad," she says. I don't know how she can keep smiling, considering what people have done to her.

"What do their names mean?" I ask her.

She likes my question. Her smile goes superhuman, and she puts her hand on the boy's head. "Azhar," she says, "is *a face full of light*. And Perizad, yes you," she says, because the girl beams up at her. "Perizad is *born of the fairies*."

"What?" I say, and she repeats it. I feel like the police have broken into my head. I almost feel sick again.

"What does Mathilda mean?" she says.

"I don't know," I say. "I have to go."

"What's the matter?" she says. "Sit with us. Move over Peri, make room."

I shouldn't even be having a conversation with her. I don't want to get arrested or have my name put on a list. The government might end up torturing me. It used to be illegal, torture, but I don't think it is anymore. I keep my eye on the girl. She's playing with a plastic giraffe. She's making him sing a song, and even though she's shy about it I can tell she's doing it for me. Little kids always want to show you if they know a song, even if they're shy about it. Mrs. Tayssir sings a little of it with the girl to encourage her. She has a nice voice and I just let it wash over me. It's just a dumb song about picking apples, a counting song, and it had some hand-clapping to go with it, which was obviously the girl's favorite part. I make myself take a little bit more of the food as they sing. The taste's not so bad once you get used to it.

I know when a terrorist dies his mother has to cry in secret. She has to smile at the funeral and raise her hand and cheer like it's a football game. That's what I've heard anyway. The thing is, I can't imagine Mrs. Tayssir doing that. She looks like she'd have a double heart attack if anything happened to those two.

On the intercom a voice announces the next stop and Mrs.

Tayssir jumps like someone's pinched her. "Oh," she says, "that's us." She quickly packs up her things. "I'll leave you that," she says of the food.

"Goodbye," she says. "I'll tell Eyad I saw you."

A couple of men look up as she passes them. I hoped no one was going to knock her down, especially since she had those kids with her. I have to be honest though, I was sort of relieved she was gone. When she walked out the door, I checked under the seat to make sure she didn't leave any suspicious packages behind. I didn't mean it as an insult, it's just what I've been trained to do.

When I look out the window, born of the fairies is staring back at me, holding up her plastic giraffe. How can she have that name? It's like she stole it from me. And I was suddenly furious at Ma and Da for never telling me what my own name means. They probably don't even know, they probably just liked the sound of it. But the funny thing is, I was only angry for about two seconds because then I remembered *Lufwa* and the way Anna said it to me, and all I wanted was to die in her arms. It was the lightning bolt of love all over again. I wondered what exactly the white nun had put inside me, and how long would it last. Was I going to be falling over every five minutes from these stupid heart attacks of love? They weren't such a pleasant thing, considering that everyone I was thinking of had basically been ripped out of my life.

Outside, Mrs. Tayssir and the kids are now surrounded by other women dressed exactly like Mrs. Tayssir. I wonder if they're her sisters come to meet her. The train starts to pull away and I watch them disappear. What are they going to do? I wonder. Bow down and pray somewhere in the hills? Secretly hatch their plans? Or will they just go back to someone's house and watch television and tell jokes like normal people? Like sisters everywhere.

I'm almost there. I close my eyes and let the train take me. Farther and farther away from everyone. Alone, I think. A.L.O.N.E. Enola backwards. Like the first plane of evil a long time ago. The first important bomb fell out of its belly. But that was a different war, ancient history. Everything was in black and white. Which made it a lot easier to watch.

38

Even though I didn't have a giraffe I had plenty of plastic animals when I was her age. Cows and pigs and horses, all miniature. There were lions and bears and even dinosaurs and woolly mammoths. Plus I had two tiny men, a cowboy and a caveman. I guess it must have been a bunch of different sets mixed together. I used to arrange them on the kitchen table and sometimes, if I was in the mood, I made hills and caves out of clay. One time Ma was cooking and she stuck a few pieces of broccoli into the lumps of clay and they were the perfect trees.

The day of the broccoli discovery Ma sat down with me and together we invented a whole new world for the animals. Ma put the caveman next to the horse in such a way that you could almost hear them talking to each other. She also made a brontosaurus fall in love with a pig. I laid a sheep down on its side and next to it I put the lion. It was the jungle and the farm and the land that time forgot all in one place. Ma and I didn't talk, we just worked like god and his assistant, doing what had to be done. We worked a pretty long time. When Da came home he walked around the table three times he was so impressed. Helene said I could get a job doing displays at the Museum of Natural History, which she went to on a school trip and which she always said was a place I'd love. "You've got a great eye," Helene said, and I told her I had a little help. When I said that, Ma came over and put her arm around me. I felt like Lewis and Clark, the two of us famous on the front page.

That night, the four of us ate in the living room because no one wanted to destroy the world of the animals. Later, when everyone was asleep, I got up and I went into the kitchen to look at it again. I didn't turn on the light. Instead I got a flashlight and I shined it on the table. It was like a miracle. It was like looking at the world from outer space, from the eyes of the aliens, and seeing the secret lives of all the creatures. I thought of going upstairs to wake Ma, to show her how it looked with the flashlight. But I didn't want to be a baby about it. So I just let her sleep.

In the morning it was gone and breakfast was on the table. I wasn't mad because I thought to myself, Ma and I will make another one. But we never did. We just never got around to it. I made a few worlds myself after that, but they never had the mark of genius and so I always crushed them right after I was done.

Desmond sort of looks like someone made it out of clay and broccoli. There're hills and trees but something's not exactly right. It's like a fairy tale that's fallen on hard times. Even the big old houses look like shacks. The air is clean but all the cars are farting pickup trucks. I don't know why Helene would want to come here. If I was going to tell the story of Helene's life I wouldn't put a ticket to Desmond in her pocket. I'd put a ticket to Paris or Hong Kong or something. Someplace interesting. You know the game, what would you do if you had a million dollars? Helene and I used to play it once in a while. Half the time Helene's answers were pretty boring, all about how she was going to use the money to help other people, strangers even. But one time when she was braiding my hair I asked her how she'd spend the big bucks and she said she'd live on the top floor of a glass skyscraper and order room service for every meal, either a vanilla milkshake or chicken français, which used to be one of Ma's signature dishes. It did sound like heaven. Helene said there wouldn't be any walls, just windows. I asked if I could come live with her there, and she said yes. But once I get married, she said, I'll have to kick you out. That's fine, I said. I told her I'd move to the apartment just below her on the 99th floor, and we both agreed that would be the perfect arrangement.

There weren't any skyscrapers in Desmond, that's for sure. There wasn't much of anything. The streets were fairly deserted, and I couldn't decide if that made it dangerous or safe. It kept going back and forth. One minute it was *Friday the 13th* and the next minute it was *The Wind in the Willows*. I went into a candy story because I needed directions. A handmade cardboard heart was hanging in the window and on the heart someone had scrawled OPEN with a black magic marker. When I walked in a bell rang. A real bell, not a tone. I'm telling you, it was the candy store time forgot. All the candy was in glass jars and the whole place was a little stinky because of all the dried fruit they were trying to peddle.

An old man came out from behind a curtain. It was really just a bedsheet in a doorway, and when he walked through it I could see an old lady in the back drinking a cup of something and watching television. An electric heater was glowing down at her feet. She was glued to the TV and I could tell it was the war just coming on because I could hear the theme music.

When I asked for directions the old man looked at me like he'd seen plenty of my type before. I figured I should buy some candy too, just in case they were poverty-stricken. "I'll have some of these too," I say, pointing to some red marbles.

"Fireballs," he says. "How many?"

"Harold!" The old lady's voice shoots out from behind the curtain. "Who's out there?!"

"Customer," Harold screams at her. The two of them were real shouters.

"Weather's gonna be on in a minute," she says. I'm glad she had her priorities straight. Who cares about the war when you've got weather.

"I'll take five," I say, and Harold takes the lid off the jar.

"You don't want those." It was the old lady standing in the doorway. "Don't give her those, Harold." She shuffles out in her slippers and makes a face at me. "Burns your mouth," she says.

"Why don't you go back inside," Harold says to her.

"You watch the weather for me," he says. But the old lady didn't budge.

"How about some of these?" she says, tapping her twiggy finger against a glass jar of squishy black fish.

"Sure," I say. "Five of those." I was hoping they weren't licorice.

And even though I only asked for five, the old lady scooped about a hundred of the black fish into a bag. Plus she ended up charging me only fifty cents. I think she sort of liked me, to tell you the truth. She was smiling at me like I'd just been born. I put two quarters on the counter. "I have more money," I tell them, just in case they wanted to sell me something else.

"Give it to the poor," the old lady says, batting her eyes. She was the glamorous type all right, in her robe and slippers. Honestly though, she could have been a silent movie star in her day. She had the face for it. Even with all the wrinkles, it was a very expressive face. It's amazing how people grow old and still they don't completely disappear. They still have something flickering in their limpy eyes. I took a good long look at them. I studied them. She was definitely a bird. And he was a lizard.

I asked what her name was and it was Lily Gold. I thought it fit her to a T.

When she asked what my name was I told her Aileen. It's an ugly name but it was the first thing that popped into my head. It's funny, the whole time I was talking to her, Harold sort of looked embarrassed. I don't know why. He kept hovering around us, pretending to dust the pretzels. I think maybe he was a little ashamed of Lily.

Before I leave, I ask for directions to 28 Larson Court. "I have a friend there," I tell them.

"It's easy," Lily Gold says. "Harold," she says, "draw the girl a map."

The old man pulls out another paper bag and starts to mark it up with a pen. When he writes the names of the streets I can tell it's the same hand that scrawled OPEN across the heart. He hands me the map and I look at it. It's practically illegible.

When I get outside I put a few dollars in their mailbox. The only thing in there was a dead brown spider. I look at the map again and my stomach does a bit of a jump. Harold's put an exclamation point after the address. 28 Larson Court!

I stroll down the street, following Harold's arrows. When I get to the end of Mercer I see that the funny curved line Harold has drawn is supposed to be a bridge, because I look up from the map and there it is. It's just a little bridge going over a stream but still, it makes me hesitate. The water was really rushing by. Plus the bridge was all stones. You couldn't be sure it wasn't going to fall apart when you were smack in the middle of it.

Protect me, I say to no one in particular, and then I go. Exactly thirty-seven steps to get across. Which adds up to ten, which is good luck according to my rules. Still, I was a nervous wreck when I got to the other side.

According to Harold's map I'm not far at all, but I stop for a minute in a hardware store, just to get warm. There's a post office inside and with my last dollar I buy a postcard with a picture of horses on it. I address it to Ma and Da, but I don't know what to put in the blank space.

"Will it say from Desmond?" I ask the lady at the counter, and she says, "Yes, on the postmark it will."

So I just send it like that, with no message.

39

I can see the 28 from across the street. Painted on the mailbox in red. There're pigeons in the trees making sounds like dreaming dogs. One fat bird is standing in the road and when a car approaches he doesn't even bother to fly. He just waddles across as fast as he can. I don't understand why he doesn't use his stupid wings. If I were a bird I'd use my wings every chance I had, even if I wasn't traveling very far.

As I walk toward the house I wish I could go invisible. My whole body going whiter and whiter until I was gone. And then I'd pass right through the walls, right into his bedroom. Who's there? he'd say, and he'd start to tremble.

It's a big house, brownish, nothing special. It could definitely use a new coat of paint. For some reason I can't knock. I just stand there like an idiot. When I finally put my fist against the door, it's pathetic, completely without power. I don't know what's wrong with me. I command myself to knock. After a few seconds my hand obeys. It pounds, one two three, but even louder than I meant. When I hear the latch turn on the door I'm afraid I'm going to pass out.

"Can I help you?"

It's a woman with long dirty hair. She looks fat but maybe it's just that she has a lot of clothes on. She's sort of bundled up. Immediately I think of a walrus.

"Who's there?" she says. She's looking at me funny, not quite at me, more to the side of me. Even though there's no dark glasses, I realize she's blind.

"I'm sorry," I say. "I just . . .

"I think I have the wrong address."

"Helene?" she says. "Is that you?" Suddenly her face lights up and she's a different person.

"No," I say, but the word gets stuck in my throat.

"Are you here to see Louis?" she says, and her hand flies to her chest like she's just won the lottery.

"I'm sorry," I tell her again. I move away from the door.

"Don't apologize," she says. "He's gonna be so glad to see you."

She shakes her head and laughs. "Miracle of miracles."

I'm taking baby steps backwards on the lawn, trying not to make a sound.

"Are you there, sugar?" Her fat arms float in the doorway like she's reaching for me. That's when I knew where I was. In the land of the dead. Everything was upside down.

"He's around the back," the walrus says, "you know where."

"Helene?"

I try to speak but nothing comes out, only a weird little noise, worse than Lucy Moon.

"Go on," she says. "He might be sleeping so knock hard." Her smile is quivery, like a candle. "He's had such a hard time lately."

Run! The word stabs me right through the skull. But the funny thing is, I start to walk around to the back of the house.

"Good girl," the walrus says. I guess she can hear my feet on the dead leaves.

I walk slowly and she watches me, the way blind people watch you. With their invisible tentacles, their secret senses.

"Cold out here," she says, stepping out of the house. She's standing on the porch now with her front door wide open. From inside her walrusy folds she pulls a pack of cigarettes. She stares up into the trees where the pigeons are. She lights a match and brings it to her face.

"We missed you," she says, blowing smoke from her mouth. I don't know if she's talking to me or the pigeons. Does my voice sound that much like Helene's? I wonder.

As I make my way around the house, the landscape gets weedier and weedier. No one's cut the grass in a long time and it's tall and brown. Strange prickly plants have popped up everywhere. Plus overgrown bushes and trees. Some of them rattle like snakes as I pass. Behind the mess of vegetation is something white. I push through a huge patch of bony pod-plants and that's when I see the little house. A shack hiding behind everything.

Then I find the path. Not a real path, just a place where someone's trampled back and forth over the grass and weeds. The closer I get the more I don't like the look of it. Behind the little house there's nothing but hills and rocks. It's not a safe place for a girl. A fort in the woods is nothing compared to this. Ma would be furious if she knew. I can hear her voice in my head. *Why don't you stay home. Stay in the yard. Play in your room.* Now that it's too late, I realize it wasn't a punishment. She was only trying to protect me.

The little house is surrounded by roses and I don't understand why they're blooming. This time of year you'd think they'd be dying. Pink roses and white ones and wide-awake reds. Big terrible bushes of them, completely out of control. I take a step closer and suddenly, from behind, someone snatches the hat right off my head. I scream. I turn with my hands punching, but it's just a stupid tree branch that's caught me. My hat is dangling in the air. I grab it back and push it down on my head. I almost start crying. I bite my lip to keep quiet, but I do it too hard and I can taste blood.

When I look back at the little house there's a man standing in the doorway. Barefoot, and with his shirt wide open. I can see the hair on his chest. The worst part is I can only see one hand.

"Who are you?" the man says.

"Nobody," I say.

"What are you screaming for? Huh? What are you doing here?" There's something mean about him, something shaky. I try not to throw up in the dead grass.

"This is private property."

"I just . . ."

"What do you want?"

I take a deep breath. I can still taste the blood on my lips.

"Is your son home?" I say. Even though he doesn't look old enough to have a son Helene's age. But I knew the man in front of me wasn't Louis. Because it wasn't just the hand that was missing. The whole left sleeve was sort of empty-looking, just hanging there.

"Who are you looking for?"

I make two fists and press them against my legs.

"Louis," I say.

"I can't hear you," the man says. He pulls his shirt closed and stares at me, but I don't back away.

"I'm Helene's sister," I say.

He takes a step back. It's one of those million years that happens in one second. We both live and die a thousand times.

"Where is she?" he says.

"Where is she?" This time when he says it, I can see he's shivering from the cold.

"Where do you think she is?" I ask him.

Please please have the right answer is the thought in my head.

"I don't know," he says. "I have no fucking idea."

He's the one with birds in his voice now. All the toughness pours out of his face. He brushes his hair away from his eyes.

"Why didn't she . . ." He blinks like he's just waking up. He rubs his eyes. I can tell he's confused.

"I've been waiting all night," he says. "Fuck."

But the real question is, who has he been waiting for? The living or the dead?

He starts to button up his shirt. I don't know how he can do it with one hand. It's like a magic trick. He looks past me like he's worried someone's watching us.

"Are you alone?" he says.

40

How do things happen? How does your life happen? Most of the time it goes too slow, and sometimes it even goes backwards. But then one day you get shot into the future and then there you are, stuck in the middle of it. It should be like water, the future, but actually it's like mud. You sort of just sink into it.

Louis is making me a cup of hot chocolate even though I said I wasn't cold. He's fussing over some cups and spoons and his body is worse than mine, shaking all over the place. While he's waiting for the water to boil he turns his back to me. He sneaks some pills from a doctor's bottle and swallows them with a can of coke.

"I'll just be a minute," he says. He's trying to act all buddy-buddy now, like it's the most natural thing in the world I'm here.

The house is surprisingly clean. There's a lot of stuff but

it's all in neat piles. CDs and folded clothes and newspapers. Paperbacks on the table stacked up like skyscrapery cartoon sandwiches. The only thing wrong is the bed. The blankets are everywhere like something's happened. A nightmare or sex or some kind of struggle. The sheets are so twisted up they look like ropes.

Before we came inside he fired a million questions at me. I didn't understand half of them and so I just kept my mouth shut. Besides, I wasn't really in such a talkative mood for some reason. Louis kept looking around like he was worried someone was hiding in the bushes. It's funny, I sort of hoped there was someone. Anyone. Someone to hold him back if he got too close. When I finally went inside it was only because he asked me ten times. And I was cold, to tell you the truth. My feet felt like they'd gone to the dentist's.

"Sit down," he says, but I don't. I just stay by the door. There's no wall between where I am and the kitchen and so I can see his every move. I think to put down my backpack but I don't want to make myself at home.

I know a fake smile when I see it and Louis had one that was working overtime. He keeps talking to me like I'm about five years old. *I like your hat. That's a cool hat. You want me to turn the heat up? You doing okay? Do your parents know you're here?* It's annoying when people talk to you like this, but on the other hand he did have a nice voice. Deep and rumbly, but sort of quiet too. Like faraway thunder.

It takes a long time to make hot chocolate with one arm. Even though he's only using a packet of mix, it's still a lot of work. Sometimes he has to use his teeth or his chin. It's like nothing I've ever seen before. And why is he still nervous? I've made it perfectly clear I've come alone. Why should he be afraid of a child? He's pouring the hot water into the cup so slowly it's like he's conducting an experiment. Watching how careful he is, I feel a little less jumpy. I actually get a whole breath into my chest.

"She showed me your letters," I say.

He's still focused on his experiment and doesn't answer me.

"She tells me everything," I say.

As soon as I say it I feel like an idiot. I couldn't even remember why I'd come here. Suddenly I didn't want to know any more about my sister. I had enough stories in my head already.

But the funny thing is, I can't stop talking. When you feel like an idiot you're supposed to shut up, but sometimes I do the opposite.

"I know all about you," I say.

Louis turns with the mug in his hand and stares right at me. He drops the smile. Something new comes into his eyes. Something sharper. They're green and, like Anna's, they're not human. When you look at them, you almost forget he's not perfect. When you look in his eyes, his other arm grows back.

I don't know if we're falling in love or preparing for war.

"Did she send you here?" he says.

I make a smile but it feels a little crooked.

"She never even said she had a sister."

When he says it I can feel my face go red. My knees almost buckle. But before I can defend myself, he's talking again. The words come so fast I can hardly follow them. All I know is something's not right about the way he's speaking to me. He's practically shouting. Every other word is Helene. Tell her this, tell her that, he keeps saying. What did he think I was, her secretary?

"I know she's angry," he says. When he hands me the cup of hot chocolate some of it spills onto the carpet. He rushes to get a dishtowel and the next thing you know he's kneeling down right in front of me. One hand scrubbing and the other limp sleeve just sagging against the floor.

How can this be Louis? I think. And not just because of the arm. He's too old. He's at least twenty-five, maybe more. He could be thirty. He already has lines on his face. I wish he'd get up off the floor. Why does every grown-up have to turn into an animal?

That's when it hits me, the perfect story. I almost fall down from the horror of it. Louis is the lover *and* the killer. He pushed her and then he followed her. He jumped. Except he didn't die. He just lost part of his body from the wheels. I get a sick feeling in my stomach looking at the evidence right in front of me. When he stands up with the chocolatey rag in his hand I can't look at his face. I back up but there's nowhere to go. He takes a step and I'm scared he's going to strike me.

"I'll take care of everything," he says. "Just tell her to call me."

He makes his buddy face again, except he messes it up by clenching his teeth. I can tell he's trying to calm himself down and put on the right kind of show for me. But whatever's inside him is too big, he can't control it. He throws the wet rag across the room. It slaps against the wall.

"I mean, why is she ignoring me? A year, a fucking year I've been waiting."

It was like myself talking. It was like looking in a mirror. The same stupid lies. Except Louis wasn't lying. It was horrible. He really didn't know Helene was dead. It made him into a monster, worse than if he *had* killed her. It was like he was a child and a monster at the same time. Awful and dumb and full of hope. I wanted to kill him. I wanted to push him into the ground to make him shut up.

"I love her," he says. *I love her.*

And then I do it. I punch him in the stomach as hard as I can. But it doesn't work. I sort of just fall into him. "Don't you know?" I scream. "Don't you know?"

"What?" he says. And then his eyes go crazy.

For a second he can't speak.

"Did she get rid of it?" he says. *"Did she?"*

"Fucking goddammit," he says. "I just told her to talk to those people. I didn't tell her to . . ."

Before I can ask him what he's talking about, he stomps over to the bed and grabs up the sheets with one fist. I can see his muscles twitch under his shirt. He drags the sheets across the floor.

"Did she kill it?" he says. He looks at me with every part of his body.

Suddenly I feel hot. I feel like the room is on fire, a thousand degrees. I don't want to pass out and so I let my coat fall to the floor. Louis stares at me like I'm naked.

"What the hell is that?" he says. "Why are you wearing that?"

The yellow dress. The one I wore on H.S.S.H. I forgot I had put it back on this morning.

"Is this some kind of joke?" Louis says.

"I gave her that dress," he says. "What the fuck is going on?" He throws down the clump of sheets and runs to the door.

"Helene!" He calls her name into the yard, and then rushes outside in his bare feet. *"Helene."*

259

An angry parent looking for a naughty child. That's how it sounds.

I stand in the doorway and watch him. There's nothing I can do. I know I've walked into another world. Obscenities and lies and twisted-up sheets. This is where grown-ups live, and suddenly I'm afraid I'll have to stay here forever. I'm afraid they won't let me go back to the other place. *A baby oh my god a baby.*

"Where are you?" Louis shouts.

I follow him outside, into the awful garden. Past the crazy roses and the weeds. It's worse than a terrorist, a dead person hiding in the bushes. I can see the blind woman at the window of the big house. It's my mother all over again.

Louis and I go farther and farther into the garden but really we're just going in circles. I think to stop him but I don't. If a person thinks his lover is alive, hiding behind a tree, it would be a crime to tell him otherwise. I don't say one word. I do for him what no one's ever done for me. I let him believe. And maybe that's the perfect magic to bring her back. Maybe the magic of a lover is stronger than the magic of a sister or a mother. It's my last chance and so I just stand there. I let Louis call for her and I wait for it to happen. Wait for my sister to walk out of the bushes straight toward us, with an apple or a dollar bill in her hand. Even though I know she never will. I'm not stupid.

A baby. Inside her. One time, not too long ago, Helene was getting ready to go out with a boy and I told her she looked like a whore. But it wasn't true. She looked beautiful. I just hated her for some reason. Sometimes you love someone so much you end up turning against them. I know it doesn't make any sense, but it's true.

260

I can't watch Louis anymore and I go back inside the little house. That's the bed it happened in. I pick up the sheets off the floor. They're cold. I carry them to the bed. When I turn around Louis is standing by the door. His eyes are wet.

"She did get rid of it," I say. "She had to."

What else can I tell him? If I let the baby live, Louis would have to be the father. He'd want to find Helene and help bring the little thing up. Which is impossible in about a hundred different ways.

"The baby's gone," I say.

Louis closes his eyes and air comes out of his mouth. Suddenly his whole face breaks open. He moans but then the moan becomes something else. It's a familiar sound and I wonder where I've heard it before. And then I remember. "Howls of Grief as Town Buries Children." It's strange, I've always wanted to hear them, I just never thought they'd come out of the mouth of a stranger.

I watch him melt and I wonder, why isn't it Ma standing there, crying like that?

I go over and touch his hand. It's amazing I don't start crying myself. But it was like Louis was doing it for me. I feel sort of shaky, and when I sit down on the bed I wonder, who is it worse for? Ma or me or Louis? Who lost more and who wins? Because when it comes to death, the biggest loser is the champion, with the crown of thorns and the blood teardrops running down his face.

"You have to forget about her," I say.

Louis moves a little bit toward the bed.

"Why has she been ignoring me?" he says, with the spit flying out of his mouth.

"She does that," I tell him. "She ignores people. One

minute she loves you and then she couldn't care less." And that's really the way she was. She kissed you good night but in the morning acted like you were a stranger. Once I was sitting with her at breakfast and she said, "I don't live here you know, none of us live here." Up till then we were just eating our cereal and everything felt perfect, the two of us dressed for school and smelling like soap. When she got up from the table she didn't even say goodbye.

"You weren't her only boyfriend," I say. Even though, considering how it all ended, he's probably the one she loved the best and hated the most.

Louis looks at me and I wonder if he can see the truth. Does he have X-ray eyes? Can he see the bones and the feathers inside my stomach?

But he can't. He's completely blind, just like the mother. Except Louis is blind from love. When you're in love, you're not too surprised when suddenly you lose everything. You're always sort of expecting it. And besides, Louis has to believe whatever I tell him. He can't fight back because the truth is, what he was doing with Helene was illegal. He can't come to our house and claim her, even if she did still exist. Then again, a person like him might be capable of anything. You could tell he was a little crazy. I can recognize crazy people, because I've lived with them. A lot of people get funny ideas. Including grown men who fall in love with sixteen-year-olds. Men like that are definitely living in some sort of fantasy world. They're a little bit off the map, when you think about it.

I have to make him forget her. It's the only way to stop him.

"She's getting married," I say.

"What?" Louis says. "That's . . ."

He shakes his head. At first I think he doesn't believe me but then I see his eyes go blurry.

"How?" he says. "To who?"

"The boy next door," I tell him. It's the first thing that comes into my head. "Someone she's known a long time," I say. "Someone from school."

Louis's face suddenly twists up into a fist. He looks like he wants to bash something with his skull. When he takes a step toward the bed, I almost scream. But all he does is sit down next to me. He covers his face with the only hand he has. The sound he makes is small, like a bird making a nest. If he's crying again it's only for himself. I almost want to get him another pill, but I was afraid to move.

It really did sound like he was breaking little twigs in his mouth. It was pretty unpleasant. My throat got tight, and I wondered if it was a mean thing to do. Telling him Helene's in love with someone else. But when you think about it, it's not mean at all. At least, for Louis, she won't be dead. Even if he never sees her again, he won't have to think of her in a box in the ground and not even know what shoes she's wearing down there. He'll never have to know the truth. Every year there's a show on television when it's the anniversary of the towers, but there won't be anything like that for Helene. Ma and Da even managed to keep her name out of the newspapers when it happened. So there's no history of Helene's death, except for us. The other history, of Helene alive, Louis can keep it going now. It'll be his job to hold her in one piece. And he'll probably do a better job than me because he won't feel sick every time he sees a train. It might be sad for him, the thought of trains, because that's how she used to come to him, but at least it won't be unbearable.

"She asked me to come and tell you," I say. "She just couldn't face you."

He looks at me and I'm not going to lie to you. He's beautiful. I glance down at his naked feet. They really would have made the perfect couple, even if there are laws against it. I can picture the green eyes looking at the red hair, and both of them barefoot in the little house. Helene was always running around without her shoes on, even outside, and it didn't matter how many times Ma warned her about splinters and ringworms and broken glass. And I bet the two of them spent a lot of time in this bed, half-naked, trying to come up with the perfect sad song to get them on the radio. You could tell he was a lot like her, one of those beautiful messed-up people who either become famous or end up living in someone's garage. I hate to say it but Helene probably would have never become a singer, not really. Who's going to hire you if you can't keep your eyes open while you're doing your number? But that's probably exactly the sort of thing that made boys fall in love with her. I wouldn't be surprised if Louis thinks about her every time he gets under the covers. He's so close I can feel the warmth of his body. I think to touch his hand again, except the arm that's next to me is the arm that's not there. I want to ask him about it. Ask him how it happened. We sit there a long while. A clock butts in, making a bomb out of the silence.

I wonder if he's relieved. That it's finally over, the waiting. I bet it wasn't easy being in love with Helene. It would be a lot of work to fall in love with a child, because the truth is that's what she still was. Sixteen's not very big at all when you think about it. It feels tinier than ever, sitting here next to Louis. But the funny thing is, she would have caught up with him sooner or later. Children are always doing that.

I can feel him still looking at me, but I stay focused on his feet. I wonder what the watchers think of this picture. Is this what they wanted, Mathilda and Louis sitting together on a bed and so close they're practically touching? Or do they want me in a different story, with someone my own age?

"You look a little like her," he says.

"Like who?" I say, even though I know who he's talking about.

"I don't look anything like her," I say. I take off my hat and show him my terrible hair. "Do I still look like her?" I say. I don't know why it comes out angry.

"I would know you were her sister," he says. It's probably the saddest thing anyone's ever said to me. After he says it I'm not even in the little house anymore. I'm in outer space where it's raining like crazy. From a million miles away Louis touches my face but the tears keep coming. The next thing I know we're holding on to each other. I'm holding him like I've never held anyone, not even my mother. I'm holding him like I have claws. After a while the tears go underground, into a cave. Louis pats me on the shoulder, and we both just sit there in the mud. I accidentally touch the empty sleeve.

"Were you born like that?" I ask him.

He laughs. It's not really a laugh, it's something else.

"No," he says.

"What happened?"

He just shakes his head. "It doesn't matter."

And it doesn't. He's right. It doesn't matter at all. I put my head down on his pillow.

"You should go," Louis says. But I can tell he doesn't mean it.

41

Hardly anyone on the train. I pretty much have the place to myself. A few men in black coats but they don't bother me. I'm scribbling away, things that happened, things that were said. But they're just words now, they can't hurt anyone. At least not *mortally*. I've heard it said that words can kill, but it's not true. You can't kill something that's already dead. Like the past is. You can't make something that's happened not happen. You just have to live with it, whether it's something you've done or something someone else has done to you.

The pen is mightier than the sword is the other famous expression. Have you heard that one? What a load of crap. Words have their place but they don't beat the sword, that's for sure. The sword'll get you one way or another. Sometimes it feels like all the stupid pen is doing is *running* from the sword, trying to keep one step ahead of it.

When I woke up in the little house, I was still in Louis's

bed. He was sitting across the room, next to the table. Something was different about him, and then I noticed his empty
sleeve was pinned up. He'd neatly folded the loose material
and attached it to his shoulder to keep it from hanging down.
I thought it was a polite thing to do but the problem was,
with the sleeve like that you could tell it wasn't the whole arm
that was missing. There was still a good chunk of it left, up
near the shoulder. I looked down at my own body, but everything was still there. I still had my clothes on. Even my shoes
hadn't been removed.

I asked Louis how long I'd been asleep for and he said not
long. He had an open shoe box in front of him. I sat up but I
wasn't exactly sure how I was going to get out. I couldn't just
walk out the door and leave him. I'd already taken my sister
from him and married her off to the boy next door. I felt like
I had to give him something in return. Plus he'd gotten himself all nicely pinned up like that. He'd even combed his hair.
I didn't think it right to just rush off. Not that I wanted to live
there or anything, but I knew that by the time I got to the station it would be getting dark already, and there's nothing
worse than waiting for a train when it's almost dark, especially when it's cold outside. And then the train comes with
its beamy lights on, and even if you have a ticket for a certain
place you're never really sure that's where they're taking you.
I've read all about it in my history books. The funny business
of trains at night.

"I guess I better go," I said with a tiny smile. I suppose I
was flirting a little, but it wasn't phony. For the first time
it felt completely natural. Louis didn't say anything and so I
didn't have any choice. I walked toward the door. My coat
was still on the floor and I picked it up. Louis's hand was mov-

ing inside the shoe box, lazily back and forth like the box was full of sand. Or like he was petting something, an animal maybe. But I could see it was photographs.

I was buttoning my coat when Louis snapped at me. "Why did you come here?"

I was pretty sure of my story now and so I just stuck with my old answer.

"She wanted you to know."

Louis looked at me funny, like he didn't quite believe me. "What were you crying about before?"

I didn't know what to tell him.

"Nothing happened to her, did it?" he said.

As soon as he said it, my hands started shaking. I looked down and noticed I was doing my buttons all wrong.

"What do you mean?" I said.

"During the operation," he said.

"No," I said. "She's fine. She just needed to rest afterwards." The stupid buttons weren't cooperating and I was making a mess of myself.

Louis was still staring at me, and so I added on that she felt pretty awful about everything, she really did. I took a deep breath and decided it was okay to be Helene's secretary. I knew exactly what she wanted me to say.

"She really is sorry."

Louis's eyes were greener than before. You wouldn't normally think of crying as a beauty secret but I guess sometimes it is. It sort of perfected the color of his eyes. It was slightly horrible. If they weren't the eyes of Jesus, they were the eyes of the Devil. Louis looked at me like it was the end of the world. Louis with one arm and green eyes and the swimmery muscles of a boy. Who was he really? He wasn't

my mother and he wasn't my father. He wasn't Anna or
Kevin or anyone I knew. He was a stranger. Which meant he
was empty. Like a baby. I wanted to pour things into him.

I didn't want her to die again.

"She had a really nice time with you," I say. "Why can't
you just be happy for her?"

It's a stupid thing to say. It doesn't work. Louis laughs his
laugh that's not really a laugh. I take two steps closer, and I
can see the photographs a little better. They're all in color
and each one is a different girl. Smiling or pouting or just
staring into space. All sorts of poses. I ask him who they are,
and Louis pushes the box across the table. My heart goes
straight to my throat. They're not different girls at all. They're
all Helene. The many moods of her. The photos were all
mixed together, it was like a magic aquarium of faces. I
thought of Rose and Violet and Daisy, covered in dust down
the basement.

I knew it was wrong for a man to have a box of photos of
a girl, sixteen and still in school. Part of me was scared, but
another part of me was strangely calm. I could see one of the
faces smiling up at me. I could see she was happy down there.

And then some sort of cloud passed over Louis. Secret
thoughts were moving around inside him. His lips mumbled
for a few seconds before any real words came out.

"I was confused," he says.

I don't ask him about what.

"I would've come around," he says. "If she'd just given
me half a chance. She didn't even . . . I mean, we could have,
she could have . . ."

I knew he was talking about the baby, and I could tell he
was angry. It wasn't really something I wanted to discuss and

so I just nodded my head. The idea of a baby inside a dead person is worse than thinking about her soul. Ma would have killed Helene. Ma would have murdered her. Ma never wanted babies. Not in the beginning anyway. She had Helene when she was too young, and she'd tell you too, straight to your face, if you asked her. Wait was always Ma's expert advice. Wait until you're older. Don't ruin your lives was the secret message. It always makes me feel a little funny to think maybe Ma wanted something else. Helene could never have told Ma the truth. Ma expected Helene to do all the great things she never did herself. The singing lessons, the piano, the art classes at the museum, it was Ma who encouraged all that. She put all her hopes and dreams inside Helene. Of course she did, who else was there?

And so when I pushed Helene I pushed Ma too. I killed both of them. I almost fall on the floor from the thought.

Why don't you? Why don't you just do it? In my head I could hear myself saying the words again. But tell me, tell me, how was I supposed to know she wasn't lying when she said she wanted to kill herself? How could something like that be true? But the thing is, there are weak people in the world and there are strong people and if there's just one rule it's that you protect things that are weaker than you, whether it's animals or whether it's humans. You have to watch out for them, no matter what. It doesn't matter if you're jealous of them or wish they'd love you more. It's my big failure, and if you want to draw a giant F on my shirt, go right ahead, I'll give you the pen.

When Louis looks up with his terrible eyes I'm afraid he recognizes me. He knows the truth. I'm the pusher. At the end of the world that's who I'll be. The man who got away.

A person's heart is a disgusting thing. You almost can't look at it.

"I'm sorry," I say. "I shouldn't have come." I'm breathing all wrong again.

Louis scratches his little chunk of arm and then quickly moves his hand away, embarrassed. Everything is shame. But for some reason we can't stop looking at each other.

"How did it happen?" I ask him. I don't mean his arm, but that's what he thinks I'm talking about. He touches it again. This time he doesn't let go.

"The army," he says.

Which doesn't make any sense. Helene hated the war. Helene was always on the side of Petronella Peacock. She would never have fallen in love with a soldier. Suddenly he's dangerous again. I call him a liar. I tell him Helene was against the war, she hated it. She thought the army was the worst thing in the world. The way it took innocent boys and turned them into criminals. Killers, she said. Animals!

"Calm down," I can hear him saying. "Why are you screaming?"

"I met her at a march," he says. "In Corinth."

Which is the town where Ma and Da teach, where their college is.

"They only have marches *against* the war in Corinth," I scream at him, and he shouts back at me, *"What the fuck do you think? Does it look like I'd come home cheering for it?"* His little arm shoots out straight toward me.

Oh god, I think, why doesn't anything make sense? The little house felt like it was flying. It could have been caught in a twister for all I knew. It could have been the house torn out of Kansas in black and white. And I just wanted to land. I wanted to be on the ground. "I'm sorry," I say. I don't want him yelling at me. If Helene fell in love with him, I can too. I do the Anna gesture of pushing my hair behind my ear, even though I don't have a lot to work with. I look right into Louis's eyes. I take his hand. "Okay," I whisper.

At first I didn't know what I was saying. I couldn't really think straight. My head felt like someone had busted open a beehive in there.

I squeeze his hand harder and I think maybe I should let him take me. Right here on the floor. Let him put the baby inside me. Maybe that's the reason I'm here. Maybe that's the grand plan of the watchers. "Okay," I whisper again, and even though I'm shaking I move closer to him.

He looks at me like I'm a jellyfish stuck to his leg. He pulls himself away. He's not the least bit interested. I can feel my face go red. I look down and I can see the box of photographs. I wonder if there are naked pictures of Helene buried underneath.

"I could have you arrested," I say.

He doesn't say anything. He knows I could.

But to tell you the truth, I actually hoped there *were* naked pictures of Helene at the bottom of the shoe box. Who knows, maybe she came over here on days she was sad and maybe he made her happy. I've heard there's a moment in sex that makes you cry out. At the end. You explode and supposedly it's a feeling that takes you straight to heaven. But you don't have to leave your body to go there. You go to heaven with your body still attached, but just for a few seconds. I wonder if you catch glimpses of dead people when you're having sex. I'll keep my eyes open when the time comes. I promise I will.

Who knows, maybe someday someone will take naked pictures of me and keep them in a shoe box. Not now, but later, when I'm beautiful. If I ever get there. In one way of thinking about it, it's disgusting, but in another, it's sort of a nice gesture.

"You won't burn them?" I say.

"Burn what?" he says.

"Nothing." I knew he wouldn't. He'd probably keep them forever. People are always doing that, saving stuff in shoe boxes, mostly to prove how great their lives were once. When Da was young he went to Stonehenge and he's still got a little piece of chipped rock he found on the ground. And even though she'd never wear them, I know Ma has Helene's earrings with the stones the color of seaweed. She keeps them in her jewelry box, in a drawer all by themselves.

When I get to the door I turn around. I don't know what to say to him, how to finish things. I ask him if they're going to give him a fake one.

"A fake what?" he says, and I say, "A fake arm."

He laughs his sad backwards laugh. It really was his trademark.

"I don't want one," he says.

"I'd get one," I say. "If I were you. They're probably giving them out for free."

And then there's silence.

And then he says, "Tell her not to write me anymore." And his face is full of stupid pride.

I nod my head.

And then I said goodbye and he said goodbye and that was it. I opened the door and I didn't look back. I knew I'd probably never see him again, and I was a little sad about that, to tell you the truth.

Outside, I made my way through the bushes and I could see the blind lady still at the window. Maybe that was her spot. Facing the little house where her son lived. Maybe she didn't even know he'd lost his arm. She'd know if she hugged him, but maybe he never let her. Maybe he thought it better to keep her in the dark.

Everything is black now and I can see myself in the window of the train. I can see my face, moony and cold in the glass. I should have asked Louis about the terrorists. If they tortured him. Or was it a bomb? He's lucky he didn't lose more. Some boys come home without legs, or even faces. He might have been able to tell me if I should hate them or not, the people who are doing this to us. We're doing it to ourselves, Helene would say. But sometimes it's just easier to believe there's an enemy, and not just some stupid war inside yourself.

You will all die. I wonder what Louis thought about that.

I never asked him about a million questions. I never asked him about the poems. The ones by Helene he mentioned in the e-mails. I should have asked him, because what did I really know about her? Probably it was just the tip of the iceberg. When a person is beautiful you never think they're really suffering, even when they are. Sick people should look sick, like in fairy tales or on television. They shouldn't be wearing sexy dresses and shaving their legs. How was I supposed to know she was about to disappear? Sometimes I wonder if secretly I'm an idiot. No better than Lucy Moon. I mean, what are people? What are they? Ma and Da and Louis and Anna and Kevin. My sister in love with a one-armed soldier. What does it mean? Most people are far away. Worse than stars. Outer space is right here, when you think about it. Outer space is your living room. You practically have to be an astronaut to live in a house on Earth.

The idea of a lover holds out a lot of hope for me. Because there's one person who will never cause you pain. Even if this person was a bed of knives you could still sleep on top of him and you wouldn't feel a thing. But I'm not a romantic or anything. I know you might never meet this person, and even if you did you might end up hating them.

I really don't know anything. I'm pretty stupid. I really am.

Do you ever think about eternity without humans? What would that be like? Would it still be the future? Infinity with no one to measure it. It doesn't sound half bad.

I put my head down on the empty seat next to me and I just let the train go wherever it goes. Home if I'm lucky. That's my secret desire. I even wish my stupid mother was on the train with me. I wouldn't even mind if she had a bottle shoved in her pocket like a wino.

I just lie there and I stroke my hair and it almost feels like someone else's hand. Because it touches me nice and easy. And it doesn't pull a single hair from my head.

42

I didn't know where to go. It was the same town I'd left a few hours ago but it felt like a foreign country. The streetlights on Liberty Avenue glowing orange and the old stone buildings sound asleep. I almost wished I had a camera. *Where were you born?* People are bound to ask me that one day, and it would be a heck of a lot easier if I could just show them a picture. Because you probably forget a lot. You probably forget most of it.

When I walked past Mool's I could see him inside, mopping the floor. The place was closed but I put my face right up to the glass. Mool came to the door and pointed to the sign. SORRY WE'RE CLOSED. But he ended up giving me a coke to go, no charge, because I told him I was thirsty. He asked me where my little blondie friend was, and I said I didn't know, I guess sleeping. He said I should be doing the same thing. He called me Missy. Good old Mool. Straight home, he said, and I said that's exactly where I was going.

But I couldn't quite get there. I walked down Ehler Drive and I saw Mrs. Bender cleaning her living room window. The lights were on inside and you could see her perfectly between the drapes. She sprayed something on the window and then wiped it in big smeary circles. Her hand was flat against the glass and it looked like she was saying goodbye to someone, but hammily, like she was saying it to a deaf person. And then I thought, no, she's saying it from the deck of a ship. And then my final thought was a Broadway musical. Farewell old chums! The big number before the curtain comes down. I almost wanted to ring her doorbell and give her the prize for best actress in a musical for deaf people.

Anna's house was totally asleep on the inside, but the little lawn lamps were on. If you squint your eyes they turn into stars. I sat on the cold grass between two of them and I looked up at the sky. They say that stars are constantly moving away from us, even though you'd never know it from down here. You just think everything's locked in place, but that's pretty much the opposite of the way things really are. All I could hope was that somehow Anna was dreaming of me with my butterfly barrettes and my old hair. The two of us on the yellow lawn chairs waiting for something stupendous to happen. I wonder what it'll be like when I see her at school. The picture in my head is the two of us passing in the hall and we don't even say a word. It seems unbelievable but what would we say? We'd be too ashamed to say anything. I just hope she knows she was the love of my life for a while. She had a big effect on me. She really did. When you're head over heels about someone, it's a real painkiller. You almost wonder why doctors don't recommend it more.

When I'm half a block from my house I notice a light on in the kitchen window. It's weird to think of life still going on in there. In some ways it's like everything that's ever happened in that house is still happening. Every room has a hundred different movies, a thousand. Like me in the bathtub, leaning back, rinsing my hair. I close my eyes and let the water tickle my ears. When I sit up, Helene's there, standing by the door. She walks right in and sits down on the hamper. She doesn't care that I'm naked, but I do, and I cover myself. "Which side of my face is better?" she says. She shows me her left and then her right. I don't see any difference and I tell her so. "Look again," she says. "One side is worse." She kneels down next to the tub and shows me both again. It's not a game. She's honestly upset, and I know I have to choose. She won't let me off the hook until I do. "Your left," I say. "Your left is better." She gets up and goes to the mirror. "That's what I think too," she says. She keeps staring into the mirror like she's lost something there. I didn't understand what the big deal was. Watching her from the tub I just thought she was vain. But now I can see it's more than that. I can see she's frightened. Helene went a little crazy on the nights she didn't have a date. But it had to do with more than boys, I think. She had this place she went to sometimes, inside of herself, and it wasn't all windows, like her dream house. It was all mirrors. When a girl starts thinking too much about the side of her face, you know she's in trouble. I wish I could go back and tell her she's perfect. And what gets me even madder is how, the whole time she was in the bathroom, I kept covering myself. What was I trying to hide? Why didn't I just let my hands float away and let my sister see me?

I move toward the house but then I change my mind. I make a detour by the big oak and go into Kevin's yard instead. I sneak around the back. The moon over the white gazebo is another perfect snapshot. Somehow things are more important in the dark. Plus the moon is a great polisher, have you noticed that? The Ryders' new swimming pool is pretty dramatic as well. It's shaped like an hourglass, and there's a dim light under the water that gives the whole thing a nice moody effect. The water is the color of Anna's eyes. I dip my hand in and it's warm. Kevin's father likes to swim even in the winter. He's a doctor and so he can afford the heat. An arm and a leg it must cost, is Da's famous remark.

As I cross the lawn the moon slips behind a cloud and I freeze. When it comes out again I keep walking. What am I, I wonder, some kind of lunar-controlled moon-bot? I share a little laugh with myself. I bet I would have made a great aunt. I'd teach her how to play moon-bot on the lawn after all the boring people had gone to bed. What would Helene have named her? "What do you think?" my sister says, and I don't hesitate. "Perizad," I say. *Born of the fairies.*

Kevin's window is dark. The whole house is dark. I wonder if he's in bed thinking of you-know-who. I almost knock on the back door but I don't want to have to deal with the parents. Why don't I just do what they do in movies? I think. And so I find a rock small enough to be safe but big enough to do the job. The first throw goes nowhere near the window, and the second throw is a perfect disaster. I actually crack the glass. The moon-bot freezes and a light comes on in Kevin's room. Suddenly he's at the window in a white shirt.

"Mathilda?" he whispers down to me. "What the hell are you doing?"

"I didn't mean to break it," I tell him.

"Shhh," he says.

"Were you sleeping?"

"Be quiet," he says. He looks confused and blind. I give him my best Romeo smile, but I don't elaborate, even though I could. *Arise fair sun and kill the envious moon, who is already sick and pale with grief, that thou her maid art far more fair than she. It is my lady, O, it is my love!*

"What?" Kevin says.

"Nothing," I say. "My father will pay for the window."

He kisses his finger like a pissed librarian. Shhh! And then he points to himself and then at me. Meaning he's coming down.

The light goes out in his room and it takes him forever to get to the back door. When he walks out he's got slippers and a blue parka on.

"Were you sleeping?" I say. "It's early."

"No it's not," he says. "It's the middle of the night." It's a funny thing to say in a blue parka and I start laughing a little. I'm just happy to be home.

"Are you okay?" he whispers. "What was happening at your house?"

I ask him what he means, and he says the police. He saw the police there earlier. My heart does a flip like a fish out of water. I'm afraid something's happened to Ma. When I fell asleep on the train, I had a dream that she was bitten by a snake. Plus, I'd started to worry about the e-mail I sent to her from Helene. What if Ma believed it? Would she try to follow my sister, even if that meant doing something terrible?

"So what happened?' Kevin says again.

"Oh it was nothing," I say. "False alarm."

"The dog," I say. "We thought someone had poisoned him but he's fine. He just ate some chocolate."

Kevin nods and zips the parka up to his neck. I'm not sure he believes me.

"Can we go to the gazebo?" I say. "I just . . . I really would like to go up there." In the moonlight it looks like a wedding cake. And the way it floats on top of the hill, I'm telling you, it's blow-your-brains-out beautiful. "Come on," I say.

"It's too cold," he says.

"Feel my hands," I say. I take off my gloves and he touches my fingers.

"They're numb," I tell him.

"What are you doing here?" he says.

I don't have a good answer.

"Oh I have a present for you," I say. I kneel down on the lawn and start digging through my backpack. I pull out the paper sack. "It's nothing much, it's just, I don't know, it made me think of . . ." For some reason I can't make myself say *you*.

"What are they?" he says.

"It's food," I say. "You can eat them."

On the train home I realized the black fish would be the perfect gift for Kevin.

"Where did you get them?"

"Some kind of candy museum." I tell him it's a long story.

He nods his head again. He doesn't say thank you.

"You don't have to eat them," I say, "if you don't want to. I'm not trying to poison you."

"Oh my god," I laugh, "I'm freezing."

Kevin turns to look at his house. The moon is making some sort of noise. It's roaring. Or maybe it's a plane or a police helicopter. I don't bother to look up.

"Can I come upstairs?" I say.

Neither of us says anything after that.

"Just to get warm," I say.

Kevin suddenly gets very interested in the bag of fish. He takes one and puts it in his mouth. "Gross," he says. He spits it out.

"I can be quiet," I tell him. "If that's what you're worried about."

Kevin spits a little more of the fish from his mouth. He wipes his face. I can see his mind doing the math of letting me in.

"You can't make a sound," he says. "You can't even breathe."

"I won't."

We make the eye agreement of a SWAT team and then we slip inside. Going upstairs it's all plush carpet and no creakers. In the hallway we pass the bedroom of his parents. The door isn't closed all the way and the two of them look like a shipwreck on the huge bed. Mrs. Ryder has her arm flung over Mr. Ryder's hairy chest. Kevin tugs at me and I keep walking. When we get inside his room the aquarium light is on just like I've always imagined. "Lock the door," I say, and he does.

Kevin goes to turn on a lamp but I tell him not to. I tell him the fish light is enough. After a while your eyes start to adjust, and it's good practice anyway. For the black days of dust and smoke. Which I've heard are coming. Perpetual Gloom, they call it. I can make out the A.S.T.O. poster on the wall.

"Arnold Schwarzenegger is technically obese," I say, and Kevin laughs. It breaks the tension. We both have a mini giggle fit. When you say something like *Arnold Schwarzenegger is technically obese* after talking about fish lights, it's what they call a non sequitur, and people often find it funny, even if you don't mean it to be.

I tell Kevin I'd like to hear some of A.S.T.O.'s music.

"Not now," he says. "I'll make you a CD if you want."

"That would be great," I say. I take off my hat and my hair goes electric. I pretend someone's just turned on the electric chair, but Kevin doesn't get the joke. He does the evil librarian again. Once I compose myself I start to relax a little. Sometimes just talking quietly to someone your own age really calms you down.

"What do your parents think of your hair?" Kevin says.

"They like it," I say. "They love it."

"I bet," he says, smiling a little.

"I used to think you could kill people with hair," I tell him.

"Voodoo," he says, and I say, "Exactly."

"It's true," he says, and he tells me about this show he saw on *Mysteries and Secrets* about people killing goats. They weren't lunatics. Apparently they needed the blood to reverse an evil spell.

"Did you know Anna's brother is coming home?" I say.

"That's good," he says.

I wait for him to ask more about Anna but he doesn't.

"Would you really go?" I ask him. "In the army?"

"Yeah," he says. "But they'd never let me."

I ask him if his parents are pacifists.

"No," he says. "But they say there's other people to do the job."

I wonder if he means poor people.

Another plane flies by. Closer this time. I ask Kevin if he remembers the towers, from when we were little.

"Not too well," he says. "I saw the movie though."

I ask him does he think they'll make a movie about the last bomb from a few months ago.

"Definitely," he says. "It was a lot of people."

"Who would be the star?" I say. But we can't decide on anyone. The blue-eyed terrorist is too much like himself to be played by anyone. He's what they call inimitable. I wonder if Kevin has nightmares about him too.

"Have you seen any other good movies lately?" I say, and he says he liked the one about the city that gets overtaken by angels, except you find out they're actually computer viruses making everyone delusional. I ask him what the angels look like and he says at first they have beautiful white feathers but then later they turn black and green and more like metal.

"Was it scary?"

"Sort of," he says. "Parts of it."

"I'm afraid to go home," I say. I pretend it's the angels that are bothering me.

"They destroy them at the end," he says, "and everyone wakes up."

"Do you mind if I get under the covers?" I say. "I'm still cold."

Kevin doesn't say yes and he doesn't say no. He turns away to feed the fish. While his back is turned I take off my coat and pull down the bedspread. The sheets are plain. Baby blue.

Kevin puts down the fish food. "I should, I should lock the door."

"You already did," I tell him.

Slowly he makes his way closer to the bed, he can't help himself. He touches my hand. "Wow," he says. "You really are cold."

"Do I have a fever?" I say, and he puts his other hand on my head. We stay in that position for a long time.

"I don't think so," he finally says.

When he climbs in, I slide over a little. At first we just lie on our backs, side by side. And then I roll toward him and put my face in his neck. He smells like crayons. Eventually his hand finds its way to my chest, but only on the outside of Helene's dress. He doesn't squeeze, he just holds the palm of his hand there and presses a little. Like he's trying to keep my heart from leaping out. Or the way doctors on *Field of Fire* sometimes have to keep their hand over a gunshot wound.

When I touch Kevin's stomach he makes a little sound, like a girl. And then there's a lot of fumbling and moving around and when he finally puts the tip of it inside me I can feel his heartbeat between my legs. It's like he's put his heart inside me and not his penis. I start to cry.

"Does it hurt?" he says. He immediately pulls back.

"No," I say.

"I have to take off this dress," I tell him. It was all bunched up and it was sort of strangling me. I unstick myself from the bed. I stand up and I take everything off.

"I don't want to make a baby," I say.

"We don't have to do anything," he says. He looks relieved.

"I don't want to hurt you," he says. "We can just sleep."

"Won't they come in?" I ask him. "In the morning?"

"No," he says. "They never come in."

Kevin stands and undresses too. It's funny, in the dark his

whole body looks blue, not just his hair. I think of Krishna again, and his overwhelming compassion for all beings. When we get back under the covers I re-tuck my face into Kevin's neck. I kiss it and he makes the little girl sound again. He snuggles up to me. His body is so warm, it's amazing. I can feel his hardness against my leg. It just rests there, he doesn't push it. I wonder if the fish are sleeping inside their cave. Fish have funny habits. I wonder if they fall in love. Probably not. Probably for them it's just the urges of biology. But who knows? Not being fish ourselves, we'll never know what makes them happy, what makes them sad. We'll never know one story from the mind of a fish. Not in a million years.

43

When I woke up something was wrong with the light. It was strangely white. And the way it was coming through the cracked window gave me the creeps. Kevin was still asleep and I eased myself out of the bed. I knew something terrible had happened. It was insanely quiet. Terror was my first thought, the white glow after a nuclear bomb or the streets filled with gas or smoke. But when I got to the window I saw that it was snow. *Snow.* I couldn't take my eyes off it. The way it was falling oh my god. It came down like it was sleeping.

I was still naked, and when I got dressed I put on Kevin's clothes instead of mine. I couldn't put on the yellow dress again. I took it with me though, and I slipped out of the room and into the hall, down the plushy stairs, straight into the kitchen and out the back door soft as a deer. I'm really quite graceful when I want to be.

Outside everything was white. It must have been snow-ing for a few hours already. The sun wasn't fully up yet but you could feel it hiding just over the hills. Snowflakes melted in the swimming pool. I looked over at my house and I prayed to god.

And then I ran into the woods. I looked for the old fort but I couldn't find even a trace of it. I knew pretty much where it should have been and I knelt on the ground and started digging, first with my hands and then I used a stick. The earth was warmer underneath. I kept digging and I didn't even know what I was doing until I stopped, and then I saw what I'd done. I'd made a grave. Not very big, but still you could fit a small dog, or a baby. Or a yellow dress. I folded it up nice and neat and packed it down into the hole. *Do it*, a voice said, only it wasn't me. It was the watchers, and I knew to trust them completely. I covered the dress with snow and dirt and leaves, and then I stuck my digging stick into the ground to mark the spot. It wasn't a very good grave but at least it was finished. A black bird flew by but it didn't cast a shadow. It *was* a shadow.

I knew my mother was dead. I stood up and brushed myself off. The footprints I'd made on my way in were already gone. The snow had filled them like I'd never been here. Like I'd never been born. This time of year, with the leaves gone, you can see straight through the trees to the houses. I took my time getting back there. The kitchen light was still on and I wondered what I was going to say to my father. How was I going to help him? Poor Da. I knew he'd end up making me a sandwich. That's just how he is. But when I looked in the window Da wasn't there. She was there. Sitting at the table in her old spot. Smoking her old cigarettes. She even had the bridges and the dragons wrapped around her. At first I didn't really believe it was her body in the kitchen, but something else. It was more like the idea of her. Her face was white. The snow should have been falling on her.

Her hair is pulled back in a tail. She looks like a girl almost. *When Helene is twenty-six, I'll be forty-six.* How old would that make her now? My mind is a jangle and I can't do the math. She keeps smoking and I wonder why she doesn't see me. Is she waiting for me to offer her an apple? If she doesn't look soon, I'll be a snowman. I'll be gone. Because how much longer am I really going to live in that house? Five years maybe. Five years at the most. It's not really a long time. *Ma.*

I hardly say the word at all, but it makes smoke come out of my mouth from the cold. Ma looks up, and smoke comes out of her mouth too. With the glass between us it's like looking in a mirror. At what you will be, what you were. Ma sees one thing and I see something else. The white smoke hangs in front of our faces and then dissolves.

Ma's hand slowly rises. That's the only part of her that moves. When I go inside I keep my distance at first. I don't ask her where she's been and she doesn't ask me. I don't say anything because I don't want to say the wrong things and make everything start all over again. Has she been waiting for me all night? I wonder. Ever since she heard the train on the telephone? Is that what made her come home?

I don't say I'm sorry. I kneel down in front of her and I put my head between her legs, right by her privates. It's an awful thing to do but I can't help myself. Ma doesn't touch me and she doesn't push me away. When I look up at her she's crying. It wasn't the Howls of Grief by any stretch. But when you think about it, the Howls of Grief aren't really her style. Instead it was just a few drops, a few diamonds down her face. Somebody should pack them up, I thought. Put them in a blue box like the one her wedding ring came in.

I felt like Houdini's assistant again. Maybe she's the one I came here to save. Maybe that's why they sent me to this place. And I don't care if she ever tells me her secrets. I certainly don't plan on telling her mine. About H and Louis and the baby. I'll keep the baby myself. *To myself.*

Everyone has two lives. Your life among people and then your secret life. Your fish life. I wondered if Da was upstairs, sleeping, dreaming of the dead.

I press my head into Ma's stomach. And then, finally, she touches my hair. When she dies, I'll be there. I have it all planned. I'll be right next to her bed. Where is your father? she'll say, but he'll already be gone. It'll just be the two of us. I'll pet her arm and hold up a glass of water to her lips, but she won't be able to drink it. She'll look at my face.

Who are you? will be her big question.

Ma, it's me, I'll say. It's your daughter. I won't give her a name. That way she can decide for herself. Or she can have both of us at the end, if she wants.

I stand up and Ma looks at me and nods. I nod back. We're agreeing on something. Except I don't know what.

Whatever you want, Ma, the answer is yes. Yes Ma, until the very end.

The Tree told me I shouldn't think about things like this. I shouldn't think about the very end or the death of my mother and father or not having enough air to breathe. Dark thoughts he called them. But he wouldn't know a dark thought if it bit him on the butt. He's an old man, he grew up when the world was all turkey dinners and long walks in the moonlight. It's a different time now. He can't compare his childhood to mine. I've seen a lot of things. All of us have. Kevin and Anna and me, and all the rest of us stuck in the future. We're different. We're not you.

But watch me, okay? That's all I'm asking. Please watch me.

Because nobody knows what's coming. Not even her. The future is the biggest secret of all and, really, what's the rush? Maybe it's not such a bad thing when someone puts his hand on your arm and says, *stop, will you stop?*

ACKNOWLEDGMENTS

I wish to thank the following people for their invaluable assistance and generosity: Courtney Hodell, David McCormick, PJ Mark, Honor Molloy, Lynn Freed, Alden Borders, Mark Krotov, Sandra Lackenbauer, Michele Conway, Karson Liegh, and Chris Rush.

For the gift of time and a beautiful place in which to write, I am grateful to the Bogliasco Foundation and the Camargo Foundation.

V.L.